EARLY PRAISE FOR THIS THEN IS WHAT COUNTS

HJ Brennan delivers this epic story of complicated love, its risky decisions, and its lingering aftermath amid beautifully-observed imagery, all impressions sharpened by violence and danger. It's a hard book to put down and even harder to forget.

— ANGELA PNEUMAN, AUTHOR OF *LAY IT ON MY HEART* AND *HOME REMEDIES*

H J Brennan's *This Then Is What Counts* is a love story in all the best and most extreme ways: the promise and anticipation of new life and the finality of death; life-long obsession, moment-by-moment joy, and cataclysmic sorrow. You will root for James and June, and as all young couples deserve, you will suffer their losses vicariously and celebrate the possibility of a happiness leavened by time and circumstance.

— DAVID BOROFKA, AUTHOR OF *A LONGING FOR IMPOSSIBLE THINGS* AND *THE END OF GOOD INTENTIONS*

H J Brennan has the ear of a jazz musician and the voice of a poet and brings these gifts to the page as the author of riveting, page-turning fiction like you rarely encounter. His unique, flawed and memorable characters become as real as the people in your life and stay with you long after you finish the last page.

— MALENA WATROUS, CONTRIBUTOR
TO THE NEW YORK TIMES AND AUTHOR
OF *IF YOU FOLLOW ME*

THIS THEN IS WHAT COUNTS

A NOVEL

H J BRENNAN

RUNNING WILD

RUNNING WILD PRESS

Paperback ISBN: 978-1-960018-03-8
eBook ISBN: 978-1-960018-04-5

For Janey, Sarah and Caitlin—
Three strong women.

There are things that'll put a hole in you. Drop you where you stand. If you make it back to your feet, you probably don't want to talk about it. You put it behind you, give it some time, throw on a fresh shirt, and things will get better. It's the story you tell yourself over and over, and the weeks pass, and the years pass, and maybe you come to believe it. But you still don't breathe right.

Maybe your life has been satisfactory. You've managed well, and things are pretty much as you planned—all the right schools, jobs, a home at the coast. Maybe you've actually done the things on your resume. Or maybe you're more like my neighbor, Erskine, who raised the eyebrows of more than one investor with his fabricated accomplishments—Rhodes Scholar, Navy Seal, the brains behind the SIM card—all glaring bull-shit, but he stared them down and got away with it.

I wasn't always sixty. I was young once—vital and in love. It's my story. If I were to tell it, I'd make it sound like a double-feature matinee with free popcorn, the best ride at the carnival, and maybe you'd wish you lived like me. I'd probably exag-gerate the good parts and take a wide path around the parts long buried. I'd tell it as if I was still there and put you on that moonlit beach, her hand in mine.

There's not time here to tell the whole story—baffled youth, gathering moss and counting the weeks until I'd be set free. Reflections of self-wounds, regrets, lost love—scattered leaves. But the cherry pickings could make a story. Bite into the low fruit—the times I got away with it, and some that I didn't—like that first night with June.

MARYLAND, 1989

Strange to be alone with her, June and me at this table. Looking around the restaurant, we're the youngest people in the room by decades. None of the other couples appear to have much to talk about. June looks somewhat as she does at the jobsite every day but in candlelight and through a different lens. Mid-twenties, crystal clean, detailed lips, coal-black eyes, and her movements echo—like a dream.

Her hands are big. She's cleaned them up, must have really scrubbed and clear-polished her short nails. Her broad, dark wrists are bangled in silver hoops. Her ears too, in not-much-smaller hoops. The sweat and musk are gone. She's sweet and dancing light patchouli—hair freed from the daily bandana, and damn, June's got a lot of hair—long, tight curls and black.

She reached for the basket and chose a roll. The knife jumped into her hand, and she drove it into the butter. Bread raised to her mouth showed light scars and live nicks on her knuckles. Glossed lips parted. June has strong, bright teeth.

We were to have been four tonight. I said something stupid to Margaret—my wife—about did she have to wear those shoes, and there I go again, and she won't be talking to me for days. She bailed at the last minute. So when June showed up at the door all smiles, like Rousseau's Technicolor gypsy in layered skirts and hyper focus, Margaret wouldn't even come down to say hello.

"I'm going, now, Margaret!" I called up the stairs. "Back by midnight!" And have a good time, Jim, I thought.

It was June's thing, her idea, this night out. A few months ago, she'd scored free tickets for a Bill Monroe concert, and her mystery man, Kane, would drive over from Maryland's Eastern Shore, and did we want to join them? I was immediately all in.

"Freaking Father-of-Bluegrass? Hell yeah, Bill Monroe!"

Margaret, not into bluegrass, resisted before finally surrendering to my coaxing—okay, prodding—and said she'd go. Though, she never signed the agreement, nor had Kane. Margaret, locked in the bedroom, Kane, a no-show.

June and I climbed into her slumped, rattled pick up, and she drove us out the slow dirt lane to the black top. I was feeling awkward, sitting this close and alone with June for the first time and actually feeling her aura—vibrating, hot. We headed eight miles south to Timber Cove. No Kane and, definitely, no Margaret.

"It's like this all the time, June. All I said was I didn't like her shoes. I mean, what the hell? Five years and it's mostly pretty good, but every now and then, Bam! She blows up."

"I don't see you two smile a lot when you're together. She's never smiled at me," June said.

"I don't think she can be happy, won't let herself. It's her parents. At the reception, her mother just glared at me—class thing."

"Maybe," she said.

Windows down, a low blood moon and the Chesapeake's negative ions bathed our moods as we twisted along the narrow-shredded strip of coast. Silhouettes of tall reeds and dock pilings passed in a syncopated rhythm along the shore. She pulled into the gravel lot and edged up to the end of a line of Volvos and Mercedes nosed to the restaurant. Her door creaked and slammed. Feet spread, she stood bent at the waist and shook out her hair ringing like all of Marrakech by the time I came around to her side.

It was early evening, not many diners. A quiet, rustic-chic place and our hostess led to a white linen table by the window over the water. The elder couples perked up dumb and tracked the statuesque, black woman in Birkenstocks, and beads and bangles from head to toe followed by a shorter, thirty-something, white guy in Chuck Taylors, clean jeans and a work shirt. The women, with forks stalled mid-flight, probably thought, "Well, the circus comes to town." The silver-haired men—one winked at me—had to be thinking, "He's too short for her, he needs a haircut, and I was born too soon."

We talked about her work on the Eastern Shore, about building wooden boats, about nutrition, dogs and music. I told her I'd love a dog, but Margaret wouldn't have it—that I loved her dogs, the way they followed her everywhere and sat at her side as she worked.

"I'd be lost without my buds," she said.

She talked about her work at the boatyard, about the precision, each surface perfectly measured, cut and honed. I, in crude contrast, was a Pennsylvania barn builder and brought up in the school of, "If it's within half an inch, nail it."

By day, we were part of a crew reconstructing a seventeenth-century Chesapeake tobacco plantation—two barns, a house and, farther off in the woods, a freedman's cottage—using period tools—broad axes, adzes and chisels—blades designed for graduated degrees of finesse. We were in year two of the three-year, state-funded project to get a clue as to how the colonists constructed their buildings. Scarred steel-toed boots laced up over thick wool socks, we walked, worked and sweated on an expansive bed of damp oak chips and shavings giving up smells of baking bread—sourdough. Six-foot oak lengths soaked in the shallow pools we'd built to keep them moist until it came time to split them open.

From a few early and rudimentary illustrations, we knew the colonists' buildings were post-and-beam constructions roofed and sided with horizontal oak—drafty siding one could peek through. By one early British traveler's account, "During winter, if you were not standing close enough to the fire to singe your clothes, you froze." All of the original structures have long since collapsed, rotted and disappeared into the earth. The project's thrust was to send a crew of contemporary builders into the forest with colonial tools and a few guidelines and see what happened. Archeologists and historians drifted in and out of our wood-chipped job site every couple weeks, interviewed the five of us, took photos and notes, then returned to their respective colleges to ponder. Most of them had no social skills, no practical skills and looked like their mothers dressed them. It's my guess not-a-one had heard of, or could spell, Mellencamp.

June had the grilled bluefish. I had a steak.

She talked, some, about her family. She said when she was a kid, she realized she was on her own—wherever she was going, she'd have to pay the ticket. A welder, her dad left when she was seven to work on the Alaska pipeline.

"He was only going to be gone for a little while, just long enough to make some money so our lives could be better—been eighteen years." She reversed the positions of the crystal salt and pepper shakers. "Reading wasn't his thing, but he could fake it, and he did. He tucked me in and told those picture books to me. Dead on his feet from eight hours welding over his head, but he read to me every night. He took my childhood with him."

That left two. And her mother, well, her mother, a striking, green-eyed and tall Cherokee, had no problem finding a series of wealthy, yacht-sailing replacements. From the time June was ten her mom would be gone, first for the weekend, then the long weekend, and by the time June entered high school, weeks on end.

It was three summers ago when she was sick of waitressing that June picked up apprentice work at Campbell's Boatyard.

"The real turning point was running into Kane at the fishing pier," she said. "I loved the pier, the water smells, the gulls and the endless space across the bay—a place where I could really breathe. It was the first time I had ridden my bike out to the end. My brakes sucked, and I ran straight into him—sent him into the water."

I chuckled and took a bite. The waitress refilled June's glass —chardonnay.

"At first I thought the big, dripping maniac was going to kill me. After he calmed down some, turns out he was between jobs and places to live. I had the house to myself, and there you have it. Maybe I was looking for a replacement for my father, who knows. Kane stayed at my place the next couple weeks until he was hired on at the boatyard. A few weeks later, he got me a job there. He loaned me some of his older tools, showed me how to care for them and kept an eye on me until I started catching on —for a price." She took a sip.

"A price," I said.

"Yeah, I should have known. Me dumbstruck by the rugged, handsome white man—forty, dark eyes, lean, mean, big and bad. He was crack to me, and I'm over it. He has a way about him, baits you good. Had my name tattooed on his shoulder like he owned me, lured me in, made me feel like I belonged. His life runs hot—the danger."

"So he's a bad mother—"

"He drinks hard, grabs what he wants, whenever he wants and blasts his way through the consequences. I was drawn to it —so alive. He's always on, always the upper hand, and he— well, you tell me how he felt. I mean, look at this." She grinned crooked, turned her head in profile, arched her back and ran her hands down her sides.

"Yeah, I get it," I said, trying to keep my distance. It was

June's nature to flirt—she flirted with other guys on the crew now and again—and I was married, after all.

"You get that I got the goods, don't you?" She winked.

"Yeah, you definitely got the goods."

"So how come you never flirt with me? Cause you're really white, and I'm really not?"

"You have Kane, I have Margaret." Where was she going with this?

"Yeah? Where?" She slid back and lifted the tablecloth. "Not under here." She blinked sad eyes and stuck out her lower lip. She slid back in and got serious. "I've been watching you, Mr. Hippy Blue-Eyes. The way you hum through life like you don't know the words. It's a little sad, but sweet, actually. And I see into you. There are some parts damaged, other parts missing."

"Missing," I said.

"My dad, too. I see some of him in you—the quiet side."

"Right." Our waitress took my empty and replaced it with a new frosted glass. The diners were livelier now. Maybe sparked by our chatty influence, or it could be the wine that was loosening them up.

"I'm totally done with Kane." She reached out the inside of her upper arm—a triangle of welted dots. "Cigarette, and you think I did that? And there are more. Sonofabitch pinned me, branded me like I was his property, his mattress."

"Damn, June. Why'd you—?"

"I tried leaving him after that first event. He found me right away, like he can smell me, or something. It was ugly."

I lowered my voice and leaned in. "The sonofabitch should be in jail."

"He cut up a guy near-to-die and went to jail. I'm finally out from under him, out of that house, too—my house, damnit!"

I glanced around, self-conscious. The other tables were tuning in.

"He's paying for it. I took his truck money and the dogs. They might miss him, but they're way closer to me. And, screw him and his bail."

"Oh hell, June," I whispered.

"Overdue rent—rent and damages. There's no going back."

1
BLUEGRASS

"Whoa, weird place for bluegrass," I said.

"Roll with it."

It was the formal auditorium of the small Catholic college. Theater seating for three hundred, house lights, an American flag stood on one side of the stage, Maryland's state flag on the other. We were early, and most seats were filled with murmuring older folks.

"Geriatric crowd," I said.

"Lot of tenured professors and their others. Brainiacs and retirees. Problem with that, James?"

"No problem."

She led me a few steps down a side aisle, spotted two empties, and we— "S'cuse me, s'cuse us"—stepped over feet and knees to the center.

The barren stage was set with mics, monitors and guitar stands. This was going to be straight up bluegrass with no fancy light show, sets or gimmicks—just the real deal.

"I'm buzzing," June said. She grabbed my wrist. "Feel my heart."

Soft. My hand rested there for a moment. Warm. I don't think I squeezed.

"You copped a feel." She unscrewed a wet, white grin. "Maybe there's hope."

"No, I . . ." I sat dazed, staring into the palm of the hand in my lap. My hand. Sure she flirts, but this was in my face.

The lights dimmed and four tall men in boots, powder-blue suits and white cowboy hats strode onto the stage. With no introductions, just a nod of the head, Bill Monroe and his Boys ripped into their high pitched and dissonant *Blue Moon of Kentucky* to the moderate applause of cultured people expressing their recognition and appreciation.

It was like someone cut the rope and June catapulted to her feet, there in the dark, both index fingers in the corners of her mouth, and shrieked out a whistle like calling the dogs from the next county. Most faces turned our way. The Bluegrass Boys smiled and nodded mid-phrase. I yanked June's skirt. She fell back into her seat laughing, grabbed both sides of my face and kissed me smack on the mouth.

"Hell, June!" Where's this night going? And holy shit, stars!

"One, two . . ." I was hearing the referee's count from June's kiss landing square on my chops. Eight-once gloves and laced shoes anchored me to the canvas. Time had slowed, mouth piece gone, and, face down, I slid a knee toward my shoulder in an attempt to stand. "Six, seven . . ." The photographers, the crowd, the corner. I woke to June's seat dancing. Her knees bounced, her hands clapped, and she sang along, ". . . *shine on the one who's gone and left me blue.*" It didn't bother me, her seat dancing—still tasting the soft warmth of her lips on mine, it hardly registered. But, by her body language, the poor under-stated lady in summer cashmere on the other side of her was being worked to a froth, being Junified. And June was just gaining her stride. Waltzes, breakdowns and two lonesome ballads later, a tall, thin Bill Monroe lowered his mandolin and stepped closer to the mic stand. He took off his hat and waved it above his head, put it back on and addressed the audience.

"I hope you folks are havin as much fun as me and the boys tonight. It's been a long time since we been in these parts, and, I gotta say, y'all make us feel right at home."

Peering in from the wings, likely college administrators in charge of this event stood, chests puffed, arms folded and proud of the success of this evening.

"We're going to change it up a bit right now. This next number is what we call a dance. And I guess if I wasn't just on the sweet side of eighty and had a partner, I'd just as soon dance as play. Anyway, here we go. Boys?"

They reeled off. June gave my hand a quick squeeze, "He wants to dance." She crouched to half her height, hands on her knees in the dark, looked left, right, and climbed over laps and out to the aisle. She quick-glanced behind her, checked her flank, then moved like a shadow down slope and out to the front and center of the first row. She stood in silhouette, stomach high to the stage. The woman had a great vertical leap —in one movement, she was onstage facing the shocked band. Legs spread, her Birkenstocks came off, kicked left, then right. She splayed her bangled gypsy arms and invited Bill Monroe to dance. He laughed into the mic while the grinning Boys continued to play.

A couple guys started out from the wings, but Mr. Monroe waved them off. He gently put down his mandolin, slowly straightened and came to June.

Now the audience clapped like they were alive. They nudged each other in the ribs witnessing two large lives in the moment.

June and Mr. Monroe touched finger tips lightly, arms wide, then eased together and began a small, gentle waltz.

PhDs clapped loudly now.

I was grinning like the Cheshire pig in shit. God, she's amazing, her Life! A woman born without filters. And, why can't I live like that? Margaret and I were Life-On-Hold compared to her.

The music rose at the bridge. Mr. Monroe might have considered that the waltz would continue in what he thought to be an acceptable cadence, but, at the key change, June was driven to double-time. They twirled to the reeling fiddle. They circled the band fore and aft, the entire stage. Skirts ablur, Mr. Bill Monroe firmly in her grasp at his armpits, his feet left the floor, and his boots struck great wide arcs. Remarkably, his hat remained in place.

The band, in its mercy, played just three of five stanzas, then slowed and stopped. June lowered Bill Monroe to his feet and held him as his inner ears settled. Finally, steadied and erect, he bowed to her. He gave her a genuine Kentucky hug and kissed her cheek. She backed away, picked up her sandals, spread her skirts and curtsied. Then a rock concert ovation as she turned, hopped off the stage and ran up the aisle.

"Well perhaps we should slow things down a bit, give this old ticker time to get that lovely young lady off its mind. This next one's a ballad, *In the Pines*.

Black girl, black girl,
Where'd you sleep last night?
Not even your daddy knows . . ."

June giant-stepped over laps in the dark, landed back in her seat, and I glowed in her current. She leaned her shoulder into me and grinned, "Smell me. I smell like Bill Monroe!"

2

KISS

The moon was high as she pulled into Inspiration Point and drove us down a single dirt lane through low brush and onto the narrow, flat, sand shore. Her door creaked. She let it hang open as she slid out of the truck and out of her sandals, hoisted her skirts between her legs, tucked them into her waist and waded out. Pretty sure this wasn't right—way wasn't right —I took off shoes and socks, followed her to the water's edge and scanned the blue, black, shimmering moon-white horizon. Her shadow swayed slow to what had to be the music in her head.

Alive. I thought. She's alive and free and goddamn sex on a shingle.

She reached into her loose skirts. Hand to her lips, she turned, waded back to me, lit the joint and offered a hit. We strolled north.

"I might head west after this project. You been west, James?"

What did she say? My mind was somewhere else. "Sorry?"

"You been west?"

"Never thought about it."

"Big country out there, not as crowded. The Rockies, Colorado, San Francisco. A new life."

"Place is a zoo, they say. Total freak show—half the city dying of AIDS, the rest marching for gay pride," I said.

Low tide, we wove around rocks and other obstacles as plain as day in the moonlight. It was a foot massage, the wet sand, and every little shell and pebble sent a spark up the back of my legs and into my groin.

June continued telling the future. "I'll just stop in, check out Haight-Ashbury, see where Janis lived, then move north or south—north. No need to see LA. Maybe Alaska. Maybe find my dad. I don't know. How about you, what are your plans?"

"No plans, really. Margaret wants to get the hell outta here and go back to school. That leaves out The West."

"There're schools out there," she said.

"Name one."

"Cal."

"I think she's thinking somewhere serious like Princeton."

"And you're just going along for the ride?" She pulled her skirts from her waist. They unfurled in the breeze.

"I got no plans right now."

She took a solid hit, held it then exhaled, "You happy, James?"

Happy? Was I? Compared to what? I thought I was. Not jumping-up-and-down like June-happy, but, okay-happy. "Sure, I guess."

She handed me the joint. "Good shit."

I took a long pull. She lightly hooked my finger and swung my hand. We stared at the horizon for what might have been five minutes, or maybe an hour. Her hand was as rough as mine. "You ever think maybe you got on the wrong train like me?" she said.

"No." This felt so good and right, so safe and warm, but it wasn't. Where we were headed was way wrong. "Gotta get home, I guess," I said to the moon.

June turned, pulled me into her and squeezed, a full body press. Her breasts firm, her lips on my forehead. She was soft on the outside, working muscles on the inside, and warm—her pubic mound pressed into me. I wrapped my arms around her and felt a rising glow against her thigh. Her lips found mine, and we kissed, for maybe an hour. Could have been more or less. Maybe ten minutes, and her neck smelled like a flower market mixed with olives and unshucked oysters and her hand in my crotch—an invitation—and mine on her breast.

"Holy whoa shit, June! This is friggin amazing, but . . ." I took a step back, bent, hands on knees and sucked in raw passion, waves and moonlight. "Hell, you know? Margaret. No shit, we gotta get outta here."

We didn't talk on our way back to the truck, just held hands grinning like first graders.

A billboard, my smile floated in the windshield as our lights fanned out the county road. I was new born. Each breath a feast, tasting of salt sea air and the smell of wisteria, and the night's warm surf rolled through the cab. Weightless, I stared at June. Green dashboard lights rose like vapor past the steering wheel to her chin, touched the edges of her lips and caught in her hair. Her eyes glistened and laughed. We were joy.

I had to think about this. This was new, what I was feeling. I mean, with my heart racing, and the bugs in my ears, and I didn't think I was making this shit up. I had taken flight and this was major nature taking over like the goddamn caterpillar and the butterfly. This was friggin complicated. "Until death do us part," and I would never cheat, right? I was dizzy and kinda sick in my stomach. I had to shower before getting into bed. Margret would smell me—June.

She dropped me off in the shadows alongside my place. I leaned into her window. A parting kiss. Not so innocent our mouths and, "Whoa, thanks," I said.

"Whoa, back, James. Sleep tight." She pulled away.

Okay and hot damn, then! That was special, and I am one lucky mother! I just had a near-affair with a beautiful woman. Friggin hella alive and young and her biological self wrapped all around me! Could we do it again, only more next time? She lived alone, right? Could I chase her out to the road? Not likely, seeing how most of my parts were jelly.

It was cool seeing June's taillights jiggle and trace, getting smaller and smaller, then poof, gone.

I took in a huge breath and turned to go in. Really quiet out here, ol white two-story above the river in the moonlight. Almost bright as day. No lights on. Big ol solitary house. Not another one for a mile. I gotta get in there and, somehow, get a shower without waking Margaret. Friggin light sleeper and fat chance. "WTF, Margaret?" is what I'll say. "I just wanted to take a shower." What time is it, anyway?

Who cares?

Yeah, who cares?

Ouu, feel that breeze just then? Warm breeze.

I hadn't realized how much support June's hand was until I tried the porch steps. They slid sideways.

"Good shit."

Just two tries at the first step, then momentum sucked me up the next three and onto the porch. Now my key. It's in my pocket. I knew that.

It's not an easy thing, holding the screen door open with your heel as you try to get the key into the deadbolt in the dark, could take a couple-a-few minutes.

"Got it."

I pushed in to a silent house.

3
BLED OUT

F our days later, I came back out pale and squinted at a
drive-in-screen of a slow-motion movie—rolling waves of
green, shadowed elms, the flickering gingko-lined dirt lane out
to the road. Behind the house, way down over the bank, the sun
glittered painfully off the river, and, from this distance, what
looked to be toy boats cut and carved in the summer wind.
Cloud pillows piled high on the blue-sky horizon, robins
chirped, and life sucks.

I had gone in through the kitchen, taken off my sneakers,
kept the lights off and, avoiding the loose floor boards, made my
way across the vast living room to the stairs. Slippery, the wide
wood stairs, from about a hundred and fifty years of polish and
traffic. I faced into the wind, the upstairs windows open all
summer, and sneaked up like a cat. Okay, the bed was empty,
hadn't been slept in. She's still pissed, probably on the sofa in
the TV room. I crossed the hall. Not there, either. She wasn't
there, and she was gone, and I looked down to the drive behind
the house and so was the truck. Back in the bedroom I turned
on the light by the bed and saw that she was seriously gone—

clothes, shoes, pictures and most of her stuff, and life had just taken a nosedive. Where? Where would she go? There was no one here for her. She hated it here. Like, I was all she had, right?

It was like someone had opened a vein. She had, Margaret had and I was drained. Four days I'd kept the doors locked, the drapes pulled and the lights off. Exile. It might have been day two I yanked the phone off the wall. All of the definitions had changed, all meanings erased. I moved from the crippled, over-stuffed upstairs chair only to change the channel, hit the head or bring up more booze. A couple times someone tried the front door. Fuck em. Fuck me.

We had a marriage, a trust, right? So maybe our love had faded some, if it had been love. Hell, I don't know. Maybe there are times I jump too quickly, don't think things through—Margaret, my shiny object. Me, hers. But she can't up and leave like that. Here one minute, then bam, gone. It couldn't really be the concert—that I went with June and didn't stay home with her. Could it? Not the concert. Hell no! Maybe her family got through to her.

"I'm rotting here." she'd said, "From the outside, in."

I thought she'd wait it out. Hadn't we talked about it? That after this project we'd follow her dream? Maybe move to New York or New Jersey for her postgrad school and my turn to be crazy in a concrete city. Yeah, she said she'd wait, is what she said, and she said it every time we talked about it. Then, she didn't.

And now, June. One stupid night. Flash in the pan. She had nothing to lose in any of this, and I had everything—everything to lose, and it looked like I already had.

I was about to head down over the bank, sit by the river and weigh both sides of rejoining the world. Hearing footsteps in the tall grass behind me, I turned to Big Tom and Little Prairie

Dog, two of the twenty-somethings from the crew. "Hey, Jimbo, been worried about you, man," Tom said.

"Margaret left," I said.

"Couple days ago, huh?" Prairie said.

"I think—"

"Let's go inside, get you a shower," Tom said. "You're ripe."

4

NEXT PAGE

Amile up the narrow country road from our jobsite, past
the sheep pastures, is The State House, the recon-
structed seat of government of Maryland's colonial capital. The
fourth English settlement in America, it's the site of a few firsts
—first effort to free religion from government in America, first
legislator of African descent in North America (Mathias de
Sousa, 1642) and first woman to petition for the right to vote in
English America (Margaret Brent, 1648). The historic park is a
curious place dotted with a smattering of locals having inher-
ited their oyster-gathering skipjacks and pastures from generations past, a small team of sniping archaeologists vying for the
next big find, a dozen-or-so state government administrators,
tourists and strings of elementary school groups, and, across the
road, the small Catholic college. That it's referred to as a city
throws nearly everyone off. There are a few seventeenth-
century reconstructions, a nature center, afore-mentioned state
house and an interpretive center, and that's about it. It's a rural
state historic park a long way from a grocery store.

The day after my self-imposed exile, June, Tom, Prairie

Dog and I sat across the road from The State House in the little college student union having lunch. Ours was a table for four—one fading tan, two very tan and one indelibly tan surrounded by hormone-stormed summer school students. Burgers and onions on the grill, fries sizzled in oil, chairs screeched, plates rattled, and large-displacement voices scrambled for position behind my eyes. Life goes on? Really?

I was shell-shocked and dehydrated. The impact of abandonment had shaken me dumb. Yeah, I went to the concert alone—with June. But we, Margaret and I, were to have gone together. It had been the plan for weeks. Really, Margaret? Really? I circled that one-question track.

Leaning over his chili to my left, Prairie Dog raised his head, "I mean, how long you guys been married?"

"Four-and-a . . . almost five years," I said.

"You guys argued a lot, hate to say. Like, maybe it was just a mistake? I mean, it's not like Margaret's evil, you know? Maybe you guys should have seen a counselor, or something," Prairie said.

"Damn, Jimbo," Tom said on my right, "Not even a note." He scratched his chin through a full beard.

"Maybe it's a test to see if you'll come after her," June said from across the table.

"Where? Come after her where? A test?" I said. "She doesn't play games."

"Another guy?" June said.

"There's no other guy. She would have told me. Just the way she is."

"Like, she's got family, man. Probably went to them," Tom said.

"Yeah. Her family's in London," I said. "Knightsbridge."

The elfin Prairie Dog stroked his short, sun-bleached beard. "Hate to say, but have a look around. You see what I see? Like, that redhead sweetie in the corner with the jocks? Could be your second chance. Reset the clock."

"I'm thirty-five, Prair! What the hell?"

"So, you called her family? See if they've heard from her, talk to her dad?" Tom said.

Tom would ask that. "Talk to her dad?" Responsible, mature for his years in mind and body—six-three, a muscular two-thirty, full blond beard, Lennon glasses, perpetual bib overalls, deep blue eyes and bald at twenty-four.

"No. I'm still reeling here. I mean it's kinda sudden. She was here, then she wasn't, and I don't know. Gotta think, give it some time to—"

"Damn, that house is stone cold. Sucked every ounce of warmth," Tom said.

"Yeah, she even took the ghosts," Prairie said.

"Hey guys, time's up." June squeezed out from the table. "Back to whackin wood."

We filed through the students and tables, dumped our trays and went back out to the sodden heat. On the way to the truck, June held me up for a second. "You goin after her, or—?"

"Or what?"

"Next page, James." She placed the heel of her hand on my forehead and lightly shoved.

"What next page? Hell, June, you see what just happened here?" I raked brown hair off my face with both hands. "I'm kinda upside down right now."

"Sorry, I'm sorry." Her hand on my shoulder.

"Yeah, okay. Okay already."

"Just saying."

5
CLIFFSNOTES

Saturday late, a couple weeks later and still feeling a quart low, I crawled off the sofa, and no way was I sleeping in our abandoned bed. I showered and rode my crap bike beneath a low western sun, over crumbling country lanes, across the concrete bridge and had to get off to push the bike up the long bitch-of-a-hill. Back in the saddle, I circled the college and another mile to June's turn off at the nineteenth-century family cemetery plot with its spiked and rusted iron fence. Hers was a tiny rental cottage at the mouth of the river and a dump-of-a-place. Belonged to the state. Sketch electricity and damp. The main room runs the length of one side of the house and a door to the little back porch—small bedroom, smaller kitchen and front entry and a much smaller bath make up the other half. In a mix of guilt and anticipation, I pedaled past plowed fields and one gone to seed. At its center, a thick cluster of trees surrounded by a wire fence, the suspected burial site of Lord Calvert—Philip Calvert, youngest son of the first Lord Baltimore and first mayor of St. Mary's City.

I bumped down the narrow dirt lane wondering, was I

driven or being pulled? Her big dogs—shepherd mixes—one white, one black, came out bark-laughing to greet and snapped playfully at my knees and hands as they raced me to her garden yard. She was stooped over, dropping string beans into a colander.

"You come for late lunch, supper, or hot chocolate and rock 'n roll?" June called, not looking up.

"How much for the hot chocolate and rock 'n roll?"

"Your heart, James. You can keep your soul, but I need your heart."

"Helluva deal." And Margaret? I thought. Were we really done?

She stood up and looked at me hard across the garden, "C'mon out back. I made sweet tea."

We sat in low canvas chairs, the dogs at our feet on her cramped back porch and watched the slow, shallow river ease into the bay.

"I called London," I said.

"I would expect you had."

"Margaret said to have a nice life."

She reached over and touched my hand briefly. "I'm sorry, James."

"Said it was all a mistake. Said she never really loved me."

"And you?"

"Hell, I don't know, June. I thought this was it."

"Is it broken love or being left behind that weighs on you?"

I stared out through low branches to where the bay met the clouds. Leave now and keep rowing, I thought. Just disappear into that silver void, and don't look back. "I've been confused since I was five—what's right, what's wrong—fairytales, parents, the church."

"Church?"

"Yeah, you know, like, Jesus loves the little children. Red

and yellow, black and white. Until it's time to scatter their remains all over Southeast Asia."

"Viet Nam. How old were you?" she said.

"Eighteen."

"You got sucked in."

I folded my arms, unfolded them and rubbed my face with both hands. "I honored my commitment and fuck that. It's over."

She glanced at me. "I'm sorry."

The next couple minutes, a wind high off the bay wove through the forest and waves advanced in our silence. Somewhere in my head, the haunting slaps of a Huey approached from a mile away, and I waited, knowing the twisted nerve behind my eyes would relax—just give it a few more seconds.

She turned in her seat and laid a hand on my chair. "You religious, James?"

Another breath and I was back. "Why?"

Her hand moved to my shoulder. "Cause we're more than flesh and blood. Everyone thinks I'm big-June-and-obvious, and that I'm all what-you-see-is-what-you-get, but no one knows what's inside."

"Yeah? What's inside?"

She faced front, folded her arms and scanned the horizon. "A woman who's made a couple mistakes, smart ass. That and the ghost of Harriet Tubman. It's who I go to when I've got to be strong—when I'm not sharing a quiet moment on my porch with a good friend who's squeezed up tighter than a gnat's ass."

"Gnat's ass."

"Show-and-tell, James. You religious?"

"I was raised in lockstep with the church—three times a week. Catechism, the whole bit. As I got older, I turned away from it—from what I thought to be theatrics, dogma, hypocrisy. Your turn." I said. "Look." I pointed to the other side of the

small river. A couple raccoons washed their hands at water's
edge.

"They're here every day," she said. "Usually not this early."

She glanced back at me, then faced out across the bay. "I've
never been in a church—I wouldn't know how to dress. When I
was a kid, I saw people coming out from a wedding—down the
steps of a little brick church and folks cheering the bride and
groom, and they were black, and she was pretty and so happy
and the flowers and her dress so white. They got into the back
of a purple Cadillac, and she waved to me as they pulled away.
I ran home and told Mom and asked about her and Dad's
wedding, and was it a big affair, and was there singing and flowers. Mom stared out the kitchen window for a long time like she
hadn't heard me. She turned, and I'd never seen her eyes so sad.
She set her cup on the table and folded her arms. She told me
that it was a small, beautiful wedding, and she had flowers in
her hair, and there were tribal elders and hippies and that Dad
was the most handsome black man on the Eastern Shore that
day. She told me I was there, too—in her belly. She said the
vows they made to each other were lovely poetry about eternity
and the sky and the sea, and they were impossible to live by.
She sniffed, thanked me for reminding her then went back to
staring out the window with her whiskey."

"Hell, June."

"Yeah, Mom has some issues.

As for religion, I've read some of *The Bible*—the *New
Testament*," she said.

"The *New Testament*," I said.

"Yeah, I tried to get into the *Old Testament*, but all the
'begots' and 'begats' wore me out," she said. "The *New Testament* is just a lot of great little stories, and Jesus and His friends
and a donkey and everybody breaking bread and making wine
and, 'You can call me Paul, or you can call me Saul,' and poor

old Peter and the cock crows thrice. Then there's the awful crucifixion, and you think it's over, but it's not, and then comes *Revelations* where the total shit hits the fan."

"Your *CliffsNotes* have an interesting slant to them," I said.

"So how do you see it?"

"I guess I have it boiled down to do unto others, and try to lead a good life."

"And 'good' being . . . ?"

"Hell if I know. Maybe say, 'please' and 'thank you?' Give to charity? Floss?" I said.

"And you think I'm slanted."

"So how is it with you—working here?" I said.

"How so?"

"Like, this colonial capitol. We're rebuilding a seventeenth-century tobacco plantation? Slaves?"

"It was mostly indentured servants in the early years," she said. "Slavery didn't really take a big bite until the eighteenth century, and now we're all stuck with it and don't know what to do about it. It buzzes around the dark room in my head like a mosquito in the middle of the night. As far as this project, I'm working on the early seventeenth-century part. I can't go near the slaves' quarters restoration. Too, too sad."

She had that right. Prairie and I were assigned to the early nineteenth-century slaves' quarters on the historic plantation my first month on the crew. The place haunted us as we worked in the tall grass above the river and applied a protective clapboard shell over the original siding. Venturing inside the shuttered single story—when we had to—in the semi-dark on that swept dirt floor, the blackened grease that stuck to the hearth made you want to cry.

The bay view from her little porch was framed on two sides by forest and her rowing dinghy tied up on the left, and on the right—along the river—her socks, shorts and underwear drying on a diagonal line from the house to a tree at the water. I guess we didn't know that June mostly wore boxer shorts. But there were a few interesting, delicate, laced things that hovered like dragonflies—purple, glimmering and iridescent among the natural cotton and wool. I wondered where or when did she wear those? What did she have on right now? No, just don't.

"What are you looking at?" she said.

"Your laundry."

"My intimates?"

"Your socks. Friggin big feet, June."

"Prick."

The sun was slowing behind us.

"You hungry? Make you supper?" she said.

"I thought I was going to have to be rude, ask what's in the fridge."

"Omelet. Cheese and herbs."

The screen door popped shut as she went in. I rose cramped and creaky and hobbled down the single step and out to the water. Our weekends were spent working out the stiffness that built up over the week of swinging axes and splitting big wood into lots of little wood. I skipped a dozen flat rocks and heard a transistor Bruce Hornsby from the house.

6

AUNT JUNIE'S SECRET TAHINI DRESSING

Dark came early at June's cottage. Once the sun dropped behind the trees and the mosquitos arrived, it was time to go in and light a few lanterns.

The dogs were already inside. She had plates, candles, flowers, heavy blue glass tumblers and a bottle of wine set on a tie-dyed sheet on the floor. She was at the sink, bare feet, and her liquid hips rolled with the music.

"You ever hear from your dad?" I said.

"You ever hear from yours?" she said.

I leaned against the kitchen door, folded my arms and watched her. Her back to me, she moved at the sink and chopping board with the honeyed ease of a pro athlete. "When I feel I have to, I visit Mom and Dad," I said. "They're still there in that little house in PA. It's oppressive being there. Takes me back to a complicated childhood—their expectations, my shortcomings, the punishments. Fried food, the church and I gotta guess they loved me. I kept my mouth shut and did as I was told. They gave me everything they never had, and I always wanted more. I go for long runs twice a day when I'm there. And why am I telling you this?"

Her back to me, she said, "Because you've had to tell it to someone, including yourself, for a long time, Mister No Feelings. And things are different with me."

She turned on the faucet, rinsed fresh-picked leaves and talked into the sink. "My dad? Have I heard from him? Couple times a year since he left, he sends a letter. Each one says he misses me, and he'll be home in a year. Pipeline was finished in '77. Said he'd be home in '78. Six months ago, he sent a letter from way up north saying he missed me, and he'd be coming home soon. Been eighteen years."

"What do you make of that, June?"

"Makin a salad—lettuce, sprouts, beans, beets, and Aunt Junie's secret tahini dressing. Please pour a glass for the cook, dear."

She threw the greens onto a towel and turned her attention to garlic in oil on the small propane range.

"Red's right with omelets?" I said.

"You're color-conscious all of a sudden?"

"No. I don't know. The wine." I poured myself a glass. "Just asking."

"Red is perfect with my omelets, James, and you're allowed to pour more than a shot at a time." She set her glass down. "Here, let's taste the dressing." She grabbed my finger, dipped it into the dressing jar and stuck my dripping digit into her mouth. "Ummm," she pulled my finger through her lips. My knees faded. I took a swig.

June being a minimalist, we ate across from each other on the floor. It was delicate, slow, and there was a special way she used her fork. I had noticed it the night of the concert, but hadn't decoded it. Now I saw what it was. Upon entry and exit of her mouth, as full lips parted and white teeth appeared, she expressed a half-smile as the fork canted slightly in her hand—always to her right.

"You're watching my mouth," she said.

"Yes."

"Why?"

"It's beautiful, and that thing you do with the fork."

"What thing?"

"That little flourish thing."

It was such contrast to the sweat and gut-wrenching days, and June worked as hard as, and stroke-for-stroke with, the guys. The last couple months, she and I seemed to be working side-by-side much of the time. If I was spudding bark, June was stripping logs just a few feet away. When I was busting logs open with steel wedges, June was busting next to me. Our daily chatter was light, not so deep as you would call intimate, but it had taken on a new timbre. And was I imagining this, flattering myself, or was she stalking me? Making it sound like a joke, I'd asked her. She said, "Now, wouldn't that be somethin?"

She refilled our glasses with the last of the wine.

"I've never had such a cared-for omelet," I said.

"Not many have. Gotta show it some love, y'all."

"You're going to tell me what's in that amazing dressing?"

"We'll share, but not that. I might bottle it someday. Trade secret." She zipped her lips. "I made brownies. You have room?" She was up and back with a white plate stacked with a chocolate pyramid. She settled at my side. "So, you're abandoned, betrayed and SOL." She leaned against me.

"Yep, shot at and missed, shit at and then some. You too," I said.

"What do you think about, laying there alone on the sofa in that big house at 3 a.m.?"

"I feel guilty. Like I betrayed her."

She bumped her shoulder into mine. "You went to a concert."

"Yeah, then we kissed—for a long time, June."

"It was a few minutes, a little peck among friends, and by then she was already gone."

"How do I know that?" I said.

"There has to be more."

"Margaret and I were attracted to each other like moths to a flame. Opposites. I the unhinged artist, she the intellectual conservative, the artist's model—her skin, the gold in her hair. She slashed and burned the canvases six months ago."

"Huh?" she said.

"'Pornographic,' is what she said. They were old school Venetian—rabbit skin glue and walnut oil—my Renaissance phase. I was all about Titian. And hell right they were nudes—mythic, romantic. Like Margaret and me. Like this was the one we each wanted ever since we were twelve. We flew right into it. Fairytale romance, the beautiful couple and—"

"Like, what the hell? She destroyed your paintings?"

"Maybe she and I have some things in common, like over-reacting sometimes. All of a sudden everything goes black, and then it's over—it's rare. Otherwise, we were solid, like, the King and Queen of the prom."

"There's your problem. Same one I had with Kane—goddamn short view and falling into that Hallmark hole way too fast and looking for something that wasn't there, and what I found was the exact opposite of what every little girl wants, and it'll burn you."

It felt like we were cut adrift from the world, sitting in the middle of that small, dimly-lit room on her square of tie-dye. Plates empty, glasses, too.

"Hallmark. Do they make a card for unconditional love? I

needed that from Margaret. I needed that from anyone. Parents."

"You want to talk parents?" she said. "You want to talk abandonment? I don't need anything! I got hands, feet and backbone, and I take care of me first. There're things I want but nothing I need. And there's no unconditional love, James. Even Jesus flipped out on the goddamn money changers. Kicked their asses right outta that temple. Long view, gotta focus on the long view."

"Right." Her voice was convincing—maybe too convincing —and I was being seriously pulled into her world, and it was breathing and alive, and I was feeling whacked. I lay down and propped my head on my hand. "Is it the wine or the brownies?"

"Both." She squeezed up behind me and rested her head on my hip. I pulled a satin pillow over from the wall and got comfortable. June's hand slipped between my knees—she hugged my leg. "So goin west young man? West with me?"

"Uh-huh, yeah, going . . . west . . . young . . ."

7

ROOMS IN DREAMS

I woke in the dark and rolled to my side. I was floating. On the bay? In a boat?

June rolled into me. "Easy there, Cap'n. It's a water bed."

She was warm lavender and her lips so close. Feathery sheets, a thread-bare web from years of washings, I reached out, turned over and felt her—us.

"You're shitting me! What? My clothes. This is your room? In your bed?"

"Something like that—my bed, in my room."

"How'd I—?"

"I dragged you in here, destroyed your shirt and pulled your pants off with my teeth, if you have to know."

"And we, I mean, did we?" I said.

"Not yet."

She kissed me. We kissed, soft, gentle, her lips, her teeth, her tongue. She floated above me. Fingers hovered and traced my face, and she whispered, "You're beautiful, you know. Almost pretty."

"Huh? How's that work, June?"

"Pretty would be too much sugar. With you, I can still taste the coffee." She rolled onto her back and pulled me along. I edged up and found her hand gripping a headboard rail. She opened it and I kissed her palm, followed my lips past her wrist, along her arm and stopped at the three raised scars.

She slid beneath me and opened rooms lit only in dreams.

8
GET EM, BOYS!

Still dark, it had to be near dawn. June snored, and the mutts growled low. I pulled out of the sheets and rolled my hundred-and-sixty pounds onto the floor. The dogs were louder now, by the front door. Feeling my way—Owww!!—I stabbed my toe into June's stone Buddha and hopped buck naked to the kitchen window. I leaned over the sink, scanned the garden—Goddamn toe!—and farther up the narrow drive. A glimmer? Way up there through the trees, like the moon off a windshield? I'd come in that way today, and there were no windshields.

"Okay fur balls. But don't tell who let you out."

I opened the door, and they launched from silent sling-shots.

"Go get em boys."

9
CRACKLING CEDAR SHAKES

S un up, we woke in the trough of her buoyant hydrobed. Elbows, knees, and hips bounced off each other like tossed wooden boats. Sunday, and, by the cacophony outside her open window, we could hear that the tide, the shore birds and the forest weren't taking the weekend off. Our clothes were a twisted mess on the floor in the corner of the room beneath her wall hooks and her scarf and hat.

"What's that?" Her brow furrowed.

"Sunshine, June. Happy Sunday."

"No, that."

"My elbow."

"The noise, James."

"The dog."

"My dog? Outside? You let him out?"

"Sorry. They said they wouldn't make a big deal of it."

"They're both out?" she said.

"Okay, my bad. I'll get em."

"We're going." She slipped a beautiful body into shorts and a T-shirt.

White Dog jumped at June's chin, snap-barking and intense. She shoved him inside and slammed the door.

"Where's Black Dog?" she said.

"Hell, June, like I know? Black Dog!" I called.

"No, let's go. They're always together."

She led up one of the drive's ruts. The summer heat was on, the humidity and insects raged. She was on a mission, a quick-march mission, and I was already sucking wind and rolling sweat. We took the trail out across the job site, past the log stack and the soaking pools black with tannin. Now off the trail and down into the cover of the ravine, the scattered remains of a rabbit along the dark creek and the shade being an easy five-degrees cooler. Her pace increased.

"June, can we back off a click? Is this really a race?"

She didn't slow or look back. "Might be."

"He's probably on the trail of something." I said. "A deer. Maybe a mile away by now." Shorter legs, I hurdled a fallen tree more awkwardly than she had. "My dad had hunting dogs —beagles—and they'd be gone sometimes for a day or two, but they'd always find their way back."

"He's not a mile away, and he's not lost," she said.

"Should we split up? I can go back up to the drive."

"We're staying together."

"Right." There was an intensity in her I hadn't seen before. Fear?

She slowed. "Okay. We're going back up. We'll go out to the road, then double back. They know not to go to the road, but . . ."

We returned to the drive and were nearly to the little ceme-tery at the road when she stopped. "No."

"Hell no!" I came up behind.

June parted tall weeds toward the fence, her broad back to me. She reached out, both hands chest-high and pulled. The crackling sounds said breaking cedar shakes. Black Dog had been impaled on the spiked iron fence. She pulled his body up and off. Sucking tears, she cradled him past me down to the house.

How long would I sit on her porch—her in the tiny bathroom with Black Dog, and it sounded like more than one in there with her talking to herself and Black Dog and crying? I had tried the door. It wouldn't budge. I pictured her curled on the floor around his body, her back against the door, and I think she said, "Just leave," muffled and quiet between sobs, then retching, and the toilet flushed.

It had to be close to an hour until the house was quiet. Another few minutes, and I went in. Lying there in the bedroom, White Dog had his nose to the space beneath the bathroom door and whined. I knocked.

Nothing.

"June?"

Silence. I felt suspended, helpless.

I kneeled with my forehead against the door. "It doesn't change anything, and it's not enough to say, but I am so sorry."

Nothing.

"If you were out here, or I was in there, I'd want to hold you right now," I said.

Brief movement behind the door. Then quiet.

"June—"

"Just shut up, okay?"

"I—"

"I, shit, James!" She yelled through the door. "This isn't about you right now. He took something too close—too goddamn deep. Fuckin bad boys is what I wanted. Why? Cause they wanted me is why, and all of a sudden I wasn't a throw-away, and I was worth something and had some badass to watch over me cause there was nobody else to, and I was their fuckin property." She was sobbing, again.

Head still against the door, I stared at the worn, cracked linoleum floor, a bit of black fur poked out beneath the door. "But, we—"

"What we?" She coughed. "What we?!" she yelled. "You're so screwed from Margaret kicking your ass, you don't know whether to shit or lay bricks, and I was just some dancing fool bouncing you on my bed and having one helluva time. Then you let my dogs out!"

Yes. I screwed up.

"Don't have a lot to say to that, do you?"

I didn't.

"Who the fuck are you, James? Are you some-day-my-prince-will-come? Are you the guy I should be falling for—should have been falling for all my life, and I think I am, and I hate you right now?"

"You're falling for me?"

"Just go!"

Mother of all headaches, my eyes felt swollen—lips and tongue numb, limbs barren. Occasional movements inside, then quiet. Rising, my hands steadied me along the way, and I was back at the small porch and the canvas chair. There was no undoing what had happened—what I had done to Black Dog, to her.

A shovel cleaving damp earth alongside the house—muffled steel against roots then sharp strikes on rocks. It might have been another hour until the front latch clicked, and I heard water in the sink. Moments later, June stood at the back door.

She sat in the little chair next to me, and she was raw. Slow light on the bay moved like it had something else on its mind.

She stretched to her side, snatched a stick from the floor, sat up and pushed her thumbs into it until it snapped. "Tall for my age, overweight and a ten-year-old girl, James. There were plenty of mixed-race kids and white teachers, but, for a couple years, while Mom was preoccupied, I had no voice. One fat, insecure girl in the back of the room." She tossed the pieces off the porch.

"Dad had left a few years earlier, and how could he? I missed him every second, and it was hard to breathe, and in the middle of the night, my crying woke me up, and I'd wet the bed. Do you know how humiliating that is?

There were reminders of him everywhere—his coffee mug, his dump of a TV chair, fingerprints in my old picture books. When no one was around, I sat in that chair. His smells. Mom wasn't one to be thinking about anything more than the next dance—she finally got rid of the mug and the chair, and hurt me all over again. I should have hidden the mug.

Then, when Mom started disappearing, I really got to thinking I was worthless—that I was a bad smell, and they'd left the doors and windows open hoping I'd just go away. I knew Mom was still around cause groceries showed up in the pantry, and her laundry and shoes clutter kept changing in her room. It was an awkward accident if I saw her, if our schedules overlapped. Then she'd be all over-the-top lovey and tell me about the box of donuts on top of the refrigerator, and there was chocolate milk, and then she'd be late for something, and, 'Bye,' and I wanted her to stay. I needed her. Didn't she know that? She's my mother!"

She rose and leaned against the skinny porch pole, her back to me.

"School was a distraction—a place with people to talk to

and things to do. I packed my lunch and laid my things out the night before and showed up each day like nothing was wrong. I bore down. Kept my notebook, studied hard for tests, did extra credit, read ahead—started getting straight A's, and it gave me recognition. I couldn't get enough of it. I wanted to be a teacher —a kind teacher."

She went quiet for a few minutes. Her quiet, her space, and I knew to stay out of it. White Dog came around from the side of the house, licked June's hand and spread out at her feet.

"My first period scared the hell out of me. I was alone and bleeding to death in my bed, and I knew what it was, and I didn't want it, and it was another betrayal, and this time it was my own body deserting me. I stayed home from school that week and did a lot of washing. Who knew where Mom was?"

"June, I'm—"

"My body changed. So did the recognition. In the next couple years, I went from a girl to a woman—shot up even taller for my age with all the right stuff in all the right places, and all the older boys were all-of-a-sudden paying attention. At first, I was insecure about it, but I grew into it."

"June . . ."

She looked back over her shoulder, then back at the bay. "Just shut up, James. I'm unloading this, then we'll see.

I did a lot of growing up at the diner. There, it was married men checking me out—gray, horny, married men. Sharon, the older waitress, kept me on track, showed me how to handle em. Said they were insecure little boys inside, and I should treat em that way.

Waitressing, money in my pocket and the older boys comin round, I didn't have much time for school anymore. I barely graduated.

Then Kane and the boat yard and learning a trade, and I

liked working with my hands—respecting the wood—keeping the tools sharp and the sense of accomplishment."

She turned to me and folded her arms. "You getting caught up? You see how I really don't have a lot, and what I do have means a lot? We're about to the part where the guy I'm getting close to lets my dogs out, and Black Dog gets killed, and White Dog and I get into my truck and just drive around for a couple hours."

I started up out of the chair. "June—"

Her hand, and just the right pressure on my shoulder as she and White Dog passed, and I dropped back into the chair. "Alone, James. I'm not interested in anything you have to say right now, and I have some shit to sort."

The front latch clicked shut.

VENICE, CA, 2015

They catch many of us by surprise, the parochial realities of others. Here, in gentrifying Venice, a construction site traffic guard was shot in broad daylight last year—shot twice and killed. There were plenty of witnesses—the killer, living his reality, in basketball shorts and a Hannibal Lecter mask. The victim in his orange safety vest, a long-time gang member, was cleaning up some equipment at the end of the day.

I know. You'll say, "But that was gang-related." Correct. But doesn't the brazen nature of it give you pause? That someone would think that a logical path of action? Okay, okay. Regarding domestic violence, consider this from an analysis of domestic violence-related homicides in Los Angeles County—

"Intimate partner violence (IPV)"—yep, IPV—"continues to be a prevalent public health issue. Recent estimates report that one in five women and one in ten men in the United States have sustained severe"—severe—"physical violence from an intimate partner over their lifetime with the most severe physical consequence of death. In the United States, over half of all females murdered (55.3%) are killed by a current or former intimate partner. Rates of female homicide do show some variation by decedent race and ethnicity. Non-Hispanic black and American Indian/Alaska Native women experience the highest rates (4.4 and 4.3 per 100,000 population) compared to their Hispanic, white, and Asian and Pacific Islander counterparts (1.8, 1.5 and 1.2 per 100,000 population) respectively."

MARYLAND, 1989

"Who would do something like that?" Tom said. "Black Dog. Damn freak."

Prairie lowered his ax and straightened up. "Hate to say, but more than one of em out there, Tomboy. Whole frigging world full. It's why we're here keeping it simple, staying away from all the crazy stuff. Now it's found us."

Grief and the chill of pissed-off still at her hard edges, June glanced at me, then away—there was something she was keeping from us. As much as I had wanted to help, June wouldn't let me. She'd dug Black Dog's grave alone, and it wasn't until a week later that she allowed me to build a rail fence around it. She was warming to me a little at a time.

In one hand, she held a razor-sharp, long-handled chisel. In the other, her handmade wooden mallet. She'd been carving an oak tenon. The craftsmanship—it looked like a gleaming, glass-surfaced watch part. When our foreman, John Boy, was around, he frequently had to remind June that we weren't building a boat—that we were building a tobacco barn, and a barn didn't have to hold water, and it was okay if it was drafty—in fact, tobacco barns are supposed to be drafty. Way different working around June now. It was tangled up for a number of reasons. One, we might, or might not, be a thing. I'd figured it out—that it was I who had been betrayed, abandoned, and I had been granted a new start. The hurt was still there, but so was the hope. I was certainly reborn, my senses piqued—her voice, the touch of her hand, her smells—triggers. My colors brighter and the sounds off the bay and through the forest in soaring harmony. I wanted to be back on that beach every night. And, we'd had our honeymoon for Chrissake. I was still limping, and I never thought a guy could have a sore ass from straight sex. Two, Black Dog's gone, and it was totally my fault. Three, it might have been Kane—that he's out of jail and was in her driveway that night is what June thinks.

10

SIN, CONFESS, KNEEL

"It's Kane. I either fight hard, run hard, or I'm screwed," she said. She was finishing up her work on an oak tenon with a bullnose plane—perfecting the surfaces so they'd slide easily into the mortise when the time came.

"What's with this guy?" Tom said from across the site.

"It was a priest threw him over the edge—middle school," June said. "Sin, confess, kneel—sin, confess, kneel. Until it was just too much sinning and kneeling, and Kane goes berserk and breaks his hand on the guy's face. From then on, no one was safe. He hated everyone. They put him away for a while. Rehabilitation. That just made it worse. When he got out, he came home and burned their house down. He ended up in the care of the state."

"Damn."

She set the plane aside, undid the heavy steel clamp holding the oak in place and laid the stud on the stack. "Yeah, so we're both orphans. He caught me reading *The Bible*, once." She shook her head. "That wasn't good. What's that look? What are you thinking, James?"

"Or it's the weirdo next door," I said.

"Down at the cove? That guy? Hee-haw, white bread rodent with yellow fingernails and shit stains down his pants? You think he got a hand on Black Dog?"

"Maybe Kane," I said.

"Yeah, maybe Kane."

The job site was a hundred yards from June's cottage. A crew of five, we showed up on bicycles and rusted-out Toyota trucks each morning ten minutes on either side of seven. The crew—John Boy was laid up at home, Tom, Prairie Dog, June and me. Personal things and tools we carried in backpacks, plastic buckets and long, narrow, shoulder-strapped wooden boxes. In the cool, moist shadows of those mornings, we took the time we needed. We spent nearly the first hour in the long, three-sided work shed easing our tools from their soft leather pouches and sharpening with files and whetstones—the only other sounds being wind through the surrounding forest, birds and lapping waves. It was a healing time for the tools and us—bringing the blades back to perfection and easing ourselves into a new day. Chisels and plane blades ground to fifteen degrees, broad axes and adzes at somewhere thereabouts. That and setting up our workspaces, depending on what lay ahead—removing bark, cutting lengths, splitting logs, shaving clapboard siding and carving beams, mortises and tenons.

Months later, when the white oak and iron-hard locust was prepared, there would be the digging of trenches and holes to sink some of that wood into. And how would the seventeenth century colonists get half-ton white oak beams into the air spanning posts on either side of a barn? We know they didn't use draft animals, which roamed wild in and around their settlement. So Prairie was tasked with building two wooden A-frame cranes operating with a series of wooden blocks (pulleys) and tackle (ropes)—presumably from the *Ark* and the smaller *Dove*, the ships on which the colonists sailed. One crane by design was smaller than the other, and for reasons known only to him, he referred to them as "bates." The minor and the master. Taut ropes and thousand-pound beams, balance was of primary concern, but the blocks and tackle did the heavy lifting. When it came time to plant the barn posts, on which the beams were to sit, three-to-four feet deep in the soil, we intended to cheat and bring in a backhoe auger.

11

OUR LIVES CHANGED

L ittle Prair and big Tom pulled T-shirts over tans and sweat to truck over to the college for lunch.

"You guys coming?" Prairie said.

"Nah, gonna eat here," I said. June was already a hundred yards away in her cottage kitchen.

"See ya in an hour, then," Prairie called. They tumbled the truck through the weeds and up the drive.

The day after that awful day we found Black Dog, I moved my bike and sleeping bag to June's cottage. I was responsible. I'd sleep in the side room in the name of security—two heads, two sets of eyes. Sure, we'd had that first circumstantial romp, but we agreed we'd sleep and shower separately, step at a time, take it slow until we figured who or what we were. That lasted about an hour.

Our lives changed. June's boiler glowed red. Her engine raced on tortured tracks, and I was sucked beneath her wheels. Mornings we rocked. Noons we rolled. What had once been our work and daily chores was now a series of healing respites— pauses between rounds of rail-splitting sex. It was carnal, pagan and beyond consent—it was coal-fed and oxygen-fueled. We consumed each other—her eyes, my ears, her toes, and we lay twisted in sheets soaked with salt lemon sweat. That, and we kept White Dog on a shorter leash.

"You think Kane was really here?"

"You're shitting me, right, James?"

I didn't know Kane. I had him pegged like the motivation-challenged, bad-choice locals up the road at our watering hole. Just then, I couldn't grasp what she knew as unavoidable.

12

SEVENTEENTH-CENTURY
WOUNDS

"Ah, shit!" I dropped the broad ax, fell to my side and grabbed my shin. "Tom, First Aid!"

He left his blade stuck in a log and charged for the cottage as he had for scrambling quarterbacks—a college bowl defensive end. By the time he returned with the gauze patch and peroxide, June held my leg elevated and offered soft words of humor and consolation. "Your way of calling it a day, James? Too hot out here for this cultured white man? No worries, sugar, I'll finish picking your row."

Prairie held his shirt over me for shade.

"We're going to need more than that Tomboy," I said from the ground.

He took a quick glance at the gaping slice in my shin. "Damn, be right back." He shot to the house.

Tom poured most of the bottle into the wound, wrapped it, and my lights were starting to dim. June and Tom brushed me off and helped me into the truck. Prairie pulled his shirt on, jumped in behind the wheel, slammed the door, handed me a joint, and we were off to the county med center. "You okay? I mean, of course you're not. Am I driving too fast? Hate to say, but the seatbelts don't work. I can slow down, but we gotta get you there soon." Prairie worried.

The job had to be getting heavy for Prair. He was the one who found Tom unconscious in the woods a couple months ago. The sprung tree Tom was felling had kicked up and felled him in the process, and no one knows how long he lay there bleeding. Prair saved Tom's life, as far as anyone could tell.

"Yeah, I'm okay. I'm just kinda embarrassed that—Ow!" The truck bounced.

"Sorry, really bad piece of road. Here. Here's some water." Prair reached between his ankles and pulled a cloudy half-gallon jug from six inches of paper, plastic and crushed twelve-ounce cans.

I took a swig. "Gack! Is this your bathwater?"

"No, sorry, it's fresh. Filled it this morning. Just gets warm in the truck. There's cookies in the glove box. Oreos."

At the med center, Prairie hovered like I was his favorite uncle. He helped me into the lobby, we met the admitting nurse, he explained what had happened, propped me in the wheelchair, filled out my forms and wrung his hands and pouted when asked to wait in the lobby. The doors to the emergency room whooshed shut. Sweet Prair.

We each had our turn at the hospital—Prairie's hand was healing nicely, and the adz nick high on the top of June's foot showed just a raised, light scar. Our foreman, John, was convalescing, and Tom was off the ice and anti-inflammatories and back in the game. Seventeenth-century wounds, twentieth-century medicine.

I was in and out the same day—irrigation, thirty-two stitches, a tetanus shot, bandage and crutches. It was a nice sharp blade, and in the humid, ninety-degree after-lunch delirium, I'd shaved a slice off the bone. The doc said to go lightly for a week, then semi-light for the next two. In the seventeenth century, I'd have been dead in days.

I spent most hours on June's little porch, leg propped, June's fresh pitcher of sweet tea with a book and White Dog snoozing—a big empty space, there on the floor next to him, where Black Dog should have been. Day three I broke out a pad of paper, brushes and my old watercolors. It had been a while since I'd turned my back on my passion to make a living. But I dropped right back into the joy that painting brought. The total immersion in the moment, the looking and actually seeing the brilliance of the bay in front of me, the colors nearly hidden in the clouds.

When the feeling of being left out got to me, I'd make my way out the lane and over to the site to chat with the crew as they worked—the accurate ax strikes, the intense light shimmering off sweat on shoulders and brows there at the edge of the forest. Those weeks, Prairie sat in the shade of a chestnut tree feathering the ends of clapboard siding with a draw knife. Not wanting to overstay my welcome, I'd return to the cottage and up the one shallow step to the porch. And, "Feeling left out?" Yeah, that had always weighed on me as a kid. Seemed that I was the only one on the block who wasn't related—every way I turned I was outnumbered by cousins, and I didn't stand a chance. That changed in the Marines where I was a critical part of a rifle squad—I had three backs to watch, and three guys had mine. Being on this crew was the first I'd felt that sense of belonging and mission since then.

13

ROCKABILLY AT THE BOATHOUSE

F riday night was happy hour, and the inseparable boys had left the jobsite early in Prairie's truck and returned to June's cottage with a few sixers. June prepared plates of veggies and hummus. Prairie, who ate every five minutes and never gained an ounce, and Tom, stuck to the jerky and chips. We hung out with laughs and song, and I was struck by how we could be work-chatting forty hours a week and still find something new to laugh at over beers Friday nights.

"So," Tom said, "Did I tell you about my trip to Scotland?"

"When were you in Scotland?" June said.

"College, summer between junior-senior years. I wouldn't be playing my last year cause of the injury, so I took the time." He popped a beer open with his knife.

"And?" she said.

"Nothing, really. Just wondered if I told you." He took a swig.

"What happened in Scotland, Tom?"

"Not a lot. Not a lot going on there. Sun doesn't shine much, but the countryside is lush green hills, and the place is calm—narrow lanes, old farms, stone fences, and the sky rolls right on down to the sea. Castles—they have castles."

"And?"

"So I met this guy in a pub. The owner, actually. Just him and me, there at the bar—middle of the day—middle of the damp cold day. There's good reason they wear wool." Tom took another swig and studied the label on the bottle.

"And?"

"I told him how I liked his place—the heavy post and beam construction, the fire in the big stone fireplace, the hand-rubbed wood bar. He said he built it himself." Tom took on a Scottish brogue. "'Built it maself I did, with ma own hands. Felled the trees, loaded em onto the wagon, hitched the horse, hauled em to the mill and had em cut to lumber.' He slapped the bar. 'But do they call ma Angus the Pub Builder? Noooo.' Then the guy points out the window and across the narrow lane. 'Ya see that wee boat anchored there on the loch? I sail that wee boat to the other side once a week and bring back supplies for ma pub and mail for the village. Been doin it for years. But do they call ma Angus the Loch Sailor? Noooo.' He pointed the other direction. 'The road you came in on, o'er the hill and through the glen. I broke ma back as I cleared the rocks, slashed the bush and felled the trees. And do they call ma Angus the Road Builder? Noooo . . . But you fuck one goat!'"

Stares and grins.

"Rockabilly at The Boat House tonight," Tom threw out.

"They charge a cover?" Prairie said.

"Three bucks, but that includes your first drink."

"Well then."

"You coming?" Tom asked June.

She glanced my way. "Hell right."

"You?" Tom looked to me.

"No. You kids run off and have fun. Just be careful, appoint a DD, and always use a condom. The door will be open. Mother and I won't wait up."

They rummaged around for the next thirty minutes, bagged empties into black plastic and set the bag outside of the kitchen door. They opened the curtain beneath the kitchen sink and stashed the bong. Wrapped in towels and barefooting out the back door and a few feet over to the river bank, they took quick turns in the outdoor shower. I sat in the "big" room in June's only inside chair, leg braced and sipped cheap whiskey. Her door cracked open, I could see her deciding on scarves and bracelets.

I hopped into the tiny bedroom, oil lamps aglow, and she turned from the mirror. Her long rough hands found the sides of my face. "Have I said I think I love you?" she said.

"Not in those words."

"I do."

"The ring please?"

She turned back to the mirror.

"Sorry. I'm getting in pretty deep, too—really deep," I said. "It's just, like, so soon. Sometimes I think maybe we ought to take a step back. I'm not sure I should fall so hard right now—rebound on the fly, and all."

"You're allowed to love. We can have this between us," she said.

"What would Jesus do?"

She turned to me. Her eyes wet. "You're weird, James. There's some kind of Martian mojo about you. Most of it's lovely."

"Most."

"Yeah, the sensitivity, the listening, the caring."

"Martian?" I said.

"Yeah, that's the part that needs work."

"Like?"

"Like I don't know. Like the not squaring up, the not fully connecting—the not just going all in with me. Hell, I don't know. Forget it. We all need work," she said.

"I been workin on the night moves—tryin to make some front-page drive-in news."

She brushed past. "Lock the door, Mister Seger, and don't let White Dog out."

14

JUNE'S INSIDE CHAIR

M an, I was tired. They were gone. I fed White Dog and let him out. I stood propped against the kitchen doorway until he came back in. I bolted the door, turned off the local FM, poured another whiskey, snuffed the lamps and collapsed into June's chair. It was an elegant-if-sagging, fan-backed wicker that once held a regal post in a hotel lobby in Atlantic City. On the side table, she had a small, framed photo of the chair from back in the day. What looked to be nine-or-ten-year-old black girl sat on the edge of the chair, hands in her lap in a pressed, short sleeve cotton dress and crossed laced anklets. When June came across the chair a couple years ago, it was on the street with a lot of other discarded stuff including the photo. She threw the wicker into the back of her truck, and here it is.

The whiskey took the edge off the exposure, the vulnerability, the un words—unfinished, unworthy and, in this case, unable. It also amped up the selfishness, the self-pity, the whoa-the-fuck-is-me, all alone and unloved. Meanwhile, June was the dance fever Belle of the Rockabilly Ball.

The pitch dark and quiet were perfect but for the ticking, gurgling appliance. I pulled up out of the chair, slid a hand behind the fridge to the house's only receptacle and unplugged the sonofabitch. Back in the chair, I rested my leg on the table. All was still, and White Dog slept. I followed.

15

LARRY HOLMES AT THE BOATHOUSE

R umors spread through this part of the county with the mail and Jolee Maye Heard, the newest mail carrier working out of Leonardtown. According to June, Jolee Maye had run a nail salon there on Main Street until her headaches and wheezing got so bad from all the acetone, and her doctor told her to get out of the business or she'd be dead in a year. Turned out the post office was hiring, and Jolee Maye had a clean driving record. In addition, she was close friends with one of the postal clerks—she'd been doing her nails for years—typically two contrasting pearlescent tones—a deep purple with whipped cream tips and a clear metallic top coat. So, Jolee Maye was a fit. She'd probably applied for the job thinking that it was somewhat like winning big on *Jeopardy*—big bucks, a uniform, and now she was somebody. But, on her first month behind the wheel of her little truck, she likely realized she had hit the double bonus round. She was pretty much privy to everyone's business. Recently divorced, fifty-seven-year-old Mary Ellen Jacobs was carrying on regular, and one might guess steamy, correspondence with a man named Deaver in

Pensacola, Florida. Eldon Hawksworthy, bachelor and church deacon, got weekly deliveries of what sure looked like video tapes—and they might well be porn—wrapped in plain brown paper from a Chicago address, and Miss Polly, tight-gray-bunned baroness of one of the small hamlets on Jolee Maye's route, received packages from a leather goods store in San Francisco. What a gold mine of red-hot-peppered-and-slathered-in-syrup speculation Jolee Maye had to share.

The rumor going around this day was that Larry Holmes would be stopping in at The Boat House tonight—that Jolee Maye had seen the former heavyweight champ and Mrs. Holmes pulled over at the mailbox by the Hardwick pasture, and they were petting the sheep. She said the champ was a gentle, funny man and that his wife, a slender woman, had the kindest and most genuine smile. She said they'd come out to enjoy the Chesapeake countryside and had been fishing on the bay and were trying to decide if they should drive home today or spend the night here in Maryland. Jolee Maye had recommended The Boat House for its homemade clam chowders—white and red—if they intended on sticking around, and the champ said it sounded like as good a reason as any, and they might just do that. This all being the God's truth, and she had the champ's autograph to prove it.

The road crew, oystermen, sheriff's deputies and retirees who were at The Boat House for the Friday Poor Man's Lobster Lunch Special—boiled haddock chunks broiled in butter, baked beans and coleslaw, $4.95—would be all abuzz, and many still hanging around, when the band moved in to set up at five.

.   .   .

Black instrument cases piled onto the small stage, a micro soundboard, wool rug and their own lights, the band—local boys and a pearl-buttoned, mostly unbuttoned round blond woman from Baltimore—traveled in a cool, unrestored Air Stream pulled by a jacked-up Dodge van parked at the side of the building. They settled in, performed sound checks and disappeared into the trailer for the next couple hours. At eight, they took the stage.

Tom, June and Prairie sat on oft-repaired arrowback chairs at a round table front and center. It was all worn-out chairs and lopsided tables on a raw wood floor at The Boat House. June was primed and tapping her chrome-toed cowboy boots as the band opened up.

16
FOOTSTEPS IN THE DARK

I woke in the chair to crunching gravel in the drive. June? Footsteps through the weeds veered off to the side of the house, then behind me and onto the back porch. It wasn't June.

Was it locked? I'd bolted the front, but the back?

White Dog lay in place on the rug building a low, quiet growl. Why wasn't he going nuts? If I stayed still in the half-moon dark, chances were that whoever peered in through the glass wouldn't see me. It was the best I could do—I sure as hell wasn't going to run. They tried the latch. It held. Then again. Quiet.

Goddamn inbred local. Probably one of the vitamin-starved cove rats. They're crazy enough to try to rob the place with me in it.

I did my inventory of the cottage—flashlight on the shelf by the stove, June's dad's Louisville Slugger by the kitchen door, knives on the magnet over the sink. That was about it. Whoever it was moved off the back porch and down to the water. The dinghy scraped and rocked. They were taking her boat? Now, a sharp blow to hard, hollow wood. Water lapped the shore. Footsteps back up alongside the house. They stopped in the drive. My nerves peaked as they came back down and tried the kitchen door. Back to the drive, there was some poking around at the trucks—what sounded like June's door creak—a *clink* of steel. Then, a couple minutes of silence, swishing through the weeds and away.

I waited. Listened at full volume. I may have heard a car start up out at the road, maybe not. Quiet. I pushed up out of the chair, pulled a crutch from the wall and went slow to the door. White Dog hadn't moved. I slid the bolt, and the door swung wide. Nothing. Not a sound. I grabbed the other crutch, closed the door and went down to the water. I expected to see her boat sunk in the shallows. It wasn't. A boning knife was driven into one of the wooden seats. Impaled there was a photo of a young June, maybe seven years old. Scrawled across it, "I saw you dance."

STABBED IN THE FACE

That night, I gotta believe The Boat House would be buzzing with good vibes. Word would have spread for thirty miles that The Champ might show up—would show up. Word was probably that he was already there by the time Jolee Maye returned to Leonardtown. Nights like that, The Boat House was packed and overflowed into the dirt lot.

It was a smoking band that played classic and contemporary covers, from Mack Rice's *Mustang Sally* to Tyler and Hamilton's *Janie's Got a Gun*. Sweet Prairie would dance with June towering over him nearly every number, and they'd meet back at the bar for refills, and I wasn't there, and weren't they just having a grand old time. Tom? Lost in the crowd. Now and again, they'd hear his banshee yelp and see his bald, sweat-glistened head above the crowd as he came off his feet. Sometime this night, June would find herself whisked into a clapping circle formed around Tom in his bibs and his Saint Vitus chicken-dance moves, and Prairie laughing to tears as June faced Tom and, just three feet apart, mirrored his every spaz.

. . .

By midnight, the crowd had pretty much given up on The Champ. So plans change. Lots of responsibility being The Champ. Maybe he got called back to his home in Pennsylvania, a family matter. Maybe his wife had a change of heart at the last minute and called it off. Whatever. They loved The Champ, but all was not lost, not by a long shot. This night was one helluva time.

There was no mistaking who was coming down the drive. They were in high spirits and having a fractured go at *Mustang Sally* with June vocally thrubbing the bass line. I hopped to the door, pulled the bolt and lit a few lamps as they tumbled out of the truck and weaved arm-in-arm across the property. They clattered into the kitchen.

"Hey there, Jim-Jiminy," June said in passing. "No champ, but a good show just the same. Goin to bed, y'all. G'night." She was probably asleep before she hit the water.

"No champ?" I said.

"Hate to say," Prairie said. "Champ had a family matter." He was at the cupboard, "Any cookies?"

Tom slumped in the chair, "Where's that whiskey, Jimbo? Being DD is trying."

I handed him the bottle then grabbed the rucksack by the back door. I pulled the knife and photo. "Look at this."

"Huh, yeah? So, what am I looking at?" Tom turned the knife in his hand.

Prairie crowded in.

"Someone pinned this picture to June's boat with that knife," I said.

"Damn, right in the face," Tom said.

"It was Kane saw her dance," Prairie said.

"Not so sure, Prair. June said he's in jail." I said.

"Who else has a picture of June? I'm not liking this," Prairie said. "*Whoever* it was also saw *me* dance."

"Okay, so this is pretty goddamn dramatic, right? So can we not scare the hell outta June right away? I'll find out where Kane is, then we'll see. Maybe the three of us have to have a talk with the bastard. What do you think?" I said.

"Damn, right in the face."

18

WE GOTTA TELL JUNE

Tom and Prairie Dog didn't like it. They held that June was going to be mighty pissed if she found out we were hiding things from her. But they agreed to keep quiet about the photo and the knife and, laying it all at my feet, said they would claim total ignorance at the reckoning. After they left that night, I bundled the photo and knife in a rag and dropped the wad down behind the fridge.

"Supply run, James!"

The sun tore through the kitchen. June had run a few miles with White Dog, they'd gone for a swim, and she was at the kitchen door fresh as a turnip when I woke.

"What do you need from Leonardtown?" she called back into the house.

"Aspirin," I said over the screaming between my eyes.

"Poor sugar. Drawer next to the sink. See ya in a few."

She and White Dog were in the truck and out the drive by the time I found the life-saving tablets.

The outdoor shower did wonders at times like this. Standing along the river, naked in God's great nature, bandaged leg duct taped in a garbage bag, morning light slipping sideways through the leaves, and I sudsed with June's homemade soap. New day, right? A time to put things in order, to unscramble this Black Dog-Kane thing, and get back to keeping it simple. Steaming jets raked scalding trails from head-to-foot. Baptism.

I single-crutched out the drive to the road. It was five minutes until a sun-leathered oysterman pulled his truck over, and I hopped a ride to the college. It was just another fifty yards to the café for coffee, toast and scrambled eggs on a paper plate with a plastic fork. The place was empty like the rest of the campus. Bikes tangled in racks, red plastic cups strewn beneath some of the trees, and in the central pond, a half-submerged Styrofoam cooler was making its way to the opposite shore. I guessed the students were out later than we were.

"Where's your buddies today?" the youngest food worker asked. Petite, tight pink uniform, cat eyes and what was probably long black hair under that net.

"Sleeping in. Saturday, you know?"

She hardly looked at the steam table as she scooped the eggs onto my plate. "What's that little one's name? The one with the fuzzy hair."

"That's Prairie Dog."

"Kinda cute. Tight shorts, all tan, pretty eyes. Like to get that one alone sometime."

"I'll tell him you said so."

"Yeah, do that." She winked. "And tell him I'm in my own place, no kids and divorced. I'm off at five."

The eggs and coffee were welcome, but incidental. This

trip had been to use the payphone outside the student union, and the call was productive. Saturday morning at the boat yard, Campbell, the owner himself, answered. Kane was out of jail. He'd come back to the yard, picked up his tools, and he hadn't seen him since.

I dropped another couple quarters, and Tom answered from sleep.

"I'm at the college. Can you get over here and bring Prair?" I said.

"Man, it's just turning noon. Later, okay?"

"We have to talk, and I need a ride. I think Kane's here."

I had given up hope, figured he'd rolled over and gone back to sleep when Tom came into the café. He was white.

"You look awful, man. What'd you do after you left June's last night?" I said.

He dropped into a chair across from me. "I just now stopped by for Prair. Deputy's at his place. Prair's in the hospital, damn near dead."

"What? No way."

"Last night. Bridge at the bottom of the hill. Just hit the bridge. Hell, I don't know. The truck's demolished. Must have hit full speed," Tom said.

"So how bad?"

"Coma."

"Prair," I said.

Tom's arms hung limp at his sides. "His parents are flying in from Montana."

Out of words, we both stared into my cup the next few seconds. We were young and immortal. Cuts, scrapes, wrong turns, we'd always bounce back, right? The next scene was supposed to be Prair and the steam table woman in her own place, no kids and divorced.

"Run me down to June's," I said.

"Yeah, we gotta tell June."

We crawled the truck down her drive. June appeared in the open doorway holding the knife bundle.

Tom shut off the motor. "Damn," under his breath.

"The refrigerator was unplugged," she called. "When I slid it out to plug it in, I found this. Belong to anyone I know?"

We left the truck doors open and stepped into the hottest part of the day.

"Damn."

The doorway was narrow and narrower, now, with June in it. We avoided her eyes as we slid past, but I felt her heat.

"Speak, James."

I propped my crutch in the corner and sank to the floor. Tom leaned, arms extended, hands on each side of the window and stared out at the bay. So it was at my feet.

"Prairie Dog's in the hospital, in a coma," I said.

"Bullshit."

"He is," Tom said to the window.

She lowered the knife to the side table. "What happened?"

"Lost control at the bottom of Tobacco Hill. Hit the bridge," Tom said.

"Lost control? He drives ten miles an hour when he drinks."

"Hit full speed," Tom said.

"Is he—what do they think?"

"It's not good. Pretty busted up."

June sank to the floor and stared at me. I let out a long

breath and took another. This was it. "It's Kane, June. He's out of jail—quit the boatyard."

She got to her feet and joined Tom's stare at the bay. Behind us, the refrigerator ticked.

Her voice unsteady, "How long . . .? How long have you known, James?"

"This morning. I called the boatyard, talked to Campbell. I found the knife and picture last night—stuck to your boat. I hid them so you wouldn't get freaked—until I found out where Kane was."

Her breathing wound up slowly, gained its strength, paused and cut loose. "He was here last night!" She turned to me. "At The Boat House and at this house. My house, goddamn it! You can't be keeping this from me! I knew it was Kane since Black Dog. Now Prairie. You're fucking with something you don't know!"

"What's Prairie have to do with it?" Tom said.

"I think someone—Kane—was messing with Prairie's truck last night," I said.

"Why?" Tom said.

"Because he saw Prairie dance with me all night," she said. "He thinks Prair's my new roll. It's my truck he should have screwed with!"

"June, he's a man like anyone else. He can be stopped," I said.

"I wish."

"So we go to the sheriff." Tom said.

"Yeah, it's time," I said.

"Won't help," she said. "Not saying we shouldn't, but I got issues with the law, and Kane's going to continue to destroy everything around me, then me. He's playing with me, and *that's* why he didn't do my truck. He's sick, and when he gets pissed he goes balls out, and this possessive shit is nothing new with him. When they were kids, his little brother took his bike without asking. He sliced off the end of the kid's finger in the middle of the night."

"Damn," Tom whispered.

"Cops don't bother Kane. They'll just slow him down. He's patient and smart. He'll wait until they're distracted. I have to leave."

"You have issues with the law?" I said.

She turned back to the window and the distant horizon.

"His own brother," Tom said.

19

BLOOD AND WATER

The three of us were a crowd in June's little kitchen. "How long are you going to hide? You said Kane's patient about punishment," I said.

"As long as I have to. I'm his new scab, James. I have to go where he thinks I won't. Leave no signs."

"So that'd be where? When?"

She stared at me, turned and went into her room.

"Damn," Tom whispered.

"Yeah, this project's just been gutted—Prair in the hospital, John Boy still laid-up at home, June and me gone. That leaves you, Tom."

"You're going, too?" he said.

I would have been happy staying—the fresh mornings by the bay, bringing the tools back to life and clearing our heads—the work, the sense of accomplishment, the banter, the weekends at The Boat House, tender moments, and love under the stars and in the bay and nearly drowning with the most amazing woman I'd ever known. I would have been happy staying if any of that was. "Maybe headed west, but don't quote me on that."

"You hooked, Jimbo?"

What? Was I? Wasn't I a free agent? Yeah, but this feeling with her . . . "Nah, I'm just going with her for soul support—help with the driving, a shoulder to cry on."

"You guys want a wing man?"

"Tom, this project—you love it. Hell, I love it."

"It's whackin wood. It's what we do. We can do that anywhere—all of us, including Prair, soon as he gets better."

I held my hand up, "Give me a minute."

I went into her room. Her back to me, she jammed socks and underwear into a pack. "Right now? You're leaving already?" I said.

She turned—there were tears—and she was shaking. She sniffed. "This is fucking serious like I said. You have no idea." She turned back to packing.

"June." I gently grabbed both of her shoulders.

"Don't, James. And give me room cause I may be sick."

I stepped back. "We're going with you—Tom and me."

Her packing slowed, then sped up. "No."

"We got your back, June. We're going."

She lowered the pack, turned and pushed me out to the front room. She scanned us back and forth and stopped at Tom. "You don't need this in your life, Tom. And what about Prairie? He's like your twin. I have to leave. You don't."

"I'll be back for him," Tom said.

"It's your job, your livelihood, and you love it here," she said.

"Blood and water," he said.

She turned her focus back to me for a few beats, exhausted a long breath and gave in. "Get busy. I'm outta here in the hour." She spun back to her room.

"I have to get my stuff, get to the bank, stop by the hospital. Where shall I meet you guys?" Tom said.

"The bridge in an hour. Pack light, leave most," she called.

Tom was parked on the dirt shoulder on the other side of the concrete bridge. June slowed, and there it was—one side of the bridge and the road surface crumbled and streaked with Prair's faded blue paint. There were damp stains, black oil, coolant, and one I tried not to see. We drifted across the solemn surface, and I watched from the passenger door mirror as Tom pulled onto the road behind. June and I hadn't spoken since we left the cottage.

"Where're you thinking?" I said.

"North."

"How far?"

"Somewhere with more soul, where I'm not so obvious—DC, Baltimore, maybe. I'll start there. Then who knows. San Francisco. Hell, maybe Alaska."

She kept it at fifty—Tom never drove over fifty. We didn't talk for the next hour-and-a-half—White Dog between us—and, from the pressure in the cab, I could tell June's headache was as big as mine. Were we really doing this? Just packing up and gone? The jobsite was going to be empty tomorrow and John Boy still healing at home and left holding the bag. The project would be delayed until he could find our replacements. None of us were huge on doing this to John. He was the dad among us—the guy who had hired us partly for our skills, but, as importantly, he'd said, "Because you're creative types, and we're going to have to make some of this construction up as we go." Now, though, in the measure of things, and her thinking this was life and death, what could we do but leave with June? I'd call in to the office at Annapolis on Monday and inform

them of the sudden illness in my family and hope they'd understand that Tom and June had driven me home to Pennsylvania.
If Kane was looking for us, that would throw him off. And did I
believe he'd be looking for us? If it was him, hadn't he done
enough? Nose to the windshield, both hands high on the wheel,
Tom shadowed us without a clue as to where we were going.

We'd set out on a meandering series of two-lanes with little
traffic and spotted with feral fields, slumped bungalows and
small billboards promoting used tire stores. But it wasn't long
until we were sucked back into the buzzing gravity surrounding
every major city as we passed cloned exits with the same gas
stations, same big box stores, same fast food, and we were
passed by young "A" types in late-model Euro sedans doing
nearly twice our speed. It was going to take a while to acclimate
to this.

Strung out and inside the beltway, we pulled up to a forlorn
motor inn on the southeast border of the nation's capital. We
dropped our packs into two cheap rooms—one canned-peas
green, one puke-orange. June's and mine looked like someone
had been murdered on the sofa. White dog sniffed it and chose
the bed. We locked him in, and the three of us went across four
lanes for pizza and beer.

Tom poured three from the pitcher and lifted his glass, "To
Prairie."

"To Prairie," we said.

He squeezed foam from his mustache, smoothed his beard
and said, "Tomorrow, June? Then what?"

She leaned back in the corner of the booth, pulled off her
bandana, fanned out her hair and deep scratched her head with
both hands. "Tomorrow, we go downtown and get lost in all the
hustle and noise. We find a cheap place to live, find work and
build a stash for the next move."

VENICE, CA, 2015

Erskine came over this morning. Early. It's always about him, my impulsive neighbor. He knows I like my space, waking up slow, time to read some full-of-itself novel or what's new-and-so-goddamn-interesting in *The New Yorker*. He burst in, all the same, saluted, whirred past and out to the kitchen.

"Good, you have coffee. Where's the sugar? Last time you had sugar out here."

Drawers slammed, spoons rattled.

"If you must have sugar in my coffee, you could have brought some with you," I called from the miniature living room.

"Everyone has sugar. Where's yours?"

"I think there's some honey out there somewhere—not that I'd recommend it."

"Hah! Found it."

"Honey?"

"Yes dear?"

He came in, plowed aside a clutter of magazines and parked his seventy-something, skinny ass on the loveseat.

"Your cup's going to leave a ring on that table," I said over the top of my glasses.

"Just fattening your collection, Jimmy."

"You're breaking my solitude because?"

"Taxes. I've been doing mine and got to thinking about where all the money goes—graft, payola, assassinations. I've seen it all, Jimmy. From inside, The Company."

"You were CIA?" I said.

"Dark Ops, and that doesn't leave this room."

"Erskine, weren't you in kitchen gadgets?"

"A beard."

I let it slide. "I guess some of the money goes to folks like us —the old, the lame and the lazy," I said.

"I'm still in pretty good shape, not like when I was twenty, but not bad. I can still crank out the push-ups. Watch this." He lifted his cup to move the table aside.

"No, never mind. I get it."

"No brag, just fact." He settled back into the cushions.

This was it, the event of the day, the thing that would wear me out and send me off to a nap right after an early lunch of chicken soup and a chunk of peasant bread. Mint chip ice cream with Christiane Amanpour and her guests. Then out to the box. Ah, sunshine, ah, clouds, ah, whatever. Riffle through the bills and junk mail, and back to the house. Nap, beer, more soup, bed, then start again tomorrow. One live Erskine event a day is about all I'm good for—a single tasker. I wish he'd not come barging in as he does, and surely not as frequently—show some respect for my space. How had I become this surrendered hermit? I've taken personality tests plenty of times. Always came out a healthy extrovert, creative type, uphill and into the wind.

"You see what's movin in across the street?" he said.

"No."

"Chinese. More Chinese movin in everyday if ya get what I'm saying."

"I don't believe I do."

"Think about it. Newest blue water navy in the world. And to go where?"

"Here?" I said.

"Bingo."

"Venice. The Chinese want to come to Venice?"

"You got it—Venice, Santa Monica, Inglewood, Long Beach, Pasadena. Not Beverly Hills. Japanese in Beverly Hills

—they hate each other. Check my facts. They're moving in faster than the Mexicans. You see what's happening with the food trucks?"

"Chinese?" I said.

"Dim sum on every corner. It's all changing as we speak. Try and find a taco truck."

Last month it was the Russians. Borscht and pirozhki trucks on every corner, money laundering, dealing only in cash. I put my book aside, the moment lost, and went out to the kitchen as he began reeling off another one.

"So, like I was about to say, we're on The President's plane and he brings up the recent assassinations and—"

"Erskine, more coffee?" I called.

"Sure, thanks. So The President asks me to close his office door so we can have a little privacy and—"

"I'll be right back. Gotta walk down to the store. I'm out of filters."

"Yeah, right—okay. So pick me up a pack of those morning buns while you're there, extra icing, no raisins. That and one of those jumbo double packs of toilet paper. Two ply."

I don't like being on the sidewalks this time of day. Kids on bikes, skateboards, walking, running in droves, to public, private and Catholic schools. They come at me from every direction—one's Chinese. I'm invisible as they brush by. Women talk about when they became invisible. How, up to a certain age, whenever they walked into a bar, every head turned and stayed turned. Then came that day when they walked in, every head turned, then turned back as though thinking, huh, thought I heard something. Men all become the same old man—the generic, baggy-assed, thrift-store-flannel guy.

I wonder if I'll ever know Erskine. We're friends, of sorts—familiar, anyway. Neighbors. But I haven't a goddamn clue who he really is. I once told him I think I have a child somewhere. I wonder if he remembers.

20

THE ONE-ARMED PRICK

WASHINGTON, DC, 1989

Deep on Eighth Street SE was Charlie's Place. On one side of the bar was a dry cleaner, on the other a liquor store, and, looking back up toward the higher-rent Pennsylvania Avenue, the shops, bars and restaurants improved measurably with each block. There was a sputtering green Rolling Rock sign in the nicotine and fly-specked window and a ten-foot-high expandable steel gate locked across the narrow brick front of the building. The large desk lady at the motor lodge had told us about it and that we should go see her cousin Charlie.

"Charlie knows everybody. Go see Charlie. Tell im I sent ya, the little one-arm prick."

I got a hand in through the gate, shaded the glass and looked inside. Ten in the morning and there were people at the bar. Tom knocked.

Chains released, deadbolts clicked and the door opened.

"Whatta ya want?" the man asked through the gate. Pasty

white, bald, overweight and average height—mine—this was probably the third day since his last shave. His once-white poly-ester shirt was wrinkled, stained, a sleeve rolled up and pinned at the shoulder, ". . . the little one-arm prick."

"You Charlie?" Tom said.

"Who's askin?"

"Your cousin Mary told us to look you up. Says you can point us at a place to live and maybe a place to work. Can we come in?"

"Mary sent you?"

"We stayed at her motel last night."

"That ain't a motel. Damn flop house. She charge by the hour?" He slapped the doorjamb and coughed a deep, wet laugh. He turned to the bar, "They stayed at Mary's, and she charged by the hour!" He was joined by a small chorus of mumbles and coughs.

"We'll buy a round. Can you help us?" Tom said.

"Maybe." He checked out the three of us. "What's with the dark one? Don't let darkies in here."

My leg still tender, I cut June off at the pass. "She's Native American," I said, "Cherokee. Lots of sun."

"Cherokee. Yeah, well, I'll be keepin an eye on you," he said to June as he took the lock off the gate. He slid it aside just enough for us to file in, then relocked everything.

"Darkies?" June whispered.

It was a long, narrow, high-ceilinged room with no imagina-tion. St. Patrick's Day fifteen years ago may have been the last time it had been cleaned and decorated. Behind the bar, next to the open cash register, the yellow light of a shade-less table lamp soaked into the dark and smoke-greased odors of the place. The far wall was ancient, exposed brick in front of which a piano sat upright on a small stage. The patrons, six androgy-nous figures, slumped on tottery wooden stools over beer mugs, full ashtrays and a few shot glasses. Five of them wore truckers' caps, and I think more than one was a woman. Lumping Charlie in with them, their collective age was decades beyond five hundred years.

"Hippies," a patron piped.

"Hipsters," said another.

"No, hipsters wear suits. Shiny cars. These guys are hippies. Pot heads." The skinny guy with his pants pulled up to his chest actually turned and pointed at us.

"Hipsters smoke pot."

"Hippies are rats."

"Rat Pack, those guys're hip. They still around? Like, Sinatra? Sinatra's a hippy hipster. No fuckin around there, Frankie baby."

"I played for im, I did. Played for Ol Blue Eyes once." The voice garbled out of a chain-smoked woman.

"Not this again," said the skinny, pants guy next to her.

Charlie was on the phone. "Yeah, they're some friends of Mary's, just got into town. Smart kids. Two young guys and a Cherokee. Huh? No, that'd be a bird. This is a Cherokee. They say, 'Lots of sun.' Tall. Suspicious lookin."

Tom wandered over to the woman. "You played for Sinatra?"

"Sure did. Played for im once."

"How'd that happen? You were with the band?" he said.

"Nope. Played at the hotel where he was stayin. His pianist got sick. They panicked. Asked me could I read music. I had a look at it. No problem. Drove me to the theater in a limo, they did. That was some night. Yep."

Charlie was off the phone. "So where's that round, then maybe we'll talk."

Tom pulled a wad from deep in his bibs, unfolded a few bills and put them on the bar.

"Make that gin, Charlie, on the rocks, the good stuff," the woman said.

"A double for the lady," Tom said. "Drafts for me and the crew."

"Thanks, dear," she said.

"So do you still play?" Tom said.

"Now and again. When it feels right."

Charlie sat a tall clinking glass in front of her. He came back with three foaming mugs. June reached between Tom and his new date and grabbed two. She and I stood away from the bar in shadow.

"So what'd you play for Sinatra?" Tom said.

She took a long swig, "Lotta stuff."

"You remember any of the numbers? Like, maybe play one for us now?"

She slid both hands forward, arms' length on the bar and flexed her fingers. She drew them back in to her barrel body, took another pull on the gin and began to topple. Tom righted her.

"Thanks, dear. Sure, why not."

"Easy on them steps, Betty," Charlie said. "No more sprained ankle, ya know?"

"I got an escort." She winked at Tom.

June and I watched fascinated as Tom helped her off her stool. It shot out from under her and slid to the door.

"Oops," Betty laughed.

Tom kept an arm around her waist and cleared sheet music from the bench as she settled onto her perch. He reached up and turned on the piano light.

"So what are you going to play, Betty?" Tom said.

"I'll sing the way it was writ. Frank changed it around. This is how it's s'pose ta sound—

Well, a good man is hard to find

You always find the other kind
Just when you think that he's your pal
You find him foolin round some other little gal."

It was a manic keyboard light show as the little stage bounced to her stride pounding, and shadows sputtered and flicked around them. Tom rocked out on the bench with Betty, his bear paw on her shoulder, and offered up spirited, horrible harmony. June helped me up the steps, and we joined in. June frequently played the Bessie Smith rendition of Eddie Green's song on her little record player. Final lines, the patrons tapped their glasses on the bar, one clapped, and it was like someone pulled her plug. Betty listed and sagged. Tom caught her, and the three of us stumbled her down to a chair at the closest table. He slid in across from her. Betty supported her chin on her hand and stared—lights out.

"Damn, Betty, that was great! Frank Sinatra, lady. You nailed it!" Tom said.

Betty snored.

Charlie came from behind the bar. "Okay, like I was sayin, I made a few calls. You got a place, third floor a couple blocks from here if ya want it. It's cheap, but the neighborhood's got some undesirables. Owner's a friend—a businesswoman. Got properties, and could use a hand. You in?" he said.

We looked to June. She nodded.

"Yeah, we're in," Tom said.

"Here's the address—she's there now." Charlie handed Tom a slip. "Say's she ain't hangin around all day, so if I was you, I'd get over there."

Back on the street, the daylight was painful.

"Through the looking glass," I said.

"'Lots of sun,' my ass. And he doesn't fuckin let darkies in!" June said.

VENICE, CA, 2015

Far from the rural Chesapeake, Venice is bracketed by the Santa Monica Pier a bit to the north and the large pleasure boats in the marinas to the south—ocean on one side, Mar Vista and vintage planes and private jets at the Santa Monica Airport on the other. It's bracketed by those, conspicuous wealth and wretched poverty. The Santa Monica Pier is a size ten-and-a-half microcosm of manufactured fun and sparkling confections crammed into a size eight. There's the Ferris wheel, the mini roller coaster, the arcade and nearly all the sweet and greasy food you can imagine. If you can find your way beyond all that, there's a refreshing walk out to the end of the pier in the sanity-restoring breeze and a cantina to sit and enjoy the sunset. I've been there once, a few years ago. These days, I'm fine with seeing the pier from a distance. In the marina south of here, there are superyachts with helicopters on them. I hear they belong to some of the world's princes and CEOs. An owner in carefully-chosen deck shoes and slacks likely flies in and lands aboard once or twice a year with whomever he or she wants to cement a deal or substantially impress. They putter out to Catalina Island, have lunch on board served by two young men in white waist coats, putter back, and there—they've taken the boat out, and it's a done deal. And, any day or night, Main Street sidewalks crawl with enterprising locals, sidewalk hustlers, domestic and international visitors, convention revelers, alluring pros, surfers, cyclists, and the deep-fried, burned-out artifacts from the sixties.

When I arrived twenty years ago, the town was going through one of its many transitions. The crack gangs were moving out to Inglewood, and the place was just starting a massive gentrification. A few fashion designers were signing leases to rundown first floors beneath low-cost apartments and turning them into show-lit-and-chic gallery showrooms. Recent culinary institute grads were taking over abandoned sandwich shops and closed-down bars and reopening with valet parking, hip menus and names like Chez Tex, Poponn Inn, Fizz City and The LearnEd Lizard. Interior designers were hanging out their shingles next to surf shacks, and coffee shops were springing up on every block. The Rose Café was a place to hang out and watch for under-dressed and down-played stars who hoped not to be noticed, or otherwise.

The timing was good for me, inheriting my uncle's little 1940s bungalow with its Lilliputian refrigerator and stove in avocado green. But first there was a lot of moving out that I had to do. Uncle Elmer was a hoarder—a paper hoarder. The newspaper bundles, magazines, tax returns, yellowed appliance manuals, receipts and service records from every car he'd owned were easy enough to get rid of. Then there were the living room shelves of hundreds of aged and brittle scores— compositions for clarinet—duets, trios, quartets, concertos, sonatas and rhapsodies. Some crumbled in my hands as they were pulled from the shelves. Uncle Elmer was in conservatory when the war broke out. He fought in Europe and came home bitter, reclusive, a die-hard bachelor and generally a pain in the neck to be around. He had never finished at conservatory, but he'd joined the musician's union and played all over the city when shows, studios or ensembles needed a fill in. It had to be a hard way to make a living—not knowing from day-to-day if you were going to have work. Going through his things and deciding what to keep and what to donate or toss, I came upon the box of delicately hand-addressed envelops in his bottom desk drawer. They were scribed in a wonderfully quilled script. Curious, I brought a cup of coffee in from the Hobbit-of-a-kitchen and settled at his desk. There were dozens of letters from a woman—Dorothy—in Suffolk, England in the village of

Clare. The earliest of the letters was heartbreaking—desperate over separation and loss. Weeks later, a letter feigned courage, and she wrote that, as painful as it was, she would move on with her life as he advised. The next week, another letter of sorrowful hope. Then came word that she had married. He was a nice man, a widower, a good provider, and he loved their daughter, my cousin, as his own. Then, the letters stopped.

Had my uncle continued writing, hoping to hear more about her life, about their daughter whom he would likely never meet? How long did it take for it to set in—that it was over? Had he felt betrayed by his own hand? Did he wish he'd taken different action, all those years ago in Clare—that he had stayed with her, or found a way to bring her here? Or, after a few weeks of wrestling with the whole thing, did he conclude that her marrying was for the best? Was he relieved? Was he now able to leave this little cottage, stroll past the shopkeepers hosing down their walks and continue north to the pier unbound and breathe the sea air anew? He'd told her he played his clarinet every day and that it was only in the music that his tortured heart was soothed. Had he continued to play once the letters ceased? Was it requiems?

21

YOU THE CHEROKEE?

WASHINGTON, DC, 1989

The address Charlie gave us was on a cracked and forgotten surface street shaded by an overhead expressway. The roar of traffic above us was breath-sucking. Most of the block's two-and three-story brick facades were boarded up or missing windows, broken glass and bottles everywhere, and there were no cars on the street. What were we getting into?

"Weird, that we can park right out front," Tom said coming up the steps. "Think I ought to stay out here and watch the trucks?"

"You really want to?" I said.

"Maybe not."

June rang the bell. No response. She rang again. Bolts slid, chains moved. A thin nose, intense eyes and pursed lips appeared in the narrow opening.

"You the Cherokee?"

"Huh? Sorry, the traffic." June pointed.

"The Cherokee?! That's you?" The face raised its voice.

"Yeah, right!" June looked at me and scowled.

"Those are your trucks?!" The chin pointed.

"Yeah?"

"Move them around back." Three long fingers appeared in the opening. "There's a stall—number three. Back door's three, too. Ring when you're ready." The door slammed.

Back at the trucks, Tom said, "Heroin."

"Maybe," June said.

The woman let us in the back door, through a spotless, white enamel and red Formica kitchen and down a narrow, glistening hallway to the front room. Straight to a chrome and leather Breuer chair, she sat with her back to the window shades and told us, "Sit." We sat across from her on a pristine mid-century sofa.

She was affected—skeletal, fifty-something and fidgety. Mid-length mouse hair, pale lips, her skin said pink and blue, and her palms were on fire. Edvard Munch would have had a good time painting her. She jittered as she lit a cigarette. She tossed the match into a giant turquoise ashtray, and a jet stream of smoke left the corner of her mouth. "Charlie says you're looking for work and a place to live, that you're smart and a little desperate, like you're running from something. But, basically, he thinks you're honest. Charlie reads people." She reached behind her and pulled a cord. The sunlight careened off the glass table between us.

Squinting, I said, "Yeah, we just got into town and—"

"I have a few properties and need someone to keep an eye on things. Someone smart, honest, awake and on my side. That'd be the three of you?"

"What kind of properties?" Tom said.

"Bar, parking lot and hotel. I'm diversified."

"Who's watching them now?" I said.

She picked a fleck of tobacco off the tip of her tongue, leaned forward and flicked it into the ashtray. "People I don't trust. Stealing me blind."

"I'm June." She stood, eased around the table and offered her hand—her shade a relief.

Thin pink hands in her lap, the woman peeked around June to Tom and me, dart-glanced side-to-side, leaned forward, tipped her ash and gave June's hand a single shake. "I'm Pat."

"This is Tom and James." June stood aside. We waved into the glare, and June returned to the sofa.

"I'll pay minimum wage—cash—and you can live rent-free upstairs, third floor. Bobbi and I live on the first two. There's no heat up there, by the way. The house has some problems—electrical, heat. But we keep it pretty toasty down here in the winter, if you're still around."

"Bobby?" June said.

"My partner—Barbara, actually. You have a problem with that and we can part now."

"Of course not," June said. Tom and I shook our heads.

"So. You want to see upstairs? It's a steep climb, and maybe you're not up for it." She glanced at my leg.

"I'll make it."

We passed through the second floor, a vast, mirrored, open space—a dance studio—and on to the third floor. The view of the elevated expressway was eye-level-intimate through tall, double-hung windows, and there was an upside to the top floor —given a couple weeks, it wouldn't be hard to improve. The space smoofed and crumbled with broken down boxes, cast aside clothing, junk mail, shredded pet toys, and it was a tinder box. We'd either be shoveling the remains of birds, bats, other small carcasses and the leave-behinds of forty years of woe-begotten tenants onto the sidewalk three stories below, or we'd be making dozens of trips on the stairs. June said, "Nice. Shall we visit your properties?"

They were a couple miles away in Georgetown.

"You live in Southeast, but your businesses are up here?" Tom said. We got out of Pat's car at the parking lot.

"Just the way it is," she said. "Gram's place. Building's been in the family three generations. Expressway's what screwed up the neighborhood. Used to be a pretty great place to live—a few blocks from The Capitol, Jefferson's Marine Barracks, the Navy Yard, shops, restaurants, gay and lesbian bars and all. Whole block's deserted. Bobbi and I are the only ones left. So, which one of you does the parking lot?"

"What's 'doing the parking lot' mean?" Tom said.

"Sit in that booth where Stealing Earl sits, take their money, make change, ask how long they're staying, and assign a space. Most of the time, we don't allow in and out privileges, but sometimes we make exceptions for regulars. That's your call, and you'll soon see what a headache it is. At the end of the night, run the report, stick the tape in the cash drawer, put the drawer in the canvas bag, and bring it to me—until I get to know you."

"Got it. I'll do the parking lot," Tom said.

"Okay, let's get some lunch." She led us up the narrow walk sparkling with students, tourists and hurried, important-looking people in fresh haircuts, suits and shoes. We dodged a cab, slid sideways between blinking, double-parked delivery trucks, and we were on the other side of the street and into a bar—The Pewter Pint.

The shaved-head, portly bartender had just landed a lunch platter on the bar in front of a customer. His eyes shifted to Pat as we made our way to a corner table. No smile, just a glance.

But for electricity and central plumbing, Thomas Jefferson would have been right at home in The Pint—low, hand-hewn, exposed-beam ceiling, white wainscoting, ancient fireplace, beautifully-crafted and finished dark wood bar back, polished brass and a worn, white marble bar top. A bit dressy for us and it was nearly full.

"Hello, Vicki," Pat smiled at our waitress—small, young and pretty. "My friends and I will have the special."

Vicki quickly took our drink orders and vanished.

"Part of the deal is you can eat here free once a day—the special. Order something else and it's on your dime."

We nodded.

"So who's doing the bar?" she said.

June pointed across the table at me, "He's experienced."

I shifted in my chair and folded my arms. Thanks, June. "Last year of art school, I managed a small-town bar," I said. "Night shift. College students, some townies. It was mostly shots and beers—once-in-a-while, a grasshopper or Manhattan. There was this older—"

"This isn't small town." Pat turned her drill into me. "This is high volume, high fashion, high money. Big dogs from Capitol Hill and their gym-toned girlfriends stirred in with entitled, trust-fund college kids. They each expect to be treated like the star of the show, but they're not. This is your show, and you run it that way—your guests on your show."

"Got it. When do I start?"

"After lunch, we'll tour the hotel, then come back mid-afternoon when things slow down. I'll introduce you to the arrogant guy behind the bar who thinks he owns the place. You'll dress like him, walk like him, talk like him, and be his helper for a week—follow his every move. Then I fire his inflated, back-talking ass."

What could possibly go wrong? And I didn't like it—me

being a part of her wicked plan and that guy's—that arrogant guy's—termination. If he got wise to it, things could get ugly.

Crab cakes and four cucumber salads later, we went next door and into the small lobby.

"Boys, have a seat. June, come with me," Pat said.

We chose two leather wing chairs on the Turkish rug by the fireplace and put our feet up. Pat led June around a huge floral spray on the desk and through a side door. The desk manager looked over every couple minutes from whatever he was doing, gave us the evil eye and tsk'd. Chill out, dude, I thought. Our boots were strategically placed atop magazines. Three everlouder tsks later, Tom glanced over to me, and we gave in. Our boots off the table and onto the floor, June and Pat came out of the office, around the desk and crossed the lobby to the carpeted stairs.

"It was originally two town homes, converted to a hotel in the 1860's," Pat said over her shoulder as she led June up the narrow stairs. June looked back and waved.

Pat and I were in The Pint's small but competent commercial kitchen with her portly, arrogant bartender and he wasn't digging it.

"James is my nephew," Pat said. "He just got into town, and he's going to help out part-time behind the bar to earn a few bucks."

"Like that's what we need, Pat, another person behind the bar. No offense." He sneered at me. Yep, it was going to be ugly.

"It's just the way it is. He starts tonight, six until ten."

He folded his arms. "Right."

I'M LIKING YOU IN A SUIT

My leg felt like the second day on crutches by the time I got back from The Pint and up to the third floor that night. I had to get off it for the next twelve hours. And bless their hearts if June and Tom hadn't seen that coming. They had somewhat cleaned two of the rooms, June had made a bed of sleeping bags and blankets on our floor, and Tom hung a hammock in his room. "Pat had it in the cellar, brand new and still in the Sears box. Says she couldn't care less if I screwed a couple eyebolts into the walls. Told me to bring in a ton of sand, buy a ukulele, and make it a goddamn beach. You ought to see the crap she has down there—a rotted Cushman scooter, set of mag wheels, two sousaphones . . ."

Exploring the cellar a couple days later, I retrieved a sixties vintage steel bike frame in my size, a Masi. A Masi from back when Faliero Masi was building steel bikes in Milano for the likes of Tour de France legend Eddy "The Cannibal" Merckx —back in the day when boys were men. I would bring it to life in the coming weeks.

I flopped onto June's blankets. "How was work, James?" She brought in two sweating beers and joined me on the floor.

"Pat's bartender's an officious, insecure, self-serving dick, but he's not stupid. He knows I'm his replacement, so he's not making it easy."

"I'm sorry to hear."

"Yeah, well it's okay. He makes a ton of money every night. Like three or four times what we made busting wood," I said.

"Pat said, 'Minimum wage.' "

"Tips, June. He makes it in tips."

"Hmm." She squeezed my butt. "I wonder how I could make tips at the hotel?"

"Can you not even kid about that?"

"Ouu, a tender spot—the real you?" she said.

"No, I just—"

"No worries, buddy. I'll be behind the desk—suit, pantyhose, blouse buttoned to the neck like a good white girl and a-yes-sir'n, and a-yes-ma'am'n, and so uptight eight-hours-a-day, no tellin what I'll do when we're alone."

"I'm liking you in a suit."

The next morning, Rachmaninoff's *Piano Concerto #2* rumbled up through the floor. I curled deeper into the pillow and covers. "June, make it stop. June?" Morning traffic crawled past our windows, and I was alone. I hobbled out of the sheets, got to my feet and tenderly made it out to the hall. Downstairs on the stereo, Vladimir Ashkenazy was in full swing at the Steinway, and I had to take a piss. Out of the dank bathroom, I limped down the hall past our tools and stacks of reclaimed southern-pine flooring and sat on the landing. Below, through the stair rails, colors passed in pastel waves—yellow, pink, yellow, blue, yellow again. I edged down a few steps on my butt. It was Pat.

Her pink hands poked out from the ends of a white leotard. Her long bare feet pointed and whirred, skipped and skimmed on the polished maple floor. Her hands spun long wispy scarves like smoke trailing behind and swirling all around. Her back arched accenting her ribs as she accelerated forward and arced out to a camel back as she flitted in reverse. Pat's world. I went back to bed.

A week later, I was the night manager at The Pewter Pint and June was in training at the hotel. Tom and his bibs were squeezed into a ticket booth at the mouth of a small parking lot half-a-block off M street. His broad shoulders nearly spanned the top third of the tiny shack. A couple feet below, a shallow shelf held a keyboard, a monitor placed off to the side and a small radio. The talk radio and his daily, unanswered notes to Prairie saved his sanity. We each had the late shifts, so it was the mid mornings that we shoveled out the debris from our floor through a make-shift chute directly into our truck beds three stories below.

White Dog liked the rides to the waste transfer station on the other side of town. It was right next to an expansive sports field complex, and he was getting damned good at snagging the Frisbee. The trash gone and the rotted bathroom rebuilt in the first couple weeks, we continued those trips to the sports complex. Work, White-Dog-Frisbee trips and hanging out at our third-floor Barbados, poking around D.C., the restaurants, the bars—it was starting to grow on me, and I wanted to stay there—but June assured me we couldn't.

VENICE, CA, 2015

Living near the ocean on this quiet side street—in my uncle's mini-bungalow—it's easy to get into a rut repeating the same day every day. I think I mentioned the morning coffee, *The New Yorker*, soup for lunch, Amanpour and a nap. I do break it up once in a while. Wednesdays, I teach figure drawing and painting at The Rose Art Academy a couple blocks away. I say teach, but that may be stretching things. In this case, teach means I instruct, then oversee and comment on student attempts. The real teach implies learning, and I'm not sure that happens.

The classes include teens-to-retirees, and each age brings their predisposed cargo. The teens are uninhibited and impatient. They expect it all just to happen as soon as they lay charcoal or paint to surface, possibly the influence of their preschool successes with splatter art and glitter glue. Many of the middle-aged, too—especially those eccentrically-dressed, of artistic temperament and with the most expensive supplies— impatient and deluded. They figure if I can't appreciate the disproportionate and impossible limbs on their figures, it's my fault, my lack of imagination. And those of a certain age—mine —are there to do just as they damn well please, happy in their own ruts. They nod politely during my comments and critiques, then continue with whatever they had been doing, essentially saying, "Go to hell, I'm old, and I don't care." Alternatives to the ten-thousand-hours-to-mastery concept.

At least once a week, I forego the early morning reading and walk a couple blocks to the beach. Shop owners are out, each hosing down their thirty feet of walkway. It's early enough that the hawkers have not arrived with their macramé plant hangers and velvet Jimi, Janis and Elvises. I see annealed homeless early risers and the delivery people carting coffee, food and beer to the cafés. I walk the paved path north along the beach and admire the young joggers, avoid the serious runners and cyclists, wonder at acrobatic yoga devotees and the gymnastic prowess of small groups taking turns on the flying rings. Muscle Beach is empty this time of day, but as the sun rises, those enamored with, and dedicated to, engorged flesh will arrive to work out and pose. Seeing the Santa Monica Pier in the distance, I turn and head back—back to my solo cottage—back to where I hole up. I must sound a bit depressed. I think of it more as resigned. Resigned and not so much looking forward as looking back. Looking back to that one year when I was thirty-five and June was twenty-five, and, if only *wishing* was *being*. She once said, "There's no going back." If I *were* to go back, to try and find her . . . Shameless. Audacious at best. Last I saw her, she was in wrist restraints and stepping into the back of a cop car headed for Anchorage. I have to think she's in Maryland, now, but who knows. She and maybe our grown child. A daughter? Tall, dark and beautiful like her? Perhaps a strapping son? I suspect he'd be strapping if he has her genes. He's short with plenty of second thoughts and balding if he has mine.

23

I HAVE TO TOUCH HER CROTCH!

June was antsy. There weren't enough miles between her and Kane and she was getting twitchier by the day. We'd likely be leaving soon.

Tom sunk in his hammock with an umbrella drink. June, White Dog and I spread out on the bamboo mat. Tom had found travel posters in the storage closet at the hotel, and we were surrounded with idyllic views of Jamaica and St. Croix with Jimmy Buffett and *Changes in Latitudes* on the box. Preferring the laid-back beach lifestyle, White Dog had moved in with Tom.

"How about we head for the islands?" Tom said.

"That's not west," June said.

"Suppose Prair wakes up? We take him with?"

"Yes, Tom. We'll take Prair."

"So where next?" he said.

"Californy. Right, June?" I got up and headed down the hall. The bathroom was cleaner than it had been in decades.

Our tools were the first things out of the trucks after White Dog. We'd ripped up the disgusting, dry-rotted floor down to the joists and replaced it with salvaged yellow pine from a reclamation facility in Anacostia. That, and a wall-to-wall mirror over the sink reflecting a polished claw-foot-and-a-bitch-to-move tub along the opposite wall. I had painted a ceiling border of mermaids and dolphins, and the room was hippy-dippy styling.

Tom and June were deep into travel plans as I came out of the bathroom, passed his door and went on to the stairs. My images circled and gathered like a funnel as I crossed the mirrored dance studio to the door leading to the first floor. Echoing up the stairs and through the door were agitated voices —Pat and Bobbi. I knocked and started down.

"I have to touch her crotch, Bobbi. I have to lift her. It's a dance!"

"You loved it," Bobbi said.

"Yeah, that too. So what?"

"So lift me, not her."

"I can't lift you, for Chrissake!"

"There it is, again. I'm fat, and you're not," Bobbi said.

I stood in the hallway outside of the kitchen, took a breath and, "Knock, knock?"

"What?" they both said.

I stepped in, "Er, hey. You guys got some coffee or something? Tea?" I rubbed my head.

"On the counter," Pat said.

My back to them, I poured in silence. I found the milk, replaced it and turned to them at the table. They sat stiff and glared.

"Can I get you guys something? While I'm up?"

"Thank you, no." Total ice from Pat.

"Mind if I sit?"

"Sit," they both said.

Bobbi was a short, largish woman, but you wouldn't call her fat—solid, stocky maybe. Early-forties, pale, black pixie cut and small, intense-just-now features. There was a fearlessness about her—former 82nd Airborne. They faced off at the ends of the table. I sat my mug in the table's DMZ and straddled a chair between them.

"Sorry I'm interrupting. Just needed a break. Guess I was getting island fever up there."

They were bottled up. Pat tore confetti bits from a knotted paper napkin, her skinny neck aflame. Bobbi turned to me and stabbed an index finger onto the table. A single tear splashed on her shirt. "I drive a bus. I sit all day and drive a bus. I like driving a bus, helping people get to where they have to go—to work, to school, to the doctor, to visit a friend. Not a lot of people like riding the bus, but they have to because that's the only way they can get where they're going, or they wouldn't even be on my bus. But they are, and I take them where they want to go, sometimes for free."

To my left, I felt Pat uncoil.

"It's stressful, every route, every shift. There's a lot of responsibility, and traffic isn't getting any better, no way."

Pat got up quietly and went over to the counter.

"My passengers never even think about it, but I get them safely through a lot of close calls every day. They have no idea."

Pat placed a Kleenex box in front of Bobbi and returned to her seat. Bobbi blew her nose and tossed the wadded tissue into the corner basket without missing a beat.

"How much exercise do you think I get sitting in that cushy seat and turning the power-steering? And I have to eat, right? She dances all day—aerobics, yoga, jazz—she can eat anything she wants."

"Bobbi's not fat," Pat said. "She doesn't listen when I say it."

"I try to watch what I eat. I pack my lunch—healthy. I pack whole wheat, turkey-no-mayo, celery, fruit and rice cakes," Bobbi said.

I looked over to Pat. She nodded.

"I'm big boned. She used to swing me off my feet dancing at *JoAnn's*. She used to lift me in the air. Tell her. Tell her she used to swing me off my feet."

"Tell her I was younger," Pat said.

"Tell her we both were. Go on, tell her," Bobbi said.

I looked at Pat. She sat straight, palms down on the table.

"You guys were younger then, Pat," I said.

Pat glanced at Bobbi then drilled back at me. "So, we're old now? It's all over? Tuck us away in a chair with a warm blanket on our laps? Oatmeal drooling down our chins and staring at Oprah?"

Now it was Bobbi's turn, "What do you think, that we're a couple of spinsters who never knew love? We're in love, still. We have our moments, still. Tell him, Pat."

"We do. Our love has grown. Once it was all passion. Now, it's passion plus." She looked to Bobbi as she pulled another Kleenex from the box. "Why are we even telling him this, Bobbi? Who's he to us?"

Bobbi blew hard and *swish,* nothing but net. "I haven't a clue, Pat"

"Look, I'm sorry," I said.

"Let's get some lunch," Pat said.

"You got it, Hon."

They rose and swept out of the kitchen like Fred and Ginger. The back door slammed. What had been a merry-go-round, the kitchen slowed and stopped.

I took a breath, took a sip and thought, Mad Hatters. They

had all the dials set to "Frenetic." How and when had that come about? For sure, they lived in a world hostile to lesbian and gay relations. And there was likely that Midwest-and-come-to-Jesus-tent-show baggage they were hauling from their childhoods and whatever might have happened to them—if something *had* happened. Pat was definitely damaged. Had she always been so intense, even as a child, with every fraying catgut nerve about to snap? Her parents. Did they wonder at the doll heads they found torn from their bodies and strewn about her room? Did they think ballet lessons might help with her identity? If that's how it happened, it worked. She seemed to find release in dance. Perhaps she opens the storm shutters and communes with what's left of that little girl from before whatever might have happened might have happened.

Bobbi, too. For just a moment, here at the table, she'd been sharing, genuine. I wonder had she been talking to me, or through me to Pat? I'd come down to give them a heads-up—that we'd probably be leaving in the next couple months. I'd have to pick another time—maybe try one-on-one with Pat. In the same room together, they could wear you out.

VENICE, CA, 2015

Fortunate as I am to have a small house in Venice, the walls do crowd in on me now and again. That's when I just have to get out to reassure myself that I'm still connected with humanity. I'm sitting here alone at this square table-for-two in The Rose Café, just now, with a latte and an almond croissant—great combination. It's an up place, The Rose—colorful pastries in the case, paper doilies on the serving plates beneath powdered confections, warm, flattering lighting and eighties music from the ceiling. Right now, it's Wham's *Wake Me Up Before You Go-Go*. I watch the young couples enter and leave. Most are gay, joyous and at the beginning of their careers, and I page back to the relationships I was in at their ages. First Margaret— a double false start and five-year disqualification. It had taken more than a few calls to get through to Margaret after she left. Her family had me pegged as a finally-rid-of pathetic parasite and hung up each time I called. I continued to stick my hand into the wood chipper until Margaret finally answered. With a civil tone, she told me she'd never return, that I had been a mistake, that I'd be getting papers to sign, that she was going back to Oxford, and I should, "Have a nice life."

Huh, look at that young couple over by the window sitting side-by-side. Their hands have found each other beneath the table, and they lean into each other when they laugh. Their electric attraction about to crackle into love. Her crooked smile and uninhibited and exploring stare into his. Not unlike June's. My love unshakeable—a bigger loss I'll never know.

A few years after June was gone came Natalie. Dear sweet Natalie—my Florence Nightingale. Our marriage didn't get a chance to fail, but likely would have given enough time and my M.O. I'm sure I'd have found a way to either slowly drive her mad or, from out of left field, release some catastrophic betrayal.

The Roman Church's immaculate Natalie and I had shared the settled years, the grown up, mow-the-lawn-and-buy-a-small-aquarium years—all two of them. She found me to be "wandering in circles," as she said. She said she thought I was funny in an unintentional, unkempt way. That I was basically well meaning, and, with careful training and a cardigan, I'd be just right. I was taken by her ivory beauty. She was even-keeled and ran at a pace I had never known. Not a sprinter, she was enduring. I never saw her sweat. It was a curious change for me, sensible, and I took to thinking I had finally grown up. You could say I liked her a lot. She worked as a saint at the community elder activities center, and I rode off each morning with a bag lunch to photo-edit the little local newspaper. We had dual incomes, direct deposit and the world at our feet. We ate healthy, I laid up the bottle and weed, we dressed well, and she died. Her God took her in her sleep. No warning and she was gone. In her place was an unrelenting sadness for years. Her family felt for me, and I for them. For a few months, I had gone to church with them, kneeled at the alter on a purple cushion and made a varnished attempt at praying over our losses—their daughter and my best friend. As the months passed into years, I stuffed down my feelings a little at a time, as I had as a kid.

Then, Eva, my third and last wife, the fair-skinned blond with the toned legs and active lifestyle. That and a pathological attraction to the ever-changing landscape of dietary rituals, higher consciousness and self-improvement tapes. A textbook chameleon, which is how we fell for each other.

I was in my mid-forties and had been single for a few years. I was in what I thought of as the winding down of my working years. With my small inheritance, I had stepped off the hamster wheel. A resigned, graying hermit who, to maintain a pulse, substitute taught in a couple private high schools. I worked two days a week, which suited me fine. The kids spanned smart-to-smarmy, and I didn't mind it all that much. There were times that it was actually fulfilling, or, at least, entertaining. I'd show up at eight, and I was out of there at three. I had no commitments, no relationships, and my life was shrinking but not my waist. I'd been adding holes to my belt. I decided I probably ought to get out of the easy chair and plug the pipe spewing beer and ice cream—get ahead of the paunch and the old man gaining on me. I bought a bike.

"I'm not racing, or anything," I told the energetic young whippet in the bike shop. "I just want a bicycle for fitness, exercise. Loved bikes as a kid, couldn't get enough. Built up an original Masi frame a long time ago."

He said he dug my old-school sneakers. He said something about the quality of the riding experience, the responsiveness, hi-mod carbon lay-up, gear ratios, power transfer, blah, blah. Then he went into pedals, shoes and clothing. He said a typical road ride is twenty-thousand pedal strokes—up, down, up, down. And how heavy did I want my pedals and shoes to be? "Just like the bikes, *Dude*, the less they weigh, the more they cost." Forty-five-hundred dollars later, I left with a road bike that weighed less than my toaster. That and a spandex outfit that looked like something from *Marvel Comics*, size "L."

I had forgotten how much fun, how freeing it is to simply ride a bicycle. Those next few months, there was no place I'd rather be than on that bike. I squeezed into medium spandex.

The go-to ride was up into Santa Monica, along the ocean down through Redondo Beach, up through Palos Verdes and back—about forty miles. Going out at the same time each day, I'd see the same faces and the same asses—all ages, shapes and sizes. A few months into it, a new ass appeared. About every third ride, I'd see her streak past, tucked down into her aero bars and pedaling an easy five mph faster than me. Bright blue spandex, white Colnago and a long blond braid. Gotta get on her wheel one of these times, I thought. Gotta find out who that tuned-up demon is. All this riding had reawakened me—maybe I wasn't ready to sit down just yet.

It's a sorry thing, but I started watching for her, checking over my shoulder. If I was going to ride with her, catch her wheel, I'd have to be going closer to her speed as she passed. A week into my new obsession, I saw her coming. Lousy timing. I'd taken a different route the day before and did a lot of climbing in Topanga Canyon. My legs were baked. I picked up my cadence.

She passed a bit slower than usual and looked over. "Thinking of making a ride?" she said. Petite, wonderful accent, great smile. Bike glasses and helmet covered the rest.

"If ya don't mind. But I'm kinda tired today."

"Hang on, I pull!" She picked up the pace as we hit a long flat stretch. I was inches off her wheel and, in her draft for the next mile, getting hints of something fragrant in her sweat and a lot of sand in her wake. And I was paying the price. The woman was an oiled machine turned up to "Red Hot" and "Angry." I was reaching the edge and, any second now, would be throwing up on my bike. I dropped off.

"Bye-bye," she called.

"Yeah, thanks for the pull."

Our first date.

A short, older couple wearing berets—his black, hers magenta—walked into the cafe a couple minutes ago. Her arm in his. Polite, soft-spoken, and the girl behind the pastry case had to ask them to repeat everything. He pointed at the lemon cake and his wife or girlfriend—they look to be my age—nodded. Their sunsets numbered and counting backwards, they took the table next to the young couple holding hands.

Eva and I shared the road a few more times until I suggested we stop in for a coffee. It was a small shop in a quiet neighborhood with outside tables, the perfect temperature, and we sat beneath an umbrella with our bikes sparkling in the sun. She laid her glasses on the table—two-hundred-dollar Oakleys. Feline green eyes and her fresh cream skin. She said she'd have whatever I was having. Trying for hip, I ordered Chai tea with soy milk and a non-fat scone. People passed and stared at the ripped, middle-aged woman, the colorful spandex, the bikes and, skeptically, at me.

"I'm Jim." I offered my hand.

"I am Eva." We shook.

"So you're training for an event?" I said.

"Maybe. You are?"

"Nah, I just ride. I don't care much for the noise and the crowds."

"Me too. No noise and crowds, I just ride," she said.

"How do you like your Colnago? Had it long?"

"It is good, not long. I think I like your Trek. Maybe I get one soon."

"Yeah, the Trek's pretty sweet."

"Sweet," she said.

"Hey, you ever ride up PCH, up through Malibu? Want to go Sunday?" I said.

"I love that! Yes. Sunday."

It was too easy—a real date.

You might have guessed that Eva was putty and socially adrift. No friends, she had just moved to LA from Sweden, was a tri-athlete, a yoga devotee and divorced.

We rode together a few times a week. Within six months, we had matching Treks, and she'd moved in with me. I was thinking she was a keeper. My place was—is—far left of Bohemian in décor and attitude, and she didn't seem to notice or care. Four months later, our shoes, socks and underwear formed the same pile in the bedroom, and we were married. It's one of my more foolish moments, but I was truly enjoying this honeymoon period of our friendship. I had recovered romance.

We settled into playing house and bicycles for the next six months—I was middle-aged crazy and she seemed to enjoy my laissez faire ways. I introduced Eva to Mexican food and micro-brews, single malts and sushi, and we partied as hard as she rode until she changed nutritionists.

I returned my cup to the girl at the counter, thanked her and put a couple bucks in the tip jar. Tina's *What's Love Got to Do with It?* played from the ceiling. I turned at the door before leaving. The old couple was still there glowing. The young couple's table had been cleared and awaited the next customers. Of course, I thought. The young. They've moved on —their horizon a sunrise fantasy.

24

THE GOVERNOR

WASHINGTON, DC, 1990

I had taken Pat's initial direction to heart— "This isn't small town. This is high volume, high fashion, high money." She was right. From 10:30 until 1:00 a.m. it was quick-pace double-time at The Pewter Pint. Martinis, Silver Bullets and tequila shots flowed as from an open tap. Happy-hours across town, drinks before dinner, wine and chateaubriand at two and three-star restaurants, after dinner drinks and government contract deals—by the time our clientele got to The Pint, they were tuned, cresting the hill and firing on all cylinders. For that next two-and-a-half-hour descent, the bar remained two-to-three deep every night. Mostly male, suits, silk ties, perfect teeth, expensive eye-wear and heavy watches threw down plastic for young-and-minimalist-chic escorts.

One o'clock, and they began thinning out. The place was ripe with booze, smoke, sweat and the fruit and green tea mixes of Calvin Klein and Bvlgari. It wasn't a great time to order a sandwich, but he did.

The waitress handed me the light green slip and disappeared into the dark, "TBLT/ff." I left the two bar-backs busy gathering up glasses and soaked napkins and pushed into the kitchen.

"You still awake?" I asked Manny.

"Yeah, and?" He turned from the sink and slid the chef's knife into its slot.

"Pretty squared away in here," I said to my cycling buddy.

"And?" he said.

"Can I get a last order of the night? BLT and fries?"

"Shit, man. Look at me. I'm like halfway out the door. I just finished cleaning up, and I gotta be at UPS in a couple hours."

"Okay, okay. We'll tell them the kitchen's closed. Just asking, you know?" I said.

"Who is it, the President?"

"Civilian. I don't know, just an order. I'll check it out. Someone wants a turkey BLT."

I went back out to the bar and scanned the room. The waitress saw me and discretely pointed him out at a corner table. I went over.

"Sir, your waitress wasn't aware, but the kitchen closed a while ago. I'm sorry. There's a twenty-four-hour burger joint half-a-block from here if you're starving." He was a tall, handsome man—blazer, open collar—looked like a news anchor.

"Thank you, son, and I appreciate that. I just don't think I can make these ol Arkansas shoes take one more step. Tell you what, I'll make it worth your while. Just throw something together back there—a sandwich—Spam on toast." He pulled an expensive wallet from his jacket. "Hell, point me in the right direction, give me an apron and I'll make it myself—one for you, too. You want mustard or mayo?" He smiled.

"Be right back, sir."

"What?" Manny snapped as I swung back into the kitchen.

"Nothing, never mind, I got it. I'll clean up, after."

"So, it's the President, then?" he said.

"No, nice guy. Fat tip. I got it." I dropped two slices into the toaster.

"Okay, get the hell out of here. I have this." Manny pulled a tomato from the basket.

I was back at his table. "It'll be up in a few, sir."

"I appreciate it. You're closing?"

"Yeah, half an hour. There's a lot to do between now and lights out."

"Mind if I hang around? I just got into town—got a late start."

"No problem."

He slid his glass forward. "Then how 'bout a double?"

The bar-backs and our waitress were gone by the time June and Tom tapped on the door.

"My friends," I said over my shoulder and undid the locks.

June, in a suit and hair rolled into a bun, leaned me over backwards at the door and gave me a Panavision kiss after which Tom pinched my cheek and said, "Such a cutie." We heard a chuckle from the table.

"Come meet," I led them over. "Governor, this is June and Tom."

"Governor?" in unison.

"Hey kids," he said getting up. He grinned like a three-ringed circus and extended a large hand."

They stared.

"Tom, June, shake Governor Clinton's hand—Arkansas," I said.

"Damn," Tom whispered, shot a look at Manny, and shook the man's hand.

"Cool," June said. She pulled out a chair and sat.

"Huh. I like that in a woman—not easily impressed, keeps her distance," the Governor said.

"I'm impressed, alright. Impressed by that little buzz that goes up the back of my neck with some people. Doesn't happen often, but when it does, umm, umm . . ." June shook her head. "First time it happened, I didn't pay attention. Thought it was just an itch. I paid for that. We having a beer, James?"

"Heh, heh—well, then," the Governor said. He and Tom joined Manny and June at the table. "Shy girl."

The four of us smiled at June. She feigned a pout and blew a kiss. I went back to the bar.

"So, Manny from Nicaragua, UPS during the day and working here at night. Plans on buying his mom a house, going bike racing and getting married. And you three, what's your story?" the Governor said.

June took the high ground and spun the tale, all but the part about Kane. ". . . so we're saving up, then heading west. Maybe Alaska, eventually."

"Her dad works there." Manny slid out from the table and headed for the door. Over his shoulder he said, "Pipeline. Prudhoe Bay. Hasn't seen him in a while."

"Never been," the Governor said. "I hear it's cold. Nice meeting you, Manny."

"Night, all." Manny closed the door.

"What brings you to Washington, Governor?" Tom said.

"Gonna see a man about putting a horse in a race—ragin Cajun who knows how to pick em."

25

HAIR OF THE DOG

It was a week later that Tom teed up a cardboard coaster and snapped—it spun like a top. "I called the hospital. Talked to Prair's mom."

Tom and June came over to the bar each night after work, after closing. We'd shut the shutters and hang out in the half-light of the reefers over a couple beers on Pat. It was fine with her as long as we turned everything off, cleaned and locked up behind us.

"How's he doing?" I said. I sat two pints in front of them.

"We should be there with him, you know? And he's showing some good signs, but that's not the only news." He snapped the coaster back into spin.

"What's the other news?" June said.

"Your dad," he grinned. "Your dad was there to pay his respects—looking for you."

"What?" Hope flashed in her eyes, then died.

"Your dad told Prair's mom not to tell, that he wanted to surprise you and your friends. But she says she's such a home-grown busy bee, she just can't keep a secret."

"She knows where we are?" She turned to him, bumped his beer and it flooded the bar.

"Damn, June!"

I grabbed a couple towels and absorbed the shock.

"Not really," Tom said. "I told her I was working at a parking lot a couple weeks ago. Seemed okay. Such a nice lady. No harm done."

June's color darkened, "Never, ever, say where we are or where we're going!"

"Right, right," Tom blushed. "My bad."

June took in a frustrated breath. "Sorry I spilled your beer. And my dad was there, in the hospital? With Prairie, with her?"

"That's what she said. Said he was finally back from Alaska and had a lot of catching up to do with his little girl."

"Did she mention he's black?"

"Never came up." Tom said.

"June, your dad," I said. "Maybe—"

"I don't think so."

Our planned stay in DC had been abbreviated. June was convinced Kane had been at the hospital and that he knew Tom was working in Georgetown. We'd be leaving in two weeks. The next Sunday, Tom came up gone.

That Sunday, it was Ravel's *Bolero* and Eugene Ormandy and The Philadelphia Orchestra drumming up through the floor and the noon sun torching sleep.

"June." I rolled over, and there were her feet. The woman dreamed a lot and got physical in her dreams, though this was the first time I found her upside down in the sheets.

"June." I grabbed her toes.

"Hey bunkie, top of the morning."

"You sleep?" I said.

"Upside down and full of dreams," she said.

"You remember any?"

"Something about an approaching storm and getting outta Dodge. You?" she said.

"Yeah, full color—us clearing out our tent site with the wind and rain coming up—taking down lines, pulling out stakes, shoving the cooler into the back of the truck, and I was doing a last sweep of the site, and you stood by the truck in the rain with our kid on your hip. Next thing I know you and the truck are gone, and I'm standing there with an empty plastic jug and an open bag of Pepperidge Farm chocolate chip cookies."

"Don't even dream of me leaving you, James. Or you leaving me. Right?"

"Right."

"And, our kid?" she said.

"Yeah." I laughed. "Crazy, right? Like, us?"

"Girl or boy?" she said.

"What?"

"In the dream, a girl or boy?"

"Good question," I said.

"I don't know how I feel about that—having a kid. Maybe a chance to do it right, I guess—a redo."

Redo."

"Yeah, like always be there for her, tuck her in, make her breakfast, fix her hair, walk her to school—love her. Maybe give Mom a shot at being a good Gramma."

"You'd want your mom involved?"

She swung her feet around next to mine and laid her head on my chest. "She's still my mother, James—issues and all. One of these days she's going to realize I'm all the family she has left, and I'm going to be there for her." She sat up and looked down at me. "First, I'll tell her what a shit she's been, then I'll be there. Let's get outta here. Breakfast, coffee or something."

"Rescue Tom from the island?" I said.

"Yep."

We rolled out onto the floor, she picked up her cluster of yesterday's clothes and headed to the bathroom.

She was back in a minute and agitated as I climbed into my jeans. "Nobody home on St. Thomas," she said.

"Maybe visiting with the ladies?"

"No. Tom's gone, James. Tom and White Dog."

"They took a walk," I said.

"Right. This neighborhood, walk-by shootings and they just went out for a stroll."

We found the note pinned to the wall inside his door, "Gone to see Prair."

"Let's go," she said. "We catch him before he gets there or join him and try to control whatever's about to happen."

"You concerned about Tom or White Dog?" I said.

No answer.

We were following Tom back into the jaws of the beast—we were pretty sure Kane was near. There was nothing Tom or we could do for Prairie. Nothing we could do about Prairie's coma, his grieving parents or the Jello the hospital kitchen continued delivering every night or the daily prayer cards from The Chapel by the Bay. If you had to choose who in and around that little hospital was in a coma, would Prairie be your only pick?

We pulled into the hospital lot behind Tom. He saw us in his mirror, and I didn't have to see his lips. Damn. White Dog smiled at us through the back window.

June chose a space, shut off her wheezing vehicle, slammed

her door and crunched through the landscape to Tom's open
window. He stared straight ahead.

"Hair of the dog?" she said.

"Huh?" He turned and looked up at her.

"Back for a nip of what killed Black Dog, nearly killed
Prairie and might kill us?"

"We ran out on him, June. We should be here. He's starting
to come round, and we're family—visit, at least."

"Once and done, Tom? We take this stupid chance, visit
Prairie, give our condolences to his parents then get the hell out
of here forever? Or do I take White Dog right now, kiss you on
the forehead and leave you in the fire?"

"Kane's not after me."

"He'll hurt you to hurt me," she said.

"It would hurt you if I was hurt?"

"We're here now. Let's get this over with."

He rolled his windows up three-quarters, locked the
passenger door and got out. Her arms pinned at her sides, he
smother-hugged her.

The cleaning-to-medical staff ratio must have been three-to-
one. The green linoleum halls were buffed to a mirror finish,
and the cool stringent air stung with disinfectant. I felt legions
of germs leap from my skin, scream in their descent and die
before hitting the floor. Tom and June felt it, too. Leading the
way to Prairie's room, Tom ran his hand back and forth over his
dome, and June briskly rubbed both arms.

Room 209: Jeffery Sansome

"It's like we're visiting a stranger," June whispered at the
door— "'Jeffery Sansome?' And who's in there with him?"

Tom took off his Lennon glasses and wiped his eyes. Glasses back in place with both hands, he tugged on his bib straps. "Okay. Let's go."

He opened the door. June followed, then me.

It wasn't what I expected, the room. It was more like a hotel than a hospital—comfortable-looking chairs, tasteful side tables and lamps, neutral tones and unprovocative but sophisticated art on the walls. Fresh flowers were aflame on the windowsill overlooking the river. Two wrung-out people, a man and a woman—he asleep with a magazine in his lap, she reading a hardcover—occupied two of the chairs. In the middle of the room, a high-tech bed was jacked up, hosed, wired and hummed lowly.

She marked her book. "You must be Tom."

"Hey, yeah. Hi, Mrs. Sansome," he whispered.

She stood. "No need to whisper." They shook hands. "This is my husband, Jeff. Jeff, this is Jeffery's friend Tom. And I'll guess this is Jimbo and . . . ?"

"Nice to meet you—I'm June."

We followed Prair's mom and dad to the bed.

"How is he?" Tom said.

With the bed raised, Prairie laid nearly chest-high to me. He looked like an angel levitating there—clean, pale, content.

"There's been flinching in his fingers and toes," his mom said. "A little more movement each day."

Prair's dad went back to his chair and sunk in.

"Jeff doesn't share my hope. It's all I have."

"I do, dear," he said. "Just tired, very tired."

Prair's hands were relaxed, powder-white and soft. I put my hand on his. "There's someone waiting for you, Prair. That young hottie food worker at the student union says to tell you she thinks you're cute, and she's single. The one with the black hair and cat eyes and all her parts dancing when she walks. I wouldn't be hanging around here much longer. She says she has her own place, but I'm not sure how long she's gonna wait."

From the other side of the bed, June scowled. Mrs. Sansome looked away.

His eyelids squinched. "Name?" he whispered.

"What? Jeffery!" his mom said. "Jeff, get over here!"

"What's er name?" Prair whispered.

"Jeff! Oh my God!" She grabbed her son's hand. Prair's dad was at the foot of the bed, his eyes like saucers.

"Shit, hell if I know, Prair. Ask her yourself."

Prairie's mom ran out for a nurse, and we were whisked across the hall to a sunny waiting room. The next thirty minutes were ablur with stethoscopes, wheeled machines and multi-colored scrubs whipping in and out of Prair's room. Mr. and Mrs. Sansome joined us in the waiting room. She shook her head. "I was prepared for the worst but prayed for this—to please let him wake up." She sat down next to me on the sofa. Mr. Sansome sat between June and Tom across the room. He looked all cried out.

"June," Mrs. Sansome said, "I have to tell you something. Jeffery just asked me to tell you—some of his first words after you left the room."

June cocked her head.

"It's the strangest thing. I mean, he wasn't conscious as far as anyone can tell. Jeffery says to tell you it wasn't your dad, that the visitor we had asking about you, he wasn't your dad."

June's lips tightened. Head down, she nodded.

"That's all he said before we were shooed out of there."

"Thank you," June said. She looked up at me and then to Mrs. Sansome. "We have to go now. We're family with your son, but we have to go. Tell him we know he's going to be okay. Tell him we miss him."

Tom patted Mr. Sansome's knee, stood and shook his hand. "Nice to meet you, sir."

Mr. Sansome nodded.

June kissed his cheek, came over and pulled Mrs. Sansome to her feet. She hugged her and whispered, "Bye."

It was a stalled moment, one of those times you see yourself in the scene from above and I looked out of place—Tom's integrity and respect, June's courage and warmth and me just standing there with my hands in my pockets. The closeness of Prair's family, them sitting here day after day for as long as it takes, their love for their son, and I was envious and maybe sensing that enduring and unconditional love thing I'd never know. June had said there *was* no such thing. Maybe. We three left.

"Next week, James. We're outta DC and gone." June glowed in the sun's low light as we trucked north out of Leonardtown. "Kane probably knows Tom's working on M Street, and it won't be that much longer until he knows where we are. We have to talk to Pat, prepare her for a change. She's gonna go total ballistic, and that's why it'll be your job, Mister Smooth Talker, and I can't believe how it happened today. You just talking Prairie out of his coma like that."

"Like Mel Blanc," I said.

"Huh?"

"The guy with all the voices, like Daffy Duck and Porky Pig. Head on collision, Dead Man's Curve in L.A. Full body cast and he's in a coma. Doesn't respond to anything until one day the doctor addresses him as Bugs Bunny—asks how Bugs is doing today. Mel perks up, 'Ehh, what's up, Doc?' "

"No friggin way!"

"Shock and awe and my magic and clean living. Gets em every time," I said.

"Maybe that's why we still have all our fingers."

VENICE, CA, 2015

I had just returned from a day at the library where I got caught up on my fines, and I don't know why they choose to call them fines. Why so negative, so punitive? Haven't they shopped at Trader Joe's? Don't they see how nice and helpful those people are? How positive, funny and clever their marketing? Wouldn't "Premium Use" fees be a better way to put it? Anyway, I sensed something different at our door—citrus, vanilla, cinnamon and cloves. Inside, large candles occupied the place like sentries, and small fragrant baskets with mixtures of dried flowers, seedpods, shriveled fruit and what might have been salt-cured monkey parts squatted all over the house. The place was spotless—fragrant and spotless. Crystals hung in the windows, and the refrigerator looked like it had been taken over by a pink-smocked hospital dietician. There were stacked, shrink-wrapped cubes of gelatinous matter with names I couldn't pronounce, canisters of powders, tiny trays of green stuff—spirulina, chlorella, ogonori, and no beer. No beer! Upon deeper inspection, there was also no meat, no cheese, no eggs, and in the bread drawer were two perfectly solid and rectangular loaves of heavy, dark and densely packed what-the-hell.

I took my book into the living room and sulked in my chair, and, oh, I couldn't wait to hear about this. Eva bounced in an hour later. She'd cut her hair, and I mean short.

She was excited to tell me that this morning she'd met a guy at the beach, a charismatic guy—young, buff and charismatic. He was a musician and a poet, and he could do one-hundred pushups, and she'd counted them. He walked her over to the health food store and helped her "realign" her diet—change her life.

"And you have to change your life because?" I said.

"I lose my center."

"Maybe it's with the beer. And you cut your hair. Cute, but what's with that?"

"We must trim down, block out distortion, insulate against feedback, squelching. Focus on natural rhythms and harmony in the universe. You are hungry? I make special something with organic ingredients—bone broth, vegetables from nature market and wild rice."

"I thought maybe we'd walk down to The Crab Pot for steamers and beer," I said.

"Clams are for butter and salt—natural killers."

"And beer?"

"A bad 'B' word, like bread, butter, bratwurst, beef, bacon."

"Now I'm really hungry. I'm going to The Crab Pot." I stood. "You coming?"

"I change my ways. I realign the center. I choose life."

I grumbled something about a life not worth living and left. I think that put us on the fast track to the end. Chances are she saw the same perfect guy the next morning at the beach, counted his push-ups, and this time they had me for lunch. I don't know where Eva is. I hope she's happy, centered and squelch-free.

In the acid sting of daylight, it appears that in sixty years I have dedicated eight or nine to what were intended to be ever-lasting relationships. I may have commitment issues.

A NEW REGULAR

WASHINGTON, DC, 1990

There was a new regular at Charlie's Place. Big guy with scarred knuckles and chin. He'd been there each night for the past two weeks. Same stool, the first one by the door. He didn't talk, just sipped his shots and side of water, filled his ashtray, listened, watched and waited. He was the kind of customer Charlie liked having around. The kind of customer who kept to himself. Came in, pulled up a stool, put a couple twenties on the bar and gave instructions one time. Told him to keep the glasses full, both of them and the goddamn ashtray empty. The customer who didn't mess with you, and you didn't mess with him. Maybe he'd spent years aboard a merchant ship, maybe a long-haul trucker, maybe prison. Charlie liked having the big guy there. He saw the bone handle of a knife sticking out from his vest, once, when the guy leaned in toward the pretzels. Charlie liked that, too. Free security. Insurance against the undesirables.

27

GLASSPACKS

We sold the two trucks to a couple questionable young guys in the alley behind Pat's who didn't give a damn that the registrations were due, the timing belts hadn't been replaced, the brakes squealed, and the tires were bald. I made my best effort to fill out the transfer of title and ownership forms per code. They watched me like they were watching a cooking show, unspooled a roll of cash, took the papers, very carefully placed them into a folder and drove off. Our serial numbers would likely be on a couple other vehicles come morning.

June and Tom had been standing a few feet away, not so much as backup but as witnesses in the event things went south. We were truckless, now. I turned to them and held out the cash. "Mercedes, anyone?" June snatched the wad and went inside.

A bit depressed at seeing his rat Toyota pull away, Tom retreated upstairs to Barbados. I stopped in at the kitchen doorway. It was happy hour, and Pat and Bobbi had their routine.

Two bottles of red were corked, and Pat drank from a small glass. "It's how they do it in Italy," she said.

Bobbi poured from her bottle over ice in a tall ceramic mug. "It's how you do it when you don't want to get caught," she said.

Bobbi counted the bills. "Okay, looks like you guys get the van." She'd been storing her low-mile '82 Dodge Ram Van at the back of the transit company lot for the past three years, up on blocks and under a tented tarp. Each spring and fall, she'd jump start it and run it for a while. Then put it back to sleep. The company had been after her to get the thing out of there for some time. Then, for no reason apparent to Bobbi, we needed something that could get us west.

"The wheels are in the cellar," Bobbi said. "I took them down, you can bring them up. You'll probably want to take turns riding in the back—there's just two captain's chairs in the front. You'll have to buy a battery, change the oil, and that's about it. You're gonna love her—dual glasspacks, mag wheels and a suicide knob. Bolt the wheels on, and drive her away."

"Suicide knob, glasspacks?" June said.

"Very cool sound—custom exhaust," I said.

"Must be a guy thing. No offense." She looked to Bobbi.

"I'm going to miss that gal," Pat said. "Some wild times in the passion pit."

"Camping," Bobbi said.

"Cape Cod, the back doors open to the ocean, you, me and the moon," Pat said. "We listened to Williamson's *Sweet Woman*, how many times?"

"And trippy Gloria. You remember Gloria—*that* sweet woman? I almost left you right then and there." Bobbi said.

"It was innocent, Bobbi, and you said you'd never bring it up again."

"You're the one brought it up, getting all moony-eyed over there," Bobbi said.

Pat looked to June and placed both palms on the table, "Gloria was just a kid."

"A senior. She was a college senior, June," Bobbi said.

Now they both stared at her.

"What, you guys?" June looked back and forth. "Like I'm getting pulled into this whatever it is between you two, or is it three, and it's your business, and do I really care?"

"You don't care?" Pat said.

"That we nearly broke up, and you don't care?" Bobbi said.

"Like we don't count for anything because we're just a couple dried up hacks? Maybe just take us out to an ice floe and leave us?" Pat turned up the heat.

"Ah-hem." I entered. "Hey, Aunt Junie, let's get those wheels, eh?"

"Right." She stood from the table.

"She doesn't care?" I heard as we started down.

28

IT'S NOT ABOUT THE BIKE

P at and I sat cross-legged on the polished studio floor. Mirrors all around, she looked dancerly from every angle. I didn't. She was in lavender Danskin and dark blue silk at her neck. I was in grubby jeans and too many days in this T-shirt. Maybe time for a laundry. I showered daily, but my clothes suffered.

"You have to save me here. That's why I brought you on—to run my businesses." She grabbed at her hair, pulled it up into a high, tight bun then hugged boney shoulders.

"We will, and we are."

"Says you." Palms slapped flat on the floor at her sides. "I look up tomorrow, and you guys are on a beach somewhere, and I'm holding the bag! I thought you'd work with me, and it's only been seven months."

"We have. And, like, you can keep the bike. I mean, it's yours anyway."

"What? What in the hell are you talking about? The bike?"

"The Eddy Merckx bike, the Masi, I mean, it's yours."

"Will you stop?" She swiveled up, stomped barefoot to the door and slammed it five times. "It's-Not-About-The-Bike!"

I'd seen her do this door thing before. The first time was shocking.

"Okay, Pat. Okay, already. Look, we've found our replacements. I found a great guy to replace me."

Arms folded tight, she glared at herself in the mirrors as she paced the edges of the room.

"He knows everything about The Pint, inside and out. He's bright, honest, personable, has a great smile, and the customers are going to love him."

"Who?" she said.

"Manny."

"Are you out of your mind? Manny's the cook, damnit!" She spun around at the far end of the room.

"He's watched me every night for the past three weeks. He's promoted his assistant, and he knows the bar, the ordering, the security, the reporting, the kitchen. Hell, he knows more than I do!"

"No."

"Why not?" I said.

"He's foreign."

"He's not."

"He's from Nicaragua," she said.

"And?"

"He's brown."

"You just heard that, right?" I left her in the studio fuming with her racist reflections.

It took a couple days of Bobbi and me working with Pat at the kitchen table. She hired Manny, but not without a fight.

"Pat, two-thirds of this city is brown," Bobbi said.

"Not our clientele."

"June is brown," I said.

"Cherokee."

"Cleveland has a football team named 'The Browns.' "

"This isn't Cleveland, and that team sucks," Pat said.

"What if Manny was Denzel Washington?" I said.

"Hired," Pat said.

"Denzel's brown, Pat," Bobbi said.

"So?"

"Pat, Manny's handsome and brown," I said.

"So?"

"You don't see anything wrong with this?" I said.

"Are we hiring Denzel, or what?"

We hadn't been back to one-armed Charlie's Place. Not since that first time with Betty at the piano. Sunday night, we drove the Ram Van over and found a space a block away. We'd be leaving in a week—time for thanks and goodbyes.

"Not sure about just leaving it here," Tom said.

"There are other cars parked all up and down the street," I said.

"Yeah, but the one six cars back is up on blocks, wheels gone."

"No one's going to want wheels off a van."

"Mags?"

Tom led through the door. "Hey Charlie, came by to say thanks." He waved.

Charlie was washing a one-armed glass. He looked up, squinted, shook his head and added the glass to an erratic pyramid on the drying rack. The three of us squeezed in, alternating between five chain-smoking regulars.

"Just wanted to thank you for introducing us to Bobbi and Pat, finding us a place to live, and all. Things worked out great. Hey, Betty!" Tom walked to the end of the bar. "How're you doing? You playing for us tonight? Somethin from Ol Blue Eyes?"

She stared, "Huh? Wha?"

"You know, like Frank Sinatra? *A Good Man is Hard to Find?*"

"Who *are* you?"

"Uh, sorry, never mind. Thought you were someone else, I guess?" Tom said.

Charlie grunted.

"Anyway, Charlie," Tom piped up, "Great gals, Bobbi and Pat. Thanks for turning us on. Like living with a couple loveable aunts. We're family, already. Hate to leave them, but we have be moving on."

No response.

"Well okay, then." Tom rapped twice on the bar. "Be seeing you, Charlie. When you see your cousin Mary, give her a kiss for us."

"Huh." Charlie waved once like batting a fly. He turned and fussed with the change in the register drawer.

We followed Tom to the door past stools of shoulder-to-shoulder hump-backed beings. There was spatial relief at the end of the bar. The last stool was unoccupied, though the space was taken—a jacket over the back, shot glass full, side of water. June glanced at the keys on the bar, then stutter stepped, looked over her shoulder and picked up the pace. Tom opened the door, and a chilled night blew in.

29

TOSS OF THE DICE

Hours later, Bobbi rose from the table in their Fifties kitchen, put her cup in the sink and filled her thermos at the coffeemaker. Tom, in his bibs, straddled a padded chair, hunched over the back, chin on his fists and barely awake. The three of us sat with Bobbi in the Monday pre-dawn. She'd be out the door any minute now—early shift this week. Pat wouldn't be up until noon.

"Bobbi, we're going to miss you guys," I said.

"Me too," she said, her blue uniformed back to me. "I thought you'd be leaving in a week, and now, all-of-a-sudden, and for some unspecified reason, you're leaving this morning, and you don't really know where you're going?"

June glanced at me. "Toss of the dice," she said. "We'll decide on the road. Maybe Canada."

"Canada." Bobbi turned around and screwed the lid on her thermos. "There's nothing there, like, in Canada. I mean, trees and, what, beavers? Sergeant Preston of the Yukon and his dog, Yukon King, and as much maple syrup as anyone can stand?"

"Toronto," June said. "Major city, like D.C."

"Except it's full of Canadians, right?" She leaned a hand and hip on the red Formica counter and shifted her weight to one leg.

"Well, yeah, I guess," June said.

"They're helpless when they come here, Canadian tourists. Play money, too many vowels, don't know one bus from the next, spinning in circles and following each other down the walk like a family of ducks."

"I guess we look funny to them, too. Like we're wound tighter than a golf ball and haven't taken a good dump in years," June said.

"Trees and beavers."

"We're going to miss you, Bobbi."

"Yeah, me too. See ya on the way back," she said. We hugged all around, and she was out the door.

30

82ND AIRBORNE

Bobbi stood at the sink in men's pajamas, gray with cream piping and buttons. It was 8 p.m., and she brushed her teeth. She turned to the full-length mirror on the door, reached her free hand behind her, sucked in her tummy and pulled the pajama-top tight. She would never be willowy, petite. It wasn't like she bulged out all over, she was just stocky—still in okay shape compared to some. She turned to the sink, leaned over and spit. Head sideways beneath the running faucet, she gulped, spit and gulped. Pat would be stretched and warmed up by now. Dance class every Monday night at that Dance Place over in Brookland. She would be sound asleep by the time Pat got home. She preferred the second shift. These first shift weeks were killers.

She woke in the dark to a Clunk! The clock glowed 10:45. The sound had come from the cellar, just below her. Probably rats. No, it was followed by a sandy, slow grinding sound. Steel threads on steel grooves and a wrench on a pipe. She hadn't moved. Short breaths, her senses gathered all their focus to hearing. There was someone down there.

She rolled over slowly and eased the drawer of the night-stand. She lifted the .45 from its terrycloth bed and rose without a sound. It all came back to her, her training and the 82nd Airborne. If she hadn't met Pat, she'd still be wearing that uniform. Safety off, she slipped bare feet across the room feeling every seam in the floor, the long hallway's worn wool runner and finally, slowly, to the cellar door. She put her ear against the door and listened, waited. Nothing. She breathed deep, one last time as she had before her first jump. She pressed on the knob as she twisted to keep it from squeaking and slowly pulled the door open. Pitch dark. Gas? She moved her fingers from the doorknob and brought her hand up to her weapon. The .45 at the side of her face, she extended a bare foot to the first step, then followed it down, slowly, listening. Now, the other foot, another step. The musty damp of the centuries-old cellar and the rotting founda-tion dissolved in her sweat. Another step.

Pat was bursting to get home, wake Bobbi and share the news. They'd been invited to spend as long as they liked at Edmond's beach hut in Jamaica. That's what he called it. The director of Dance Place called his property, "The Hut." But it wasn't a hut at all, as far as she could tell from the pictures. It was a charm-ing, primitive stone house on five lush acres and a secluded lagoon just a couple miles from Ocho Rios. And for just thirty dollars a day, his elderly and spry Aunt Maud would cook for them.

Pat shut off the ignition, swung out and locked the door. She hustled to the dark house, bounded up every-other step and stuck the key in the back door. She pushed it open and flipped the switch. The flash and impact blew her off the porch and flat onto the hood of the car.

NOT A BAD DAY OF TRAVEL

ACROSS OHIO, 1990

A clown's manic grin loomed over us. It probably scared the hell out of kids, as it punctuated the entrance to Conneaut Lake Park, near the Ohio border and across from Camperland, our first night's destination. The dark thick with summer crickets, Tom crawled our headlights over roots and through the gate.

We endured cold showers and wrapped in thin towels for a gritty barefoot walk back to the van. A dozen campfires sparked and cracked in the near distance and cast smoldering oak shadows across our path. S'mores sweetened the air. We dressed in the van, where Tom couldn't avoid an eyeful of June. He squeezed past me and out the back to strap up his bibs and whispered, "Damn."

Fresh, relaxed, and our backs to Pennsylvania, we strolled out through the grounds and down the country road a half-mile to the tiny Pelican Inn. A concrete block bunker, and, but for its sign, it had the genderless personality of a rural post office. A bell tinkled above the door as we entered the linoleum and Formica diner-turned-after-hours-bar. From the ceiling, blue sparkle lights weaved through fishing nets, and a small, mirrored ball spun the place like an abbreviated roller rink. The jukebox played country. A few older couples embraced and shuffled slow to the music but stopped and tracked June as we entered. The young local crowd at the Bud Light counter was caught up in boisterous gaiety and ignored us. We found a table, and I went off for a trio of twelve-ounce long necks.

"Not a bad day of travel." I was back with the beers.

"Same day, tomorrow. South Bend," June said. "Hard to think that life goes on as usual back there without us—The Pint, the hotel, the parking lot. Charlie and his 'no darkies.' Neanderthal cracker, one-armed prick!"

"Piano Betty," Tom said.

We both looked at him and took a swig. June grinned wet. "Uh-huh, and you got it bad for her, don't you, Tomboy."

He chuckled and looked up. The TV across the room reflected miniature in his Lennon glasses. He took them off, wiped them with his napkin and, with both hands, worked the wires back over his ears. "Damn," he whispered.

We followed his gaze to the TV.

"That's our block."

In the foreground, hair stuck to her face, the reporter sweated and told the story to the camera. She looked back over her shoulder from time-to-time and pointed through the night at the blazing buildings, firefighters hauling hoses, moving barricades and tending to valves on scattered trucks. On the screen beneath her, a white caption rolled on a blue band— ". . . five-alarm fire consumes a nearly-abandoned neighborhood just blocks from The Capitol. There are two confirmed resident fatalities, and three firefighters have been evacuated to MedStar with injuries sustained during a roof collapse."

June's chair fell out from her. She bolted to the door. When I caught up, she was on her hands and knees in the parking lot. Her back arched, she retched and choked. Between violent heaves, she sobbed, "I did this!"

32
ENOUGH

It was a long, silent, half-mile return to the van. June opened the back doors, climbed into the dark and collapsed onto the floor. Then Tom. I closed the doors behind me and, shoulder-to-shoulder with June, felt for her hand. She pulled it away.

I sat drifting, helpless, logic erased. Was it June's heart pounding through her back against the side of the van, or my own?

Breaking into that dark rhythm, Tom coughed as dry as sand. "Enough."

A minute passed.

"Yeah, okay," I said.

Next to me, June sniffed.

"Kane," I said. "So, enough."

"We call the DC police. We call tonight," Tom said.

33

KANE'S PLAYING WITH US

Over the next couple hours, sitting there, inches apart, we unfolded and refolded it, Tom and I. "She can't go back. He's a monster. Even if they lock him up, he'll find a way."

"Black Dog, Prairie, Pat and Bobbi." His voice strained like a dull blade.

"Like, we say what? We think this guy's running loose, wreaking havoc, killing and maiming just 'cause we think so? We think he blew up a city block because June danced with Prairie?"

"It's gotta stop, Jimbo."

"No argument."

"So, we call."

"We call, anonymous."

"Whatever," he said.

"It's not you, Tom. You don't carry any of this. It's June, and me—June and me, he's after."

"I'm married to Kane," her voice as small as I've ever heard. "Thirty dollars at the courthouse and a clerk pronounced us married. On our wedding trip, we robbed a gas station in Florida."

"June, I—"

"Damn," Tom whispered.

"He was there," June said. "At Charlie's—he was there. He's playing with us."

34

LITTLE SUCKER'S UP

Pat and Bobbi. Broken, we drove in silence. Gas stops, rest stops, we drifted with dead eyes. We had lost track of why we drove, we just drove past dots on the map—South Bend, Joliet, Davenport, Des Moines, Omaha . . . We hated fast food, but it was all we ate—fuel. Tom and I shared a few beers around the fire each night, voices low, as we tried to guess what came next, and what could we do about it. It amounted to everything we'd chewed over a dozen times before—go to the police, keep running, turn and fight . . . June? Mute in the van. What was ripping through her head right now? Like, she totally owned all this mayhem and her world had squeezed in from three sides, and there was only one short path left, and she was near the end of it? She looked resigned, like she was ready to jump. Could I pull her back? Save her—us?

There was no sharing the blame. Each held to it tightly, owned it in our lungs, breathing shallow and quick that our guilt would not escape. The Ram Van's cockpit blew dark and cold, and we spoke only as needed in machine-speak. Tom. He'd made a bad choice signing on for this trip. Avoiding our eyes when we three were together, he stared out the side window and moved around us with the caution of a two-hundred-pounder on spring ice. It was only in White Dog that he found relief—his panting smile, the Frisbee acrobatics. Then, for a moment, at a gas station west of Omaha, the sun broke through.

"Prairie's walking!" Tom shouted on his way back from the phone booth. "His mom says he's wobbly, but walking."

"Hell yeah!" I returned the hose to the pump.

"They're moving him back to Montana in a couple weeks," he said.

"Prairie?" June asked coming back from the restroom. Fingers spread shoulder high, she shook water from her hands. "Prairie?" She flashed that wonderful, one-wheel-in-the-gutter grin.

"Yep, little sucker's up and moving around. They're taking him home."

"Prair." Her eyes filled.

35

KANE DOESN'T OWN US

NORFOLK, NE, 1990

We passed a college on the outskirts of Norfolk, Nebraska and continued into town. If there had been mountains, it could have been a more affluent small-town Pennsylvania. Slow and quiet, about twenty-thousand people, the downtown was less than a mile of shops, then a spattering of single residences mingled with a few churches, insurance offices, barber shop, veterinary clinic, auto repair. June pulled up to a liquor-convenience store, and we went in for a paper.

"Hi guys." She was a young, together-looking blond with a palomino braid, probably an "A" student, college senior. "Can I help you find something?" she said, coming out from the counter. Tan, toned and athletic, white sports bra, red basketball shorts with a big white "N" and nearly Tom's height. She went right for him. "Fishin tackle, feed caps, flip-flops, six-packs, pork rinds, Slim Jim's, onion dip and tater skins, any size wanna-be, Corn Huskers poly 'T.' You want it, we got it. What do you need?"

Tom looked over to me, then back at her. "Poly T."

"This way, hon. You'd be an 'XL.' " She reeled him to the back of the shop. "Where you guys from, Omaha or somethin? You're not from around here. Kinda cute in those eyes and bibs and all."

He turned a quick look back and arched his eyebrows on his way to the T-shirts. June came over and grabbed my hand. "Whole milk and corn fed."

"And?" I said.

"Nothing. Just saying. Tom's kind of lady, and I fucking miss you." She spun me to her and kissed me, physical. Our teeth clicked. I pulled back.

"That hurt, June." I tasted blood.

"Love stinks, baby. It's destructive, murderous, and we're blind. We don't know where or when or who's next, and you can climb out and up onto the bank any time you want. Get up to the road, stick out a thumb and hitch a ride outta here. Forget Margaret, forget me, and you're gone. I can't leave. I'm the goddamn bulls-eye! Shackled, wrists and ankles and stuck in the middle of this and no way out."

"I'm in—right here with you. Always. You're not alone. Maybe we stand and fight. Tom's in, too. Kane can be stopped. He doesn't own us."

Fists hard at her sides, she glared. She jammed her hands on her hips, "He owns me!" She spun and moved to the back of the store, to Tom.

"What? June!" I called to her back.

She hooked her arm in Tom's and leaned into him.

36
THIS PLACE?

I went out to the crumbling lot. Beyond was a two-lane, tar-snaked macadam—no traffic but for a pick-up every thirty seconds. An array of grain elevators paralleled the tracks on the other side of the road, their suffocating dust mixed with stringent manure from somewhere out across the golden waves to the gathering dark horizon.

We were in a quiet town in Middle America, far from the water, the oystermen, boat builders and Kane. No way he could know where we were, right?

The call to the DC police had been a catharsis, lightened the tension for a moment. Like the whole thing—he—was now in someone else's hands. That wore off by the next day. "Who are we shitting?" June said as she drove us past Ashtabula. She leaned across the center console and turned off Bible radio. "He's probably in Pennsylvania by now."

Tom and June came out of the convenience store and into the van's shadow an hour later. I sat depressed in the open side door. Tom had a folded paper under his arm. "Perri pointed out a few apartment rentals that look encouraging," he said. "I'm thinking, stay a while. Maybe take some courses at that college this summer."

"Perri?" I said.

He blushed.

"Tom-boy's love agent," June said. "The future Mrs. Thomas Hardware and a line of towheads tagging along."

"In my dreams," he said. "She let us use the phone. These people are really nice around here."

"These people," June said.

"You guys, too. Hang out here, put down for a while, save up some travel dough? I'm staying," he said.

June shrugged.

"Anyway, we can go look at a couple places tonight, five and five-thirty. They're a quarter mile from each other in town," he said.

"These people." June went around to the driver's door. "It's twenty-to-five. Shall we?"

"Here? We're staying here?" I said. "What the hell's this place?"

"You have other plans, James?"

"No plans."

37
YOU LET DARKIES IN?

A very tan, short, sixty-something with a perfect black pageboy and pressed khaki shorts led us up the steep outside stairs to her second-floor apartment. Her sneakers were strikingly white. She opened the door to high ceilings, inlaid hardwood and what she said were seven rooms. She started most sentences with, No. "No stomping on the stairs. Come and go quietly—I live on the first floor. No shoes inside and no marking up the floors—they've just been refinished. No smoking. No stereos. No foul cooking odors. No feminine products in the toilet." We knew the rest. No dogs, no dope, no fun.

At five-thirty, we pulled up to the front of a well-kept, gray, hip-roofed clapboard bungalow and detached single garage on a half-acre lot. A large patch of dark earth along the side of the house had recently been rototilled. From the street berm, a crushed granite path bordered with marigolds meandered to the front porch.

He sat there on one of the two white ladder-back rockers. Lean and calm with thick, short-cropped gray hair and spitting into a jelly glass—the landlord.

We filed up to the first porch step behind our largest asset.

"Hey," Tom chose his best opening.

The landlord rocked forward and spit.

"Come to see your place and if you'll have us," Tom said.

"So, that's what you look like. Didn't look like that on the phone," he said.

"Yeah, we're thinner in person," Tom said.

"You're a big young fella. Bald already. Strong, too, eh?"

"I'm okay. Yeah, stronger than some."

"Educated?" he said.

"Some college, got hurt—football—never finished." Tom lowered his eyes.

"Hey, relax. I'm just askin. Come here and sit. Name's Nolan." He held out his hand.

Tom shook the hand and took the rocker. June and I settled on the floor, our backs against two recently-painted porch poles.

Nolan spit, placed the jelly glass between his thighs, produced a half-pint of Wild Turkey from his shirt, unscrewed the lid and took a pull. "Ahh." He handed it to Tom.

"See out there?" He pointed with his nod. "Beyond them hills to the northwest? Way out there is where there was Lakotas. They thought they owned that land cause the US Government made up a Fort Laramie Treaty with em. Said no whites would ever settle there. Well, gold was discovered and whites did settle on Indian land and the Lakotas tried to drive em off. US Government didn't like that, and one day they sent General George Custer and about three hundred cavalry out there to whip their ass. The Lakotas killed him, his horse and all his men. Whatta ya think of that?"

June turned to me, "I like this guy." She hugged her knees and asked him, "You let darkies in?"

· · ·

June and I enrolled in a couple classes. Out of the blue, she was intent on getting certified as a commercial truck driver.

"Really?" I said. "A truck driver?"

"Think about it, James. Seeing all the hidden parts of this country from inside an air-conditioned cab, stereo cranked up and getting paid to do it."

"There might be more to it than that," I said.

"Thank you, Mister Adventure."

I marked time in a cartooning class. The class was a far cry from the musty, darkly serious, self-important academy training I'd been through. We dissected political cartoons, practiced illustrating and exaggerating expressions, learned caricature, depicted movement, represented the passing of time . . . It was fun, and I volunteered to draw cartoons for the school paper. My real interest, though, was staying close to June and gaining part-time employment at the college.

38
WOULDN'T HAVE BET ON THAT

It was a beautiful Nebraska Saturday, and Nolan and I stood on the other side of the house, away from June laying down new rows of winter vegetable seeds in the garden. Turns out that Nolan was a survivalist and a bow hunter. He handed me one of his bows. It was a simple one, compared to the robotic transformer bow he'd been shooting with dead accuracy.

"Square up," he said. "Feet slightly spread." The bow was a lot lighter than it looked. He came around behind me. Over my shoulder, a carbon fiber arrow appeared. "Place it," he said. "Like I told you."

I did.

"Okay, three fingers, arm extended. No, not hyper extended, just straight. Elbow up. Draw back and anchor—corner of your mouth. Look down the arrow. Breathe, aim, aim—"

The arrow slipped off its perch and, still attached to the string, went all awobble and sideways.

"Okay, let's regroup," he said. "Start from the top."

I slowly released the bowstring and lowered the bow.

"Feet," he said. "Square. Place the arrow. Yeah, like that. That's right, draw, anchor, corner of your mouth, look down the arrow, breathe, breathe, release."

The arrow cut straight to the target, ricocheted off the top and launched into the blue. I may have punctured a tire in Oklahoma.

"Probably enough for one day. That's a fifteen-dollar arrow out there somewhere. You can give it back next time ya see me." He took the bow, patted my shoulder and disappeared around back.

I walked over to the edge of the field behind the house— winter wheat for miles.

The longer I waited, the worse it was going to get. At the moment, the wheat was green and just a couple inches.

Get out there, find the arrow, I thought.

Hell no. Just give Nolan the fifteen bucks, and be done with it.

Right, and that's what he'd expect from an Easterner.

What do you care? You going to spend the next day-and-a-half looking for that arrow? For fifteen bucks?

The light was on in the kitchen, the first stars in the sky and garlic and onions in the air. Perri's bike leaned at the back door with our three garage-sale finds. We had separate schedules, now, and just one van. It spent most of the time in the garage. We pedaled all over that small town and up to the college. I stepped into the kitchen.

Tom and Perri were at the stove and sink, frying chicken and prepping salad. Perri made hot-damn garlic-fried chicken. Nolan leaned on his forearms and spun an empty rattling Bud on the table.

"Guilty until proved innocent, extinct until proved living is how the government sees it," Nolan said.

I laid the arrow on the table and went to the fridge.

"Ask the Ponca tribe. One day back in the Sixties—the Nineteen-Sixties—the government up and decides they don't exist. Just like that. Them and about a hundred other tribes. Oh, and did I mention their land? Since the tribes don't exist, they can't own any land, can they? About one-and-a-half million acres, I'd say."

"Beer, Nolan?" I said.

"Right, and you found the arrow. Wouldn't have bet on that."

"You're into archery, Jimbo?" Tom said.

"Not exactly."

"He's a natural, just have work out a few kinks," Nolan said.

I took Nolan's empty and set down a cold one.

"The Arapaho, local boys, just west of here. They had their day. Their day and their say. Roamed and fought in every direction at once. Pawnee, Crow, Blackfoot, Arikara—means 'people whose jaws break in pieces,' if *that* ain't a clue—the Cre and the Nakota. They fought the Cheyenne, Sioux, Kiowa, Apache, Comanche and the Navajo. Just couldn't sit still, them Arapaho. James, remind me next weekend. I'll take you and June down to the river to see a friend of mine—Arapaho. I'd invite you two," he leaned back and held his bottle up to Perri and Tom, "But, I'm sure you'll be—ah, busy." He winked at me.

Their backs to us, Perri stepped to her right and kissed Tom on the shoulder.

I looked over to June at the table. She leaned on her elbows and fooled with Nolan's bottle cap. She glanced up at me, briefly, then back at the cap and crushed it in her fingers. I missed what Tom and Perri had, too—that free-wheeling, unfettered love. June was doing some hard work—working through the knowing and not knowing. Looking over her shoulder and feeling the pressure at her back. Knowing her intuition was dead-on and sensing Kane on our trail. I knew she'd work through it—that, in time, things would get better, and I'd do all I could to help, and I'd be here once she worked things out. Lately, it was half-asleep and the middle of the night, when the tensions relaxed, that her leg would cross over mine, and our love would be silent and slow.

Tom and Perri *were* busy. Perri at the convenience store, stopping in each day to visit her ailing grandma and tutoring Tom. Tom intended to become a nurse. He'd enrolled at the community college and was already having a hell of a time with his psych class. She'd been through it, though, with honors. She had her undergrad behind her, and, come January, she'd be starting med school in Omaha.

39

WHITE DOG TOOK SHOTGUN

Saturday, June and I were ready. White Dog and our daypack with waters, trail mix and dog biscuits lay between us. We sipped coffee on the porch rockers until Nolan's camouflage Jeep Cherokee rolled up.

"Okay, take me to the river," I said as we loaded in. White Dog took shotgun.

"Hope you came hungry," Nolan said over his shoulder. "My river buddy's quite the cook. We'll be in for something special today."

Nolan's driving skills would not be called, "solid." He talked while he drove and kept his eyes in the mirror most of the time. "That there's the Norfolk Regional Center." He pointed as we passed. The Jeep veered in that direction. "They've dressed up the name over the years. Started out as the State Hospital for the Insane in the late eighteen-hundreds." He glanced up at us. "And what they called insane back then could be just about anything—domestic trouble, intemperance, financial problems, disappointment in love, sun stroke, overwork, religious excitement and masturbation, to name a few." He placed his arm over the seat and actually turned around. "One girl was admitted over being homesick." June pointed toward the windshield. "Right, right." He faced forward and got us out of the oncoming lane. "They changed the name to the State Hospital, then, later, to the Regional Center. My buddy and me, we've done some time in there. I still go back once a month. Like I've graduated, or something, and they call it 'outpatient.'" He checked us in the mirror. "My buddy, the one we're meeting today, he says he's never going back."

We drove about ten miles southeast staying within sight of the Elkhorn River. The river did crazy things here. Like the Arapaho, it worked all directions at once. It meandered, carved, curled, spun and circled creating islands, peninsulas, tributaries and swamps. Here and there, washed out timbers and car bodies spotted the banks reminding us this river floods.

Off the main road, Nolan took us slowly down a narrow and broken, single-lane concrete strip. "Oops, missed it." He backed up and took an unmarked left. We eased, a foot-at-a-time, through tall brambles, down a Jeep's-width maze of cottonwoods and willows and into a forest clearing at river's edge. Two other vehicles were parked randomly beneath the trees—a four-wheel, rusted out nearly-colorless International Harvester with a spotlight mounted by the driver's door and a small, olive-green, mid-Seventies Toyota stake body. We came to dead stop between them, and Nolan shut er off.

The area was a flea market gone to seed—the ground sparkled with glass bits. Nearly a dozen door-less refrigerators, shot-gunned buckets, shredded tires, crippled farm equipment, shopping carts, whole and broken pottery, suspended tarps, a couple gutted sofas, and a faded American flag, that I guessed to have forty-eight stars, hung from a rusted cable sagged high between two trees. The place was overseen by a tin-roofed tar shack, and ribs were on the breeze. Nolan pushed the blanket aside and led us in.

"Hey Chief, what's for lunch?" he called.

We felt our way through dim humid light to a rough-sawn, primitive bar. Behind the bar, an array of propane camp stoves and a damaged collection of recycled five-gallon cans boiled away. Blue gas flames provided most of the light. My eyes adjusted, and we weren't alone. Eight feet down the bar, two large, mouth-breathing men stared at us.

"Hey, Junior," Nolan said. "Chief around?"

"Out back." Junior had a very small voice for a large man.

"How's Daddy today?" Nolan said.

Junior turned to the other man, looked him up and down, straightened the man's ball cap and turned back to us. "Daddy's fine."

Behind the bar, a USMC, government-issued blanket covered a doorway. It moved, and a giant stooped through sideways. His head was the size of an ice chest. He straightened up and wild, black hair skimmed the low rafters, and, but for his long, white, bib apron, he was naked.

"Hey, Chief, how're things?" Nolan said.

"Mmm." It was deep, resonant. He moved to the boiling cans, pulled a long-handled spoon from his apron pocket, knocked a mangled lid to the dirt floor and stirred.

"You got ears?" Nolan said.

"Snouts," Chief said.

"Well, we'll have three. White bread, hot sauce and three RC Colas if ya got em cold."

June shot a look at Nolan.

"Chief, these are my friends, June and James. June and James, say 'Hello' to Chief Gordon Oldshield, active-duty Arapaho and USMC vet."

I held out my hand. "Hi."

He stared at me like a python about to devour its pry. It was slow-motion as he raised his hairless boulder fist. It floated out past my hand and kept coming. His fingers unfolded and locked around my neck, and he lifted me a couple inches off the dirt. I grabbed his wrist with both hands. My chin dug hard into his grip. Okay, I thought, stay cool. Think. My eyes inflated. His eyes pulsed. Drums? Old men and kids pounding drums? He cocked his head, looked over to Nolan, then parked his stare at June. Pressure built in my head, and I was thinking, time to do something. His grip increased, and he raised me another inch.

"No!" June said.

No shit, June! Thanks, I thought.

In micro-stages, he lowered me, released his grip, and the drums stopped. A nearly silent metallic *tink* of a watch cog, and he shrugged. Then dark, and I swear, for a second, the stoves shut off. Flames flickered on, and he turned back to stirring. Stunned, we stared at his back until his shoulders quivered, he coughed once and giggled. It was helium, his giggle, inhaled and suppressed. Another couple giggles, his tank filled, and his booming laugh crashed into the room like a runaway eighteen-wheeler. Busted axles and burning brakes tore up sections of roadbed and smashed at the walls as passenger cars were thrown from the bridge. My heart rate peaked. Chief took a short breath, wiped his eyes with a wrist and tossed his spoon clattering among the boiling cans. A second semi of thundering laughter plowed into the first as he shuddered and tucked back through the blanket doorway and disappeared. We stood motionless and waited for someone to rewind what just happened.

Swallowing hard a couple times, and it hurt, I asked, "What was that?"

Nolan stood trancelike a few seconds more, then jerked awake. "He sees something in you."

"Something," June said slowly. She backed up to a crate and sat.

At the end of the bar, Junior and Daddy hadn't moved.

THE DRUMS

That night in the silence of our room, the windows open to a transcontinental breeze, I flat out asked June, "Where do you think Kane is—what's he doing right now?"

We lay beneath the sheets, she on her back, hands behind her head. She didn't respond.

"June?"

She let out a tired breath. "He's zig-zagging behind us. Probably in Indiana. He's been to Camperland at the Ohio boarder, saw that we stayed there and he's on his way."

"You're pretty sure."

"I'm pretty sure." She rolled to her side, her back to me.

The fields buzzed and crackled with night bugs.

"Chief's nuts, isn't he," I said.

"Maybe," she said.

"What was that today? Like, Chief grabbing me by the throat?"

"Not sure, but the drums," she said.

"The drums."

"Yeah, I heard the drums, and he knew it. There was something running through us there—all of us, even the locals."

"I thought it was just me hearing the drums. Like something supernatural," I said.

"Yeah, like him thinking he'd change the future," she said.

"For who?"

"For me."

VENICE, 2015

After class this afternoon, I went over to the deli for a rare and early meal out. Erskine was at a corner table scrolling his laptop. He looked up as I entered and waved me over.

"Hey Erskine."

"Pull up a chair, Jimmy."

I'd been hungry just a moment ago. Now, it left me.

"I can't really stay. I'm not actually sure why I came in here." I sat down.

"Destiny. I've been struggling with some things here, then you show up to help," he said.

"You're struggling."

"Yeah, writing an old girlfriend. I'm thinking about getting back together. I read a two-page retrospective of her deceased, studio-big-shot husband. I got to remembering how she and I, well, we had some pretty good times before I got deployed. Girl's a great dancer—wink, wink."

I felt the increased momentum and heard that horrible sucking sound reported by survivors just before being swept over the falls. Erskine—long twig of a guy—he's a primal force, and I had to get out of there. "Really, I ought to be going." I slid my chair out.

He scrolled up his screen.

"I preface all of it with sympathy, etc." He pointed. "Then

I go into recalling the good times we had and wrap it up with this, 'In remembrance of our youth, the love and the precious times we shared, I have donated my estate—the homes, the cars, the boat and the plane—to Doctors Without Borders, and I will live out my days doing good for others as a common man. Will you join me in my campaign?' Is the bit about the doctors too much? Are they still around, Doctors Without Borders?"

"When did her husband die?" I said.

"Awhile back. Big deal in *The Times*. She lives in Solana Beach. There are some damn nice places there along the ocean. Huge places."

"Erskine, I can't. Why must you do this?"

"Romance, Jimmy. Addicted to love."

"I'm sorry, Erskine. I don't have words for this."

"Yeah, it's hard to put into writing."

I left Erskine to his love letter and took the long way back to the house, up some alleys I'd never noticed. I was feeling left behind—as though life was passing me by. The alleys reveal what once was, now history—cast out appliances, bits of clothing, deflated toys, strollers, discarded tires.

Back East—small town—we played in the alleys as kids. No traffic, it was safer than playing out front. I guess the neighborhood mothers could keep an eye on us, too, from the kitchen windows. Balls and bats, marbles and four squares. Plenty of first kisses in those alleys with spin-the-bottle and the embarrassment of "Jimmy loves (name)" chalked on the dry summer surface. I was a puppy love slave from the start. Devon was my first. I must have been nine. Then Phyllis followed by Joan. The names washed away in the next rain. Erskine still plays.

Our fences weren't as high as these. I'm in a blind maze, walking these root-lumped alleys, so narrow with solid six-foot fences on each side. Times change. These fences were built not as a demarcation but to physically keep me out. Every fifth dead-bolt gate has a large, loud dog behind it—one that wants to tear me apart.

There are probably alleys where she lives in Solana Beach, but well kept. I don't suppose they're referred to as alleys. Lanes, more likely—well-lit passages with appealing names—Magnolia, Citrus, Palm.

Erskine never mentioned her name. Why hadn't I asked?

* * *

I was about to spray-paint a rusted doorstop—a half-size, cast iron Boston Terrier. One might wonder why someone would even care about a rusted doorstop or keep his underwear and socks in separate drawers and never put lettuce and mustard in the same sandwich. I placed the doorstop on a page from yesterday's newspaper before spraying—a page from the obituaries. It brought me to tears. Beautiful people. Wonderful people. Some so very young. Talented. Oh, there were a lot of the usual look-who-died-before and look-who's-survived chronicles, but some of the writing about some of those dear lives was lovely—heart-breaking. I folded the page and stuck it away in my books. I may never look at the obituaries again.

I am alone. By the looks of things, for the last time. Someone will probably find me here in this chair, a three-week old *New Yorker* open in my lap, the essence of Eva's vanilla and cinnamon long gone. Everything in the refrigerator will be spoiled, all but the beer. That'll still be okay, and I hope whoever finds me here will take it for themselves. There are no wastes so egregious as wasted beer.

I'm not what I think of as lonely. I don't want, wish or pine for companionship. After all, I live in a city of three million and change. I see people—students in my class—every week at The Rose Academy. They sometimes give me an allotment of their divided attention. The vendors on the boardwalk nod or wave from time-to-time. And there's Erskine.

I am alone in this small house—my uncle's house—within this private space. I share it with no one. Ah, there, a second thought, not so much that I'm alone—more clearly put, I don't share. I don't share chores, bills, the bathroom, the bed or the refrigerator. I don't share morning conversations over coffee. I don't share an article from *The Times*. I don't share breakfast, lunch or dinner or a funny thing I heard at the grocery store. I don't share a bottle of wine, a sunset or a frightening dream. On second second thought, I really am alone.

Would I have seen this coming? Should I? The pre-teens with their futures ahead of them pass me in the alleys, on the streets on skateboards and scooters, ripping it up on bikes and stomping about in raucous groups. I hear snippets as they pass —Cade plans on racing NASCAR for Red Bull, Denise is headed for Broadway, and Angel's "going to be a lawyer, man," and he's going to have, "one fine car." At their ages, mine were cowboy dreams—riding the range, harmonica by the fire, sleeping under the stars. Should I be embarrassed they still drift through my thoughts now-and-again?

There are millions of guys, at this moment, thinking, I need some time alone—just some me time. Guys with high-pressure jobs, too many kids, huge mortgages, buried in student loans and credit card debt, car payments and high-maintenance part-ners. They romanticize just a night out, a day, a weekend. Their idea of some time alone probably isn't this—as I live.

I never thought it would be like this—bridges crossed and not having the motivation or energy to find and cross the next one. I think I mentioned that by nature I am an extrovert. I lived my young life forever charging ahead and into the wind, as though this was all endless. Games in the alleys, art school, the military, a little boxing, barn building and, for a short while, photo editor of the *San Francisco Chronicle*, believe it or not. I shuffled friends, wives and jobs like there was no bottom to the deck. Now, as the twilight sneaks in, I think, huh, I may have had that wrong.

There's plenty written about social influences on aging and senility—on isolation's impact on mental health. PBS had a panel of experts discussing the effects of hearing loss on the aged, on how those people disengage, drop out, their screws loosen, and, soon, they're trapping pigeons and frying up squirrels—to paraphrase. Other experts discussed the uplifting, healing influence of physical contact—a peck on the cheek, a pat on the shoulder. I still have my hearing.

Margaret left while we were both young enough for a fresh start at a full life.

I've mentioned that Natalie, my second wife, was a Botticelli angel and so shall remain in memory. We didn't have enough time together for me to change her—to make her bitter.

And Eva—well, you know.

It's June. It's the weight of love lost and thoughts of our child with me in this chair. I wonder at the short young life we had and return daily to those last few days.

THIS, THEN, IS WHAT COUNTS—
A LIGHTNING REACTION

NORFOLK, NE, 1990

I n addition to being a survivalist and bow hunter, Nolan was on full disability through the VA. He and Chief had been in the same platoon back in The Nam. Where I covered it up in a fugue state—out of sight, out of mind—they struggled with the day-and-nightmares. Chief had burned out years ago, didn't like hospitals all that much and chose to self-medicate there in his tarpaper shack by the river. He made enough to get by serving up pig and cow part sandwiches—he had cousins at the slaughterhouse—and RC Cola and moonshine to a few underage locals and transient fishermen. Over that next couple months, I had a good time drawing for the campus paper and rendering bigger-than-life homework caricatures of Chief. He tacked them up outside on the back wall of his shack and wanted more— "Me fishing. Me on a tractor. Me and Elvis."

· · ·

Nolan continued to refine my archery skills. "You're a natural, and it's perfect that you don't know that." He'd brought a book over to the house a few days after I launched that expensive arrow into the void. Herrigel's, *Zen in the Art of Archery.* Standing behind me as I struggled to become one with the bow, to be the arrow, he read from the book. *The man, the art, the work, it is all one. Don't think of what you have to do, don't think of how to carry it out. The shot will only go smoothly when it takes the archer himself by surprise. This then is what counts —a lightning reaction which has no further need of conscious observation.* I was starting to get it—I mean not get it—to not will it, to just be. It worked. In my absence, the arrows sought out, and were pulled directly into, the center of that celestial black hole swirling in paper and straw about a hundred feet away.

June and I mucked out stalls at the Ag Center and at the campus farm to pay for classes, our minimal living expenses, and we were able to tuck away travel funds. Work was four hours in the early mornings and another four each night—move the tractor around, hook up the manure wagon, clean out the stalls, dump the wagon at the compost pile, clean the equip- ment and put it away. Some days work over-lapped with class schedules, and we'd split straight from work to class, sweating and a bit gamey. In a city environment, we would have been offensive. Here, we somewhat blended in.

Tom found work with the night-shift cleaning crew at the Carson Cancer Center, stopped at the gym at the end of each shift and had adapted surprisingly well to existing on a series of naps.

SECOND BEST BARREL RACER
EVER RACED

"I haven't spent much time in a solid house, a real house," Perri said. She forked up another bite of salad. The five of us sat at the kitchen table for Sunday dinner—Perri's garlic-fried chicken, June's spicy mash and Tom's Nutty Jamaican salad. Nolan and I split the wine and beer tab.

"Been in a single-wide long as I can remember. Oh, there were the dorms at school, but they're more like pass-through housing for migrant labor. This just feels so solid, permanent," Perri said. She rapped the table.

"Your mom's place ain't so bad," Nolan said. "More chicken, please?" He held his plate. Perri speared a thigh and dropped it next to his mound of spicy mash. "Tell em bout your mom."

"Tell what?"

"Best barrel racer ever raced." Nolan worked on the thigh and stared into his plate.

Perri pushed back from the table an inch, hands on her waist. "Mom might just be that," she said. She looked at Tom.

"She got injured, too. Ended her career and put her in a chair. Didn't end her spirit, though. I was three, and Mom and Dad left me with Gram and trailered their horses over to Gillette for the Grand Finals. Mom won. It was a long day and a big night. After all the ceremonies and awards, they loaded up the trailer and started back at midnight. They had to be feeling pretty great, there in the cab, with her trophy between them. Mom said they were singing along with Janis and *Me and Bobby McGee*. Dark road, black ice, and a semi flew across the median in front of them. Dad was gone. The horses had to be put down. Gram's never been the same—her only son."

"I'm sorry, Perri. Damn." Tom put his hand on hers.

The table was quiet but for forks on plates and robotic eating. After what seemed like an hour, Nolan piped up. "And now she might be the second-best barrel racer ever raced." Nolan pointed the chicken thigh at Perri.

"You didn't say you raced," Tom said. "Surprise-a-minute. When can we see you?"

"Two weeks. I'll be at an event at the Ag Center. It's not a competition, more just a demonstration—showing off—and I couldn't do it without the perfect horse. We've been a team for a few years now, and Scamp knows the routine better than I do —charge the money barrel, and find the pocket. Don't anyone blink—the whole thing's over in fifteen seconds. This event is a fund-raiser for a cause I believe in, and that's the only reason I'm even riding again. I think I'm done racing. With school, basketball and all, there's no time. Something's gotta go, and it sure isn't this guy." She shoved Tom.

Ropes & Rhinestones Barrel Bash for Wheelchairs
Northeast Community College Ag Center

Sep 2 1, 7 p.m.
Featuring Norfolk's Own
Great Lakes Nationals Champion
Perri Salter

43

SWOLLEN WATER HELL

On the afternoon of September twenty-first—in a matter of twenty minutes, at three in the afternoon—the sky swelled to a dark, opaque green, and if we were still on the East Coast I'd have said, "Refinery fire." Dark winds swept into Norfolk across the hills lit by a narrow band of thick yellow sky that crawled the horizon. West of us, there was already swollen water hell. At the National Weather Service in Hastings, meteorologist Mike Moody told the news stations that flooding was less likely east of Grand Island, but rain and other factors could complicate the situation there. "The worst of the flooding clearly is to the west, but there's going to be that debris coming through, and then those issues with near-river access roads and county roads. Those will be the problem areas," Moody said.

VENICE, CA, 2015

I read in *Popular Science* that ink jet printers and internal combustion engines rely on fluid physics—how drops move through space and what happens when they hit a surface.

When they hit uncontrolled and unpredictable, things get messy. Engines misfire and family photos smear like Francis Bacon paintings. In flash storm conditions, drops crowd into streams, creeks and rivers, flow downhill at eight-pounds-per-gallon and move weathered materials in a suspended load. These are pieces of rock that are carried as solids as the river flows. Unlike dissolved materials in their load, the size of the particle that can be carried as suspended load is determined by the velocity of the stream. As a stream flows faster, it can carry larger and larger particles. The larger the size of a particle that can be carried by a stream, the greater the stream's "competence." Twenty-five years ago, on September twenty-first at approximately 4 p.m., the Elkhorn River at Norfolk, Nebraska was quite competent. It rolled at about 8,976 gallons or 74,905 pounds-per-second.

NORFOLK, NE, 1990

Chief's place by the river? A big, naked ex-Marine combatant Arapaho doesn't get too excited about changes in the weather. Ropes, hand tools, a case of RC Cola and General George Custer's sword wrapped and duct taped in the "World News" section of a month-old *USA Today*, he packed his substantially-lifted cab-over and drove away in full disregard of roads, paths or water hazards. Chief smiled. He liked 4-wheel drive. This is all from Nolan's telling.

44

AND NOW LADIES AND
GENTLEMEN

T he Ag Center was surrounded—livestock trailers, pickups, security vehicles, maintenance carts, generator trucks and cables running in and out of the building. High above the campus, mercury vapor lights struck crystal halos in the drizzle and cast interlacing shadows of the serpentine procession of umbrellas on the sidewalks far below. They ascended from the lower parking lots—students, town folks and farming families followed the network of broad, concrete pathways uphill to the four sets of tall double doors leading into the center.

Inside, the grandstand was about a hundred and twelve percent of maximum occupancy. Dozens more spectators piled into the fenced-off, standing-room-only areas at both ends of the empty and groomed arena. Staging areas at the edges were alive with handlers, riders, animals, ropes, flags and leather, and the atmosphere stuck to your face—the loamy arena floor, steaming hot dog carts, hot buttered popcorn, horse shit and the damp audience in animated anticipation. High above, on each gable end of the building, six giant exhaust fans woofed and struggled for circulation.

At one end of the arena, June and I stood pinned against steel pipes. It was the five-feet-tall horizontal rail fence that would keep us from being trampled by large powerful animals at speed. Behind and around us, farmers, cowboys, cowgirls, students and families with toddlers and infants shuffled, squirmed, wiggled and wedged in.

Across the way, at the grandstand, a uniformed officer pushed Perri's mom into her first-row-reserved space. Tom followed. We'd never seen Tom in a cowboy hat, and it was kinda weird with his bibs and all, and June said he looked like Charlie Daniels. High-crowned white hat, his matched Perri's mom's. Tom settled in on one side of her, the cop on the other.

June could do it up either way—black-magic woman or Cherokee princess. Tonight, her hair glistened and swept back into a series of braids that culminated between her shoulders in white beads and hawk feathers with a delicate, red headband riding above turquoise shadowed eyelids. Long lashes, cheek-bones chiseled with rouge and gold dust and hammered silver hoops jangled on her ears and neck. Have a seat, Grace Jones, it's the Warrior Princess.

House lights dimmed, spot lights wove and raced through the arena, and the intro to Survivor's, *Eye of the Tiger* blared from the speakers. An, "AND-NOW-LADIES-AND-GENTLEMAN," announcer, and the evening's star-spangled spectacle of barrel racing, calf roping, bull riding, and the hoof-and-horn-evading gymnastics of the clowns was under way. This night, Perri wasn't the caring, easy-going girl passing the chicken to Nolan. She was a superhero in sequins and leather. Her back strong and straight, she sat tall in the saddle. Her hands looked bigger than before, and, by the set of her jaw, there was no question who owned the arena when she was in it.

She and her horse awed the crowd. They ripped horizontal as one and cut and pounded the deep earth around and between the three barrels like they were on a tether. I was struck by her, as I was with June—heroic, independent women, more capable than men.

At the end of the wonder-buzzed evening, and half-stepping in the lazy current toward the doors, we heard there was live music up the road at The Heifer.

"Let's do it," I said.

"I'm country-westerned out, James."

"C'mon, one dance, one drink."

"Uh-huh, like that's ever happened."

Wipers slapping, I leaned into the fogged windshield and June pointed, "That's it." In the parking lot, chrome, glass and puddles shimmered red, green and yellow from the neon signs above, around and on the warehouse box of a building. Out front, just below the large neon heifer sign, a smaller animated neon of a six-shooter shot three rapidly-flashing bullets toward "Parking." The lot was full.

We parked out by the road and hopped and splashed over small ponds and wove between rows of SUV's, pick-ups and randomly-parked big rigs. June wasn't sure. "This isn't blue-grass, James. This is red, white and country and a bunch of farming cowboys. People been in there awhile, you know? Pretty tuned up, by now."

"I get it. We'll poke our heads in, have a look. If it's bad, we're outta here."

45

THE COACH GUY

We pressed through the door and were blasted with heat, laughter and the local band working an Alabama hit. I shouted, "I'll get drinks!" June shook her head. I couldn't hear her, but I knew she was saying, "Umm, umm, umm." She aimed for the restroom across a rolling sea of truckers' caps and cowboy hats. I found a passage where someone was just leaving and climbed onto the stool. Bottles and glasses rang through the smoke, voices fought to rise above the band, and sight became the communication of choice. I waved a twenty to the closest bartender, pointed to the guy's bottle and shot glass next to me and held up two fingers on each hand. It was a U-shaped bar. Scanning, I landed on the bull-of-a-guy directly across. He looked like a former wrestler, maybe a football coach. Groomed, he was out of place—city haircut, expensive white shirt open at the neck, cuffs rolled once, big watch, rings, two martinis and manicured, clear-polished nails. What's *that* about? He smoked, glistened and glowed pink as the snout on a state fair hog. Just a few ticks from a heart attack, if you'd asked me. Probably on the road a week at a time, a high-end salesman. I whacked the two shots and chased them.

June appeared behind me. The coach guy stumped out his smoke, wiped his brow with his cocktail napkin and creep-stared our way. I handed a cold long neck back over my shoulder.

"Hey, cowboy." June's lips brushed my ear, her voice blew hot. I heard her, but the words took a while to get past the charge that shot through me. The woman's lips that close were electric.

"Keep this stool," I said. "My turn to the restroom. Damn, June, you do this every time, rattle the piss outta me."

"Precious bodily fluids." She kissed me on the forehead, squeezed my butt and slid a thigh onto the stool as I slipped off.

It was a game, getting through the crowd. A little like high school football special teams—barreling down field, bouncing off shoulders and helmets in a kinetic, foaming, white-hot melee of full-speed funk. Find a slot and shoot it. It was a tangle of hog-fed, clod-busting farm boys, trans-continental truckers, skinny-assed bull riders, retired locals and a gaggle of getting-down and getting-hot women who found them alluring. Sweat, hats, boots, tattoos, piercings, hair run wild and ripped up, ass-peeking shorts. And this was a road culture destination for freight drivers. We had seen it building to a crescendo in the truck stops along Route 80 across Ohio, Indiana and Illinois—suspect showers, cologne, dried bouquets, chocolates, cheap jewelry, sex tapes, rubbers and, aphrodisiacs—ground skink parts, mandrake root and dried chopped oysters in cleverly labeled vials. Tom said it first, "Damn, these truck stops look like they're working up to an orgy."

It wasn't an orgy. An orgy would be of singular purpose, common interest. These people wanted to strut. Strut, rut, pose, tempt, feign and compete. Single moms with nests of runny-nosed kids stashed at their neighbors' doublewides were combing the crowd for rich daddies and talent scouts, each the starlet of the evening. Each showing goddamn Junior, Harvey or Billy-Frank that she had what Hollywood wanted, and didn't he wish he hadn't run out so soon. Rumor had it there was a direct link to Hollywood in Johnny Carson's hometown of Norfolk, Nebraska, and the hopeful, but never evidenced, word was that producers and scouts came through all the time looking for the next new talent. A couple shots in me, mental edges eased and making my way back to the bar, I was thinking, push-up bras. If I had sold all the push-up bras in this place tonight, I'd be doing okay. Who sold those, anyway? Store in town? Young handsome guy like me fitting them? These women get em somewhere. Probably catalogs, but that might be a problem—not being able to try them on, and all. I oughta open a shop. I'll call it Twin Peeks. Hmm, maybe no more whiskey tonight. A bit lost in the crowd, my mind came back around, and I was re-finding my feet. I dodged a huge guy with a brass Peterbilt buckle as big as my head and ran, chest-to-gut, into a stocky bald guy.

"Sorry, my bad."

"It's okay, baby" he said and disappeared into the crowd.

I stood stunned. "Telly Savalas," I said to no one. "That was Kojak!"

I made it, shit-and-hallelujah, back to the bar. "June, I just ran into Telly Savalas!"

June's eyes were steel. She was locked and quivered small and tight like a cornered rabbit. It wouldn't have been visible if you didn't know her. Tom would have seen it and whispered, "Ohhh, damn."

. . .

The Coach stood on the other side of June. His large, manicured fingers kneaded her shoulder. Of course, she was beautiful, and he was helpless, ". . . like a bee to honey," I heard through the noise. Bastard. From his perspective, he probably thought he had a lot to offer, thought he was a cut above these locals—a successful urban businessman, a no-limit expense account and an impressive watch. Back in Omaha, I suppose he had a maid, a gardener and personal trainer who came to his house—his really-enormous house. But he had no way of knowing the pressure that had been backing up in June these past months, the strain she'd been under, her dam full, and he surely didn't see the trickle escaping through the fissures and seams. No, he didn't see the pressure on those seams. So he went on, probably thinking, a little sweet talk and he'd run this honey up the road to his room. I heard the tail end, ". . . and you being a cross-breed and me being a likeable rich, white—" I stepped around her and short hooked a left to his kidney. Shit, maybe that was over reaching. Definitely no more whiskey.

His knees folded. He released June's shoulder and grabbed the bar for support. Was he done? I guessed he was wondering that, too. He looked like he couldn't find his next breath, but he wasn't done. Nope. He raised himself up. Behind him, the bartender was speed dialing. Coach glared down at me, grabbed two fistfuls of June's braids and sniffed them. He took a long, loud, cornhusking suck. June shot a look at me, eyes wide. She trapped his wrist in her ax-handle grip, launched off the stool and, in the process, sent me to the floor. With both hands, she swung him like Thor's hammer, toppled stools and patrons, knocked tables to their sides, glasses in all directions and sent the place into shattered chaos. The bouncer charged. Still down, I caught his ankle with my foot, and he launched head-first over the bar. June had the coach on the floor, her hands clamped on his throat. Kane, Pat, Bobbi, Prair, Black Dog. She was letting it out, letting it all out, and this poor bastard just happened to be the valve. She straddled his chest. She leaned into his sweat-blue face. "Get it up, asshole. I'm going to fuck you to death!"

Three bale-tossing deputies burst into the ring that had formed around me, June and the guy she was choking. Each chose one of us. They pulled us to neutral corners. The one who drew June was a couple inches taller than her and had his hands full. The cops wrapped their arms around each of us from behind, worked our wrists into constraints and offered horse-whisperer advice, "C'mon now. Easy, there. Take a breath. Breathe, now."

"I *am* breathing, you big sonofabitch! I'm trying to get *that* fucker to *stop* breathing!" June yelled. Her boots stomped like pistons. Her restrainer looked over to his buddy holding me and grinned. He had her arms pinned to her sides and was careful to keep his most vulnerable spot out of range.

The deputies moved us to separate rooms of The Heifer. Hell if my guy, Ned, didn't turn out to be the guy we'd seen earlier at the arena. Perri's uncle! He took me to a booth, pushed me in and took the outside seat. He waved for the waitress. She brought a pitcher of ice water, and he poured a glass for each of us.

"Where's June? What's happening with June?" I said. She had to feel trapped.

"She's in good hands with my partner. Just a few questions, we write it up, then we all go home."

They didn't need much of a statement from us, Ned being family and all. They'd seen enough and wrote it up pretty much as they saw it. Nothing major. They'd file their report—damage to The Heifer, smashed furniture, broken glass, bruised patrons, etc. A server had the wind knocked out of him, and another Heifer employee, the bouncer and soon to be nominated MVP defensive lineman at the university, had some scrapes. And, not putting too fine a point on what might have been misconstrued in any other context as sexual assault—it's just that they weren't exactly sure of who was assaulting whom. The drunk and disorderly sales executive did have those bruise marks on his neck, and he'd likely be pissing blood for a couple days, but he probably didn't want any of this getting back to corporate, now, did he? So it was a wash, a minor squabble.

46

THERE WAS TROUBLE

"Article, here, about Telly Savalas being in town. Making a movie, they say." Nolan held the newspaper open broad as a barn door at the kitchen table. "Also, says, here, there was trouble at The Heifer, and you two were in it." He lowered the paper and looked at me. "Says there are conflicting stories on what started the whole thing, but you've paid for the damages." He turned the page and snapped the paper back open. "Sounds like an admission of guilt, if you ask me."

"Is that right, Jimbo?" Tom said.

"June?" Perri said.

I closed the refrigerator, sat a beer in front of Nolan, popped another and handed it to June. She sighed. "He was just trying to help. It was mostly me, and I'd do it again if I had the chance, but bigger."

"She was forced into a situation," I said. "Couldn't have gone any other way."

Nolan lowered the paper. "I guess you had your reasons." He raised the paper. "Didn't say, in the article. Just that there was trouble, and you were in it."

VENICE, CA, 2015

"Road trip, Jimmy. Pack your bags!" Erskine burst in, swept past me and trooped into my bedroom. "You ever consider making your bed? Your clothes are everywhere. Where's your suitcase—there's a saxophone in your closet? You have a suitcase, right?"

"Erskine, please come out here." I marked the book and laid it aside. "What are you doing?"

"Tomorrow morning, Jimmy. We're off to Solana Beach. Ah, here, under the bed. Damn small suitcase, but we'll just be overnight."

"Erskine?"

He appeared in the doorway and held my suitcase to his chest. A decade older, he looked younger than me just then, his face a kid's birthday surprise.

"Pour us a coffee—it's a fresh pot—come sit down, and let's talk. I bought you sugar, it's above the stove."

He sat two cups on the cluttered low table between us. "This time tomorrow, we're on the train to Solana Beach, old boy. Annie'll pick us up at the station, probably in some big bitchin Mercedes."

"Can we start from the beginning? Maybe keep in mind, who, what, where—things like that?"

"Oh, right, okay. So, remember my ex, the one with the fat-cat studio exec who screwed the pooch six months ago? You and I wrote to her from the deli? Doctors Without Borders? Lives in Solana Beach? Her name's Annie. That one?"

"I didn't know her name."

"Yeah, well, she called. Invited us down for dinner."

"Us," I said.

He looked out the window and scratched his chin. Low fan palms close to the house and, beyond, bare trunks of mature date palms measured the sky. Two young people wheeled past on rollerblades. "Well, yeah, like, I'm not going alone, all these years, and all."

"You told her you're bringing me?"

He folded his arms. "Not exactly."

"I hope you have a very nice dinner, and I'm not going. It's not fair to her, and it's just weird for me. Hell, Erskine."

He leaned forward, fists on the table. "You lend an air of authenticity, Jimmy. Kinda like a reference, someone to corroborate, and you're believable. There's, like, some kind of screwy alien innocence about you. It's arrested development or something, like maybe you should have been a priest. Were you breast-fed? Besides, it'll get you outta this dump for a couple days, into some fresh air and a good meal. God, you ever take a close look at this place?"

"No, Erskine."

"Well, if you turned the whole thing on its side and gave it a good shake—"

"No, I mean, no, I'm not going."

"Okay, what if I let her know you're coming? It'll probably put her at ease to have a third-party there. You're gonna love her, Jimmy. Legs, smile and a great cook."

47
KANE KNOWS WHERE WE ARE

NORFOLK, NE 1990

It was six days after The Heifer incident that I was at the kitchen table in my happy space and knocking out another cartoon for the campus paper. It had to be on the editor's desk in an hour. I'd be racing the bike back down there just before dark. The deadlines are the same each week, but the inspiration never hits until right on top of due. Then, I scramble, sketch, erase, curse, sketch again, and, if the gods are smiling, I ink it, wait for the ink to totally dry—or there will be hell to pay—erase the remaining pencil lines, stash it in a stiff envelope, tuck it into a messenger bag and pedal that two-ton Schwinn as fast as it'll roll.

I heard June prop her bike against the house. She took a while unlacing her boots, toppled them on the little porch and came in smelling salt-sour-damp from a hard day's work. She was gray. She dropped an envelope onto the table. "Shit's hit the fan."

"What?"

"We're outta here."

I picked up the envelope, addressed to June Slaughter, ". . . c/o Northeast Community College." It had been sent from Des Moines three days ago.

"He knows we're here!"

I opened the envelope and pulled out the torn half of a Talbot County, MD marriage license and a photo-copy of Kane's recent note to Florida's Alachua County Sheriff naming June in the robbery. Across the bottom he'd scrawled, "See you soon." The adrenalin hit. Weak in the stomach, my arms felt useless, hands fell from the table, and I dropped the envelope to the floor.

"He told the cops who I am, and he knows where we are!"

A long few seconds passed while our future detonated and scattered like shrapnel. I shook my head and stumbled through no good options. I hadn't given him enough credit—figured he'd given up, by now. The envelope was too real, his presence at our table.

48

THE RESPONSIBILITY, THE POWER, THE CHOICE

"If it was you, if you were Kane, would you really be on your way to Nebraska right now?" Tom said. "Hasn't he done enough? And telling the Florida cops about June and the robbery? He'd be implicating himself."

"Doesn't matter what I'd be doing. It matters what June thinks *he's* doing. And she says he's balls out, doesn't give a shit, and he'll deal with the Florida authorities if and when they catch him."

"Well, I'm staying in Nebraska. Perri and I'll be here on your way back. Damn, there's just a point where it starts to sound like paranoia, Jimbo, and Kane just yanking your chain."

"Sounds like psych class is starting to sink in."

"Yeah, it is, but I'm just calling it like I see it."

It was midnight and June's and my impromptu going-away gathering. As far as we knew, Kane could be but a few hours away. We planned to tandem drive forty-eight hours straight and stop at a motel on the third night for showers and food. We'd bought a double mattress from Nolan for the back of the van. He and I stood beneath the bare bulb on the front porch in front of a dozen friends and neighbors. Steve Miller and *Fly Like an Eagle* played low on Tom's boombox—"*Time keeps on slippin, into the future . . .*"

Nolan asked for silence, then took on a dramatic bent. "With the placement of this sash, I welcome James, here, to 'The Order of the Arrow.' " Nolan held the red and white Boy Scout sash open. I placed my head and arm through. He took a step back and shook my hand.

From the back of the gathering came Chief's resonant, "Arrow."

Tom had disappeared inside and was back now with a long, bulky box wrapped in brown paper. He carried it like a load of firewood to Nolan.

"And now," Nolan said, "we endow our new member of 'The Order' with the responsibility and the power and, most importantly, the choice." He hefted the package over to me. "Open it, James, your prize, your voice."

It was a helluva lot lighter than he and Tom made it look. I tore the paper away. "Whoa, Nolan! Too much." It was a bow like his—a high-tech Bear compound capable of launching an arrow at one hundred yards per second. Attached to the bow was a five-arrow quiver and four field point target arrows.

"I've put it to good use over the years, til I got the new one. That one's yours now. And, here." He handed me a business card. "My cousin out west—San Francisco. Look her up if you're out that way and need a place to stay."

Tom reached back inside the screen door. "Here's the bow rack for the van, Jimbo."

Nolan nodded toward Chief. Guests parted as Chief came forward, onto the porch barefoot in deadpan loincloth, and stopped within choking distance. He brought his broad fist from behind his back and straight-arm presented me with one more arrow—a carbon-shaft, razor-sharp, hunting broadhead.

"Thank you, Chief," I reached for the arrow. Slow to release it, he stared down at me. His eyes—the irises—were from the bottom of a lake—the darkest brown with other-worldly green and blue fragments scattered like birdshot reflecting a tiny June, in reverse, there, next to me. Tiny June and the breeze and the wheat rattle stopped, and I felt as though my feet left the ground. His hand dropped back to his side, lifeless. He nodded and returned bare-assed to his spot at the back of the gathering. Time stuttered around Chief like *Star Trek*.

"Okay, like I'm all tears here, okay?" I said. "June and I will miss you all. It's been great living here in the middle, sane swath, of America."

June, Perri, Tom and I shared long, tear-stained hugs. We had a bond. Surely this wasn't the last we'd see of each other.

VENICE, CA, 2015

I didn't go to Annie's with Erskine. But how does he do it, turn back the clock? Start over? He sent that stupid Doctors Without Borders email, Annie thought about it for a couple months, responded with an invitation and, badda-bing, they're dancing on her deck just like old times. Yeah, I know, it was all based on lies, but that's not how either of them saw it. Annie was wrapped up in the idea of Erskine, and, I'm convinced, Erskine takes for reality anything that shows up in his head.

Back in the day, it had been fun-and-games from the start, with June—a lot of personal digs and kidding on the job site— snipes, practical jokes, lunch chatter, beers after work and good-natured put-downs—all innocent. Then, about the place

where you came in, things between June and me had evolved.
"Hot chocolate and rock and roll," is how she put it. Maybe you
remember that. And, yeah, that's the moment when I started
falling in love with June. I wouldn't admit it to anyone, but I
was falling, and I had a problem with that—committing to that.
It was from when I was a little kid. When the parents who love
you slap you around and sometimes you're bruised and bleeding, it can seriously squirrel your love concept. Two other
moments stick—that "I'm-married-to-Kane," moment in the
back of the van and the attack kiss in that Nebraska convenience store. I ran my tongue over my lip thinking about it. It
was like one minute we were warm and Downey-soft folded in
love, and the next she was shaken to her foundation and
sprung-steel-and-concrete desperate.

It had been a mistake, her marriage. She said she'd been
rudderless and adrift too long and needed to tie on to something, to someone. Kane's skiff motored up, and she was fooled
by the paint job. Now she wanted to send it to the depths, sink
the marriage like it never existed.

We were being thrown about, June and me. Tom was
caught in the same gale, being swept along, but that couldn't
last. He was going to need his life back soon. I was feeling my
love for June deepen each day, and she had to know that, right?
We had history—passion and history. Castaways. She was
strong when I needed it, and I was there to help pull her boat
off the rocks. She was scared with good reason. She had said
that our senses weren't enough, that we were blind to when and
where it would strike—whatever it was. Looking back, maybe
through your eyes, how could we have been positive it was
Kane who started the DC fire? Not a great question to bring up
to June, just then.

. . .

Shit. Someone's at the door. They prey on the old and infirm, here, in this neighborhood—charities, magazine sales, Christians. This is probably another solicitor—an offer to paint my house or soccer fund-raising. Every day, it's something else. Maybe this time it's a precocious kid from some private school, his mother accompanying him just out of sight, and the little over-achiever raising money for his six-week summer-session in the third world. It'll be all over his CV as a candidate for the Senate someday, that he built schools and healed the sick in Honduras. I'll ignore the door.

It's stuffy in here—my small living room—stale here, at times, when the ocean lays flat. I imagine Tom, June and me wedged into this dark space. Of course, it wouldn't be just Tom. Perri would be here, too, the girl from the convenience store, and that would really make a crowd. The three of them might have to sleep with their feet in the hall.

She was a sweet young woman, Perri. Bright eyes, teeth, future and hooked on Tom. I don't know how she saw it all at first sight, everything we knew and felt about him—the integrity, loyalty, outer and inner strength, his sensitivity, his heart and his capacity for lasting love—but she did, and she grabbed him up. That short time until June and I left, he "boogied," as he said, "on Perri-winkle love. And, damn if I don't call her Prairie half the time!"

If I could turn things back? Redo? I'd skip the public-school years, for sure. All but the summers, but probably some of those, too. Nineteen to thirty was great—on my own, over-reacting to what I had seen as years of indenture. Nineteen to thirty—art school, out of the service and into the music, the women, the fun—daring, sinew and muscle and having a ball.

In the world, on the move and immortal. Margaret and five years of tainted love? I'd skip that one. But that year with June —that one year—I'd hover there, slow things down and hit "Repeat." There, I'd drift in the poetry of her broken smile in those times before things went dark.

49

EMERSON-BUILT WEAPON

OMAHA, NE, 1990

He was just about over all this hide-and-seek. Kane. Then, he'd figured it out. Her old man. Her dad. She needed her old man. People who needed things were sitting ducks. He sold the truck and bought a ticket. He boarded the plane in Omaha. It would be so much sweeter if she came to him. And she would come to him.

He woke as the plane touched down. He was in the tail, a crammed window seat backed to the restroom, and he was more than irritated with the chatty, anxious passengers hopping up as soon as the seatbelt sign binged off, fussing over bags, their yammering offspring, dragging their fat down coats and assorted crap out of the overhead bins. Civilians. His jacket and hat were all he'd brought aboard. He'd checked his small bag. He'd pick up a new knife somewhere in Anchorage before the puddle-jumper north. If he could find one, it would be an Emerson-built weapon. A folding knife, strong, quick release black blade and *lightweight titanium handle. A tool built for one thing—use in close quarters.*

If he'd had something like that when he was a kid, when that mama's-boy orderly put the goddamn leash on him and dragged him down the hall, he would have gutted the sonofabitch. That would have got some laughs. Yeah, but his wrists were tied. He'd have needed to work his hands free first. Then, they'd have some real fun with guts spilling out and everybody screaming and scared as hell. Yeah, an Emerson blade.

Would these assholes just form a herd and get the fuck off this plane?

ACROSS THE GREAT DIVIDE, 1990

The drive across Colorado's Rockies had stunned us. School-books and TV had come up short describing their solid, sheer, snow-patched and Goliath-stopping drama. We pulled in at the 14,000-foot Gray's Peak in the Arapaho National Forest, and it felt like the top of the world. Our gazes spread out across an open sea of frozen crests and troughs. Late afternoon and we hiked a partial out-and-back, and ours were the only shadows on a rugged trail of rock debris, micro herbs and granite outcrops. The elevation took your breath away. Way ahead and on point, White Dog frequently turned to see that we were still following.

Back in the van we continued through those twisting vertical passes, and, finally in overload, I dozed.

The Ram Van swerved and straightened. I bumped awake. Behind the wheel, June was raised out of the captain's chair, her back arched, and she reached behind her seat. She hooked her bag and brought it up to her lap.

"You okay?" I said.

She pulled an envelope from deep inside and lowered the

bag to the floor. "Something to read, James." June passed the envelope across the Pepsi-spilled, peanut-stuck hump of the van's motor console.

It was a letter from her dad addressed to her Maryland address and postmarked, Prudhoe Bay, AK. I read it a couple times—

My June,
You are a gron woman. I no you are smart. I hope you are good and in love. If you find it keep it. This world aint nothin but for love. The hi is -7 today. I dont like it. I dont think my black man Mississippi blood ever will. We do long days here. It is cold and dark. Now I work on a wirline. Me and 2 other men. 2 weeks up here in the cold 2 weeks down in a Anchorage motel. 2 weeks in Anchorage go fast. Job dont pay good like the other ones. Im bout dun it. For good June. I been down to Seward 15 times ever August for sun and samon and take a brake and warm up. After that I am rite back in the cold. I eat at the old Seward hotel if you ever com up. I miss you bad pretty lady. I look at the piksure you sent. Be good and do good.
Love, Dad xxoo

Huh, so close, yet so far. What kept him there and her here? It's like they'd agreed to this keeping apart thing, this weird, lonely dance they did. Couldn't he just get on a plane and end it tomorrow? Couldn't she?

Oh yeah? And what about the man in the mirror, my man?

Not the same. I know where I am and why.

And that would be?

Just keep on keeping on, is what I'm doing. Live for today, life in the moment—it's a Buddhist thing.

Oh, now you're Buddhist?

And will you shut up?

I turned it in my hands. The paper. It was smooth, cheap paper, probably taken from the drawer of the copier in the company office and folded, unfolded, folded again and long since dog-eared. The words. The words written in great concentration and labor, and he, knowing they were probably spelled wrong, had taken his best shot. The words made the paper priceless. It had been in his hands, in his cold hands is what he wrote. He didn't like the cold, he said. Nearly twenty years and he didn't like the cold? "Pretty lady," he called her. I lowered the letter to my lap and looked over. Her jaw twitched.

"He wants me to have a better life, so he sends checks I don't need. I deposit them for him—for when he comes back. It's always been him that I needed." She sniffed a June sniff. "I haven't shown his letters to anyone. I have all of them."

"Thanks for letting me read this. He really loves you."

"Then why didn't he come home?"

"Do you know for sure why he left? I mean, your mom and all."

"It's when I went off to first grade that things started to change with her, with them. Looking back, I guess Mom having time on her hands during the day wasn't such a good thing for the marriage, but he should have stayed. I never thought we were poor—we were fine. But if he was going to move somewhere to make big money, he should have taken us with."

"Where he was going, he couldn't. Sounds like there was something else about his leaving. Something he can't say," I said.

The next dozen miles were silent, and I thought some about my dad's fatherless and hard, young life and how he didn't have a natural grasp on the idea of childhood. Our most intimate moments were when he was doling out punishment. In his later years, he had tried to show his affection, but I still had my guard up. He kept trying, though.

Utah and Nevada's Great Basin Desert had been vacuum-baked to its bleached bones and appeared endless. We had both been born and raised in the deciduous East. Forests damp and deep in their dark humus from millennia of decay where insects, fowl, reptiles and mammals glisten and shine in unrelenting humidity. I didn't count one bird in our crossing of that barren forty-thousand- square-mile-plate—and we had a flat.

"Hell, June, look at that." It was a black, ring-shanked barn nail, half of which lay bent flat along the tread of the right rear tire. The other half, the business end, was inside. "You want to take White Dog out there in the scrub while I change this?"

"Or I could help," she said.

"Nah, I got it."

I did my best to stay in the three-foot swath of shade on that side of the van and the little relief it offered. The road surface and shoulder had been sucking up Danny Fahrenheit's degrees since sunrise ten hours ago and weren't about to be intimidated by a bit of shade from me or the Ram Van. Old wheel off, new wheel on, and a gallon jug of water later, June, White Dog and I had the A/C on full. Soaked with sweat to my roots, I was out of those blazing soles and barefoot with a fresh gallon jug in my lap as she drove. Maybe it was a bit of woozy heatstroke that blinded me for a moment.

"Hit him!" my dad said from behind me. I stood just below the step at our front door. "Go ahead, let him have it." It was an older kid from up the street who had chased me home. I faced him, a homemade whip in my hand—a short heavy stick with a lamp cord attached. I was scared, couldn't move. "What are you waiting for?" Dad said. The kid's eyes dared me, his fists clenched, his curled lip. In a fright-fueled movement, I lashed out. The whip wrapped twice around the kid's neck. He screamed and dropped to his knees. Back to his feet and running, he clawed at the cord. He shrieked terror in his flight, the whip handle banging at his knees. I wished I hadn't done it. It was awful—the kid's screams. I turned and looked up to Dad. The door closed.

50
I GOT SUCKED IN

I recovered and looked over at June. "You robbed a gas station."

Two Harleys swung out from behind and passed us—ape hangers, old guys in do-rags, sleeveless vests, women in tube tops leaned back on sissy bars.

"They're frying, out there. Going to be bacon, tonight," June said.

"Sunscreen," I said.

"There's not enough on a bike all day in a sun like this."

"Ape hangers," I said. "Really stupid." Two hands on the jug, I took a swig.

"I didn't know what was going on," she said. "We gassed up and Kane asked did I want something from inside. Cute little place—yellow—outside of Gainesville. A store and deli. Told me he'd be right out, to pull the truck up by the door. No need to shut it off. He'd just be a second." Her eyes were miles beyond the horizon. "He came back out, stood there on the stoop with a stuffed paper bag and a handle of whiskey. He stretched like he just got out of bed and looked around. Tall, tan, muscled T-shirt, a Florida Gators hat he must have just bought and perfect but for the scar on his chin—the knife scar. He smiled, grabbed the truck's door handle and was stepping in when what was probably the owner stumbled out of the store behind him. Bloody nose, an older Asian guy—his shirt torn open. The man shouted something, 'Hey, you can't—,' something." She took a long breath and sighed. "He shouldn't have grabbed onto the tailgate. Kane yelled at me to step on it. We dragged the man. We dragged him screaming until he fell off in the road. He didn't move." She glanced at me, then ahead, again. "I watched in the mirror until he was out of sight."

The new tire sounded different than the old one—different tread pattern, different air pressure. Out the side window, I watched the rocks and scrub for as far as I could see. She didn't have a choice. She had to do it. Kane, and all. She said he was nuts, and he is. So, she was a victim as much as the Asian guy, right? "I'm sorry," I said to the glass. "You got sucked in."

"Yeah, I got sucked in."

51

WINNEMUCCA

The sun was setting behind distant peaks as we pulled off the exit at Winnemucca to get the damaged tire plugged. Garish lights from gas stations, a big box store and fast food restaurants illuminated the area. I asked the guy fixing our tire —by his shirt, his name was Nash, and he looked to be nineteen and under-fed—where we might go for real food and local color. His grin should have been a hint. "First of all, I ain't Nash. Don't know who the hell Nash was. Just a shirt in the pile they make me wear. And I ain't gonna be here long enough to get my own shirt, tell you that right now. But you head down there through town and cross the tracks. Take the first left, and you'll find The Mineshaft. Little place by the tracks. My gramma hangs out there near every day." He snipped the excess off the rubber plug he'd inserted. "She's something, Gram. Fancy's herself an exotic dancer. Raised me on government checks until I was old enough to apply for my own, then she kicked me out. Didn't qualify is why I'm pluggin your tire right now, and its goddamn discrimination is what it is."

A few blocks down into town and it wasn't unlike Norfolk

—tidy houses with fenced yards, the hardware store, dress shop, thrift store, barber shop, nail salons and a sixties vintage single-screen movie theater next to the closed diner. We crossed the tracks, hung a left and came upon a squat of a building with no windows, a gaggle of Harleys backed up to it and a police cruiser along the side. Carved crudely into the steel-strapped and desert-hardened wood door was, "Mineshaft."

"Very inviting, James."

"It comes recommended."

"By Nash," she said. "The garrulous gas station gourmet. He's probably washing down a Twinkie with Mountain Dew right now."

Windows at half-mast, we locked White Dog in the van, crunched across sooty railroad dirt, and I pulled the heavy door open to a blaring AC/DC's *Highway to Hell*. We entered a large worn-out room scattered with pool tables, a juke box, bandstand, a long bar occupied by an unraveling string of men including the cop, and there was a small platform in the center of the room with a pole reaching floor to ceiling. The only other woman in the place—a petite woman —was wearing a black negligee. The bartender. We were ignored. We went down to the far end of the bar where there were no seats, near the restroom, and leaned. The bartender, in fuzzy slippers, was busy chatting up the cop at the other end.

"Whatta ya think, June?"

"You know what I think."

"It'd be pretty awkward to just walk out. Don't you think?"

"I think I'm already feeling pretty awkward, James."

"Okay, we give it a few minutes. You gotta use the restroom?"

"I'm not going in there."

"I kinda have to go," I said.

"And you're not either. I'm not going to be standing here alone with my ass in the wind."

"But—"

"Hold it."

The bartender looked our way, then went back to chatting with the cop.

"Doesn't look like they have much for food here, unless the kitchen's in a separate building," I said.

"They have jerky, chips, pretzels and that big fucking jar of pickles. That's it."

"You're in a mood."

The bartender approached. "Hey, how you folks doin down here by your lonesome? Not from around here. You ready to order, or do you need more time?"

"Hi. Could we see a menu?" I said.

She laughed. "Oh, I knew you'd be a funny one. Maybe you'd rather be seated in the dining room. What are you drinking?"

"I'd like a water, no ice," June said.

"I'm going to have to charge you for it, sweet lips. Nothin's free in here."

"Then I'll have some nothin."

I jumped in. "I'd like a draft," I said. "Local beer, micro-brew if you have it."

She cold-steel-daggered up at June, then turned to me. "Just cans, funny guy. Bud, Miller, Bud Light."

"A cold Bud sounds great."

She turned, mumbled to herself and went to the other end of the bar.

"Are you trying to get us thrown out, or what?" I said.

"She's going to charge me for a glass of water? She's pissing me off. And is there a health department in this state? I wouldn't eat anything she's touched. Ignoring us, then pulling that, 'nothing's free sweet lips.' And now she's back to talking to her cop friend and pouring him a shot, and good luck getting that Bud."

"That's it, then? We're outta here?" I said.

I sighed and followed June toward the door. "Won't be needing that, Bud." I waved to the bartender. "Going back up the hill to Denny's."

Backs to us, no one at the bar turned. "Right, funny guy. Maybe they have a draft of something loco-micro for you. That and a big glass of nothin for your Amazon girlfriend." June slowed a moment, then continued to the door. I pushed it closed behind us.

"Neanderthal pricks."

There was a parking lot for big rigs behind Denny's beyond which laid wasteland—a great spot for White Dog to stretch his legs and take a leak. And there were ground squirrels—White Dog nirvana. Early stars emerged, and I was thinking about tomorrow, crossing the Sierra Nevada and, with White Dog stops and a hike at Lake Tahoe, rolling into San Francisco probably sometime after midnight. Why had I taken us into that bar? I knew it was going to be bad. Even with getting a flat, that place was the worst part of our day. It had noticeably ruined June's day. She'd only said two words since we left.

I called White Dog. He raced back, jumped in through the side door, and we drove around to the front of the building. Windows half down, I locked the door thinking grilled chicken and mashed potatoes, side salad, oil and vinegar as an older loaded-down pick-up with Florida plates parked next to us. A slim guy, the driver climbed slowly out his window which disturbed White Dog. He barked and growled. Forty-fifty-something, the man limped over and asked, "Can your dog have some jerky?"

"Yeah, I guess," June said. "But go slow, he's a bit unscrewed right now."

He moseyed over to White Dog in our driver-side window. "Hey there buddy, you want a treat? Been hunting rabbits? You like squirrels? I got squirrel jerky here. Southern squirrel." There was integrity and calm in the man's voice, and White Dog took to it. The man continued talking to White Dog as he offered the treats. "Where you headed, boy? East? West? I'm going west. Not too sure about this new chapter, but that's where I'm pointed." White Dog's tail wagged as he lapped bits of jerky from the man's palm. "Okay, all gone, pal," the man said. He scratched White Dog behind the ear. "Maybe see ya around sometime." He moved his controlled, crooked gait toward the restaurant. He called back, "I like your dog."

52

TONIGHT WE SLEEP IN SAN FRANCISCO

The next morning, we motored up the steep dry side and down the wet side of the Sierra Nevada nine-thousand-foot peaks with snow-patch artifacts that would soon be buried in new drifts. We passed signs stating "All vehicles over 10,000 GVW must carry chains."

"This is a long drive-in good conditions. I wonder what it's like for all these big rigs in the snow?" June said.

"It would scare the hell out of me," I said. "But maybe you'll be finding out soon enough."

"I liked learning about the truck back in Norfolk—learning to drive it, snugging it up to the loading dock, getting my license. Not sure I'll use it, though. Not so sure I'd be wanting to do it every day, all day, for a living—sitting in that cushy seat and turning the power steering like . . . Bobbi."

We were quiet the next couple miles—thoughts of Pat and Bobbi.

After a few minutes, June said, "How'd the early settlers do it? Get through these granite mountains?"

"I guess some didn't," I said. Horses, mules, oxen, men,

women and children, pulling and pushing their wagons, wagons with wooden wheels and axles, loaded down with everything they owned and looking for the easiest passage and finding none, and someone heard there was a shortcut and that farther to the south there might be a river they could follow, and winter approached, and they were racing time, and time was relentless. On this very route, the Donner party lost the race. "They should have stuck to the Oregon Trail," I said.

Back down to six-thousand feet, we followed the clear Truckee River upstream to Lake Tahoe. At Tahoe City with a population of about a thousand with half as many tourists, we found a quiet spot along the lake for White Dog to harass the ducks and geese, then we toured a small museum—The Marion Steinbach Basket Museum. There were hundreds of baskets from eighty tribes spanning two centuries. Some were said to be water-tight and some were the size of wrens' nests. "They lived through the winters on pine nuts?" June said. "I'll bet those stick to your ribs. How many pine nuts would make a meal? The Washoe must have been some skinny, hard-ass people."

"According to the museum, they're still around here. Not many, but some. Been here six thousand years or more," I said.

"The only faces I've seen are white."

There was a thrift store across from the bagel shop where we had lunch. The owner told us of a remote, little-known place where the locals hike with their dogs as she wrapped June's coffee press and waffle iron in newspaper and slipped extended play, re-mastered vinyls of The Chambers Brothers, Cream and Willie Nelson into a recycled paper bag. "Just be on the lookout for bears and big cats out there," she said. "This time of year, there aren't as many people around, and the beasties get bold."

On the way back to the van, June put her foot down. "I'm

not going out into Blackwood Canyon with White Dog. If he saw a mountain lion, he'd be torn apart trying to save us."

"But she said the place is spiritual, and when have you ever seen a mountain lion . . . anywhere?" I said.

"Look, James, we saw the lake and it's beautiful. White Dog chased the ducks and no one got hurt. We both loved the baskets, and you passed on the cowboy boots at the thrift shop. Tonight, we sleep in San Francisco. Let's go."

53

PUSH THE BUTTON TO TALK

SAN FRANCISCO, 1990

"**D**o you believe it?" I said.
We took a right on I-80 and crossed the Bay Bridge at midnight with hundreds of other cars. Did that sound routine? Perhaps for the others, but we were, as June put it, "In crazy cool."

"It's like we're in a movie," I said.

"We are," she said. "This is the main screen feature attraction. Look at this place. Who lives here? What can their lives be like? Every day they wake up, and they're here." She rolled her window down, leaned out and was swept with maritime winds. For 180-degrees there was vibrant visibility, the French vanilla ice-cream moon on the bay, and it looked like Oz. Lights glittered in steel and glass towers and up one side of the bridge and down the other. Two hundred feet below, cargo ships all the way from China lit up in their wait patterns for the Oakland harbor. To the right, Alcatraz blinked, and in front of us, the city was a faceted jewel.

As we passed through the Treasure Island tunnel, Rush Limbaugh was blathering on the radio and scalding San Francisco's mayor, Art Agnos. Agnos had recently opened the city to the people, all the people regardless of color, religion, age, handicap and sexual identity. A controversial figure, a couple years ago, after a fair housing meeting, he'd taken a couple bullets in the chest from members of a black cultist group, a rogue off-shoot of The Nation of Islam. He lived because of the angle, the downward trajectory, of the bullets. Currently, he was receiving nationwide conservative flak from every angle. June turned off the radio. "Funny how it's the prayer meeting regulars that get so tweaked over a guy trying to do good," she said.

The Ram Van's deep exhaust went silent. We had taken one of the first few exits off the bridge, crossed a couple lanes and pulled up to the curb just past "Entrance." We left White Dog in the van and rang the night bell at the pink stucco, two-story motel.

"Hello and yes?" His tiny puppet voice squawked through the intercom. He peeked out at us from a doorway behind the reception desk. His door swung open some, and we saw further into the living room of the manager's apartment. It was lit by a large TV.

"Hello, can you open the door? We need a room." I waved through the glass to the small brown man. Between him and the TV, a woman in a sari carried a baby across the frame.

"Push the button to talk, please," he said.

June pointed to the side of the box.

"The button, like she showed you."

"Okay, there. Can you hear? We need a room. Can we come in?" I said.

"I only have a double-singles room left."

I pressed the button, "That'll be fine."

"Names, please?"

I pressed the button, "Can we come in? Won't that be easier?"

"Hold up I.D. please? Names?"

We dug out our licenses.

I pressed the button, "I'm Jim, this is June. We've been driving all day. We're really tired. We're from Maryland. Can we come in? This is difficult."

"Of course you may come in, and thank you." He buzzed us in.

"Thanks," I said. We took two steps to the Formica counter and laid out our licenses.

"Welcome to San Francisco, friends from Maryland. Many street people bother us." He pulled a form from below and handed me a pen. "Please fill this out." He pointed a thin finger, "License number goes here, and I will need a home address in case aliens take you in the night and I have nowhere to send the bill for your flight."

"You watch *Twilight Zone* re-runs, don't you," I said.

"It is how we acclimate to your country, watching reruns —*Twilight Zone* and *F Troop*. Very helpful." He grinned.

"Your voice sounds so normal, now," I said as I filled out the form.

"I am relieved, sir, and thank you. Yours, too.

As an amenity, we serve breakfast. There are Fruit Loops, Cheerios and bananas in the morning and coffee and tea. There is milk for Cheerios and packs of non-dairy creamer for the coffee. Please respect the other guests, and don't pour milk into your coffee. Use the creamer. You may stand here to eat. No food in the rooms, please. Also, there will be news on the television behind me in my apartment. The door will be open, and I will turn the volume up so you can hear. Breakfast is between six and six-thirty. It can be crowded, so, to get a good spot, it is best to come early."

He pointed to the end of the building, handed us a key to a first-floor room and buzzed us out to a clear, perfect night. June went straight to the room. I walked back to the van, pulled out of sight of the office and retrieved White Dog. By the time it took us to get into the room, June was asleep on top of her single. White Dog licked her hand then climbed onto the other bed. He curled up, glanced at me and covered his eyes with his tail.

I leaned in the open door and watched them—our family. The three of us, dead tired and here. We'd arrived. Nearly three-thousand miles from home and as many emotions. Bright and beautiful San Francisco and a fresh start. Maybe this is it. Maybe put down and grow up.

The night was full of traffic, music and laughter. Across the street was a leather bar, The Stud. Preferring the fresh air, I supposed, many of the patrons hung out on the sidewalk, and I saw countless versions of grab-ass. Waking later to noises that made it through our would-be air conditioner, I understood that, as closing time approached, things really came to a head at The Stud.

Ours was a room untroubled by personality. The window's heater-air-conditioner was missing all the control knobs. It hummed along at street temperature. I pulled the stuffed corner chair over, propped my feet on White Dog's bed and went black.

54

A SCOFFLAW THROWBACK

We found Nolan's cousin's place the next day, not far from the addresses where Janis, Jimi and The Dead had lived. We'd have the top floor of a Victorian just two blocks up the hill from Haight Street. It was a three-story climb to a gable-windowed trio of rooms. The view was great. Otherwise, it was essentially an attic with a small bath.

The city was booming. Hi-tech companies were taking over old warehouses, and the young and privileged were job-hopping like it was a party game. Busses, cabs and restaurants were full, and we had no problem finding jobs in those first few days. June's commute was down the hill two blocks. She'd be working at Wasteland, an upscale vintage clothing store on Haight—a place stars passed through on a regular basis. It was perfect for her—a coffee roaster next door and natural foods across the street next to the taqueria and a skate shop. I'd be tending bar at a corner on Howard, south of Market, the M&M Tavern, that boasted the highest volume of liquor poured per week in the city. No TV, no jukebox, no décor. It was worn-out, old San Francisco. It was a dark drinking place for a mix of the unemployed, blue collars and newspaper people.

It was a throwback, the M&M, to a time when zero tolerance for drinking on the job was a scofflaw. Just a couple doors down from *The Chronicle* and *The Examiner*, the M&M served the pressmen, the editors, reporters, photographers, ad people, truck drivers and maintenance crews, and they all worked round the clock. Some showed up showered and shaved before their shifts for a breakfast of an egg in a beer, having just left the bar six hours ago. Editors in polyester ties, white shirts and some in blouses and heels pounded down a few during lunch breaks, and many of them stopped in for a pop or two after work. Mixed in with the paper crowd, over-worked cops, warehouse jocks, and a few Hells Angels malcontents kept the ancient and oft-repaired stools polished.

It was a rare moment at the M&M when a patron and I chatted. Too busy. There were times though, typically mid-shifts at the papers, that things did slow down enough to restock the coolers, catch up on the glasses, empty ashtrays, wipe down the scratched surfaces and reorder stools. That aside, I'd entertain myself drawing caricatures of the long-term-parking patrons, usually with a fine felt-tip on the backs of cardboard coasters. I gave them to any of the subjects who were aware of what I was doing and cared. Most weren't and didn't. The rest, I stacked behind the cash register, and the stack grew to over a foot. One day, I was called out on it.

"Hey! What're you doin, there? You drawin me?" Far end of the bar—vodka/rocks, cigarette, thick, smudged, dark-rimmed glasses, square jaw, full nose, slack, beat-up tie, extra-large, yellow permanent-press shirt, sleeves rolled to the elbows and full, salt and pepper hair that had just wiped out of a demolition derby.

I took the coaster over to him. "Yeah, just fooling around. Here, it's yours if you want it." I busied myself with a couple guys who had just come in.

"Hey, Skeeter," he called. "C'mere." He slipped his pen back into his shirt pocket and handed me a coaster with me on it. "Whatta ya think? Good as yours?"

"Not bad," I said. "But no cigar."

"You're right. Yours is better. You have more of your work around here?"

I pulled half of the stack from behind the register and placed it by his glass.

"Nother round, double." He pushed his glass forward and pulled the stack to him.

I returned and sat his drink on the bar by his ashtray.

"These are good, damn good." He shuffled through the coasters. "Hey, that's Herb! How long's it take you, each one? Where'd you learn to draw? Do any layout? Had any college? You ever work for a paper? What's yer name, kid?" He threw out his hand, "I'm Gary."

55

IN THE HAIGHT

Up in The Haight, June was steaming wrinkles out of silk blouses, wool slacks, Hawaiian shirts and assisting the renowned window dresser. And she was star-struck. In her first month, she'd already had a great boat-building chat with Charlie Watts, pounded fists with Ruth Pointer and nodded back discretely to Axl Rose.

Late dinner at a little Mexican restaurant in The Mission, clear sky and we climbed the steps at home. "Friggin center of the action, James, and just a few blocks from our place. I love it here. Here, it's not me that's different, getting stared at. You maybe don't get it, being a white guy and all. Maybe here, you're weird cause you're just too white. Everyone's different, here. God, I love you."

"What the hell, June? You're color conscious all-of-a-sudden? And where'd I hear that before?"

"Shut up and kiss me." She snapped off the light, led me across the small kitchen and shoved me onto the bed. She climbed out of her boots and laid down next to me. "Are you happy, James?" she whispered. Her hand on my chest, she lightly nipped my ear.

A bolt shuddered through me. "Very." I moved on top of her as I wedged out of my shoes. Propped on my elbow, I traced her face with a finger—a circle round her chin, the ridged accent defining her lips, across the bridge of her nose—and I kissed silk eyelids. My lips on hers, that June scent came up—that engaged and hunting scent. She opened to my tongue and invited me in as she spread her legs, dug her heels into the mattress and arched up into me. "We're still dressed," I said.

"What can we do about that?" she whispered.

I slipped my hand under her sweater and we peeled her out of that and her bra. Then, my shirt. Blue moonlight through our attic window lit the edges of her breasts.

She drifted her fingers across my chest. "You still have builder muscles," she whispered into my neck.

"So do you."

"Prick." Her teeth flashed in the dim light, and she was grinning. Up on her knees, she undid my jeans and they came off. She moved onto her stomach and stretched out—her arms spanned the bed. She squirmed as I slid my hands beneath her, untied the waist sash of satin pants and worked them off and onto the floor.

Twenty minutes later and spent, we floated shoulder to shoulder on our backs. "I always hoped . . ." she said.

"What, June?"

"That it could be like this." She put her hands behind her head. "That I would feel so perfect, and in love and in San Francisco, of all places."

"Yeah, I get that." I moved to my side, head propped on my hand and watched the rise and fall of her moonlit breathing. "We're on a roll," I said.

"Where's it going?" she asked.

"Where's what?"

"Us, James—our roll. Where's it going?"

"Here," I said. "It's going here."

"Huh. Yeah, maybe we're on a roll."

VENICE, CA, 2015

As straight and strong as June appeared during those early San Francisco days, mid-nights changed the rules. There were a few times I'd roll over to two large staring eyes. "You okay?" I'd ask. She'd turn to her other side.

How often would she remove and reinvent herself until she could feel safe? How far would fear drive her—us? Without question, I'd follow her—my removals and reinventions shadowing hers.

She'd said she and Kane had been together for a year, and, like all predators, he'd learned her every move. She said he had a sixth sense, and, eventually, he'd figure out that they'd continued west.

"So, how's he going to know this West?" I'd said. "There are hundreds of towns up and down the coast—too many options."

"Think about it, James. Would I be in San Diego? LA? Portland? Back home, I nearly wore out Janis's *Cheap Thrills.* We can't stay here forever. He'll figure it out."

"June, there are a lot of things standing between him and us."

"Like?"

"I don't know. Money. It takes money to travel. Food, gas, lodging. Look at us. We've burned through Kane's truck money and my stash, and we're both working. He's gotta be picking up day jobs, or whatever, to pay his way. That keeps him in place for a couple weeks while we tandem drove the Ram Van. That, or he's been robbing 7-Elevens and finally got caught in

Colorado. He could be in jail in Colorado Springs, right now, awaiting trial."

"Colorado?" she said.

"Well, yeah. Kane would really stand out there. I mean, everything's pretty tidy in Colorado with the affluence, clean air, Telluride and skiing. Kane probably got pulled over for drifting through a stop sign, the officer didn't like the looks of him, checked the database, and he matched Kane to the 7-Eleven robbery that morning."

She dark-stared at me for a long five seconds. "You should write children's books."

56

AT THE CHRON

SAN FRANCISCO, 1990

"I'm thinking if you're good enough for the M&M, you're good enough for *The Chron*," Gary said. "Hell, it almost makes you family."

He hustled me down the ancient, noisy corridor and the floor rumbling from the presses two-stories below, past the plastic machine-like clacking of the reporter's pool and we burst through the antique wooden door and into another open, high-ceilinged room of forlorn beige cubicles. "Darla, this is Jimmy, our new guy in graphics."

"Hello, Ji—"

"He's legal age and a US citizen. He's never been convicted and is willing to submit to a background check. He's from Pennsylvania and just got to town a month ago. Last employer was the M&M, and why are you looking at me that way? He's straight, filing as 'single' even though he's practically married and they live at 715 Downey Street in the Haight. He starts at the bottom of the management grades. Are you taking this down, Darla?"

"Thank you, Gary. May I have a moment with Jimmy? I'll walk him back over to graphics when we're done."

"Yeah, sure, but make it quick. Unlike HR, we have deadlines." He spun and was on his way. He called back over his shoulder, "Keep her on task, Skeeter."

"I don't really know why I'm here. I have no experience," I told Darla.

"Gary must have his reasons."

"Well, yeah, I can draw."

"You must be pretty good."

"Yeah, I guess I am, but I've never worked at a paper. I've never worked in an office."

"You do now, and this is quite a paper. There are people standing in line to work here," she said.

"I'm grateful, for sure. I just don't want to screw it up for you guys."

"I'm sure you won't."

57

ALREADY YOU'RE MAKING ME LOOK BAD

I sat in front of Gary's nearly empty desk—pen in holder, open day planner with no plans and a small brass clock. Behind me, he paced his huge office. "We're going deep. We'll be taking shots at the seamy underbelly of city and state officials, inequities and championing the disenfranchised," he said. "Pete'll write it, as only he can, and you'll do the illustrations. His columns get picked up in a lot of places, and your work's going to be taped to refrigerators all over the country. People don't cut out columns, but they do cartoons. A lot of *Ka-pow!*, *Swish!*, *Riiipp!*, *Ka-boom!*"

"Like, Mullen and Ricigliano?" I turned and said.

"Huh. That college stuff rubbed off on you. Yeah, like the ink-stained jokesters. We're bringing back the fun and games and the drama department. Damn paper's been going the wrong direction ever since these hi-tech geniuses started showing up from all over the planet. No sense of place. Full of themselves, eating out every night, big German cars and so goddamn successful and thinking everything can be explained in ones and zeros. People are people. People still wanna be entertained, ya know? Go to a Wednesday afternoon Giants game and count heads. Lotta sick days, there. Those the only shoes you have?"

"I'm sorry?"

He came around front. "Your shoes. You're going to be meeting the publisher in a couple hours, and already you're making me look bad." He pulled out his wallet. "Here's a couple hundreds, and I'll expense it. Run up the street, and get some respectable shoes and pants—dress slacks. Then get back here by one. Go up to Macy's. Tell them to dress you like a professional."

Who carries hundreds in their wallet?

"And a collared shirt—something to hide that snakebite on your neck. Geesh!"

I hustled out onto Fifth Street's crowded walk and realized I didn't know where Macy's was. Up. Gary said, "Go up to Macy's." So, I wound upstream through the throngs of people in a hurry, some pulling roller luggage, Japanese tourists spread out in guided groups, and I aimed for Market Street. My head was fogged. This had all fallen into place so fast. I wasn't sure I belonged here, this city, this paper. I was a painter, a builder. Sure, I'd done cartoons for the school paper—the school paper! Day one and I was going to a meeting with my new boss, the publisher and their ace syndicated columnist. I was bush league in the pros, and it had my stomach doing flips.

58

WITH THE PUBLISHER

W orn, wide and white marble stairs led to the executive suites. I held onto the rail—slippery new soles. The Macy's threads had me feeling a bit more comfortable—at least I looked the part. We passed a dozen private executive offices, most doors open, and their muted desk lamps distinct from the harsh fluorescent hall lights. In their quiet lairs, far from the high-frequency operations on the floors below, I imagined those of power patiently planned, schemed and determined the direction of the company and the news. Gary opened one of the double doors at the end of the hall, and we entered a cavernous reception area—Persian rugs, dark wood, leather, porcelain and gleaming brass. Long, open drapes at one of the tall windows waved the city in—cabs, tourists, MUNI busses and the ring of a cable car turning at Market and Powell. Shrimp-fried rice and "Ja-eesus Christ!" A Bible-thumper passed on the street three stories below.

"Want me to close the window, Millie?" Gary said.

An ancient gray willow, she looked up and smiled. "Oh,

please, of course. Thank you, Gary. I didn't hear you come in with all of that going on. Pete's already in there. Go on in."

"Thanks. This is Jimmy, by the way. My new guy."

She stood, barely taller than when she sat, and we shook. A bird's hand, warm.

"C'mon." Gary opened a tall heavy door and led me into the publisher's suite.

In the center, a large antique table commandeered its space and proudly presented a bombastic array of orange and red flowers in a tall, blue-dragon vase. On the periphery were alcoves of assorted small tables with crystal lamps, bronzes, a couple Remingtons, full bookcases, awards and photos spanning the century. I definitely didn't belong here. Damn, Remingtons! Two stretched, trim, forty-something men at opposite ends of the room, each sunk deep into a brass-studded leather wing chair, elbows splayed, fingers laced across their chests, one in jeans and a work shirt, the other casual slacks and a polo. Both wore cowboy boots propped on frail, low tables. One looked vaguely familiar.

"Gary, thanks for coming." The one in the polo pulled his knees in and stood. Six-something, full curly-and-gelled blonde hair, gym-toned and confident, the guy could have been a model.

"Foster," Gary said. He slumped into a leather sofa just inside the door and underhand waved me like a puppy toward the publisher.

"Foster Farallon, this is Jimmy and he's got more talent in his little finger than half the tea in China."

Foster laughed and thrust a long hand, "I am pleased to meet you, Jimmy. See why Gary's not a writer? Have a seat. Pete, are you going say hello?"

"Hey, there, Jim, Gary," Pete invested two calories and raised his fingers slightly, then let them drop. It was the guy from the Denny's parking lot at Winnemucca. Narrow snake eyes, sharp features and a five o'clock shadow in the early afternoon.

I looked around for a place to sit and came up wanting.

"Jimmy, this is Pete Baxter, the most independent sonofabitch in the kennel. Pete's also our newest columnist. We coaxed his sorry excuse of a truck all the way cross country from Palm Beach—he's just now losing his tan. It took us months of persuading and a bit more than the budget to get him here."

"We've met briefly," Pete said. "Mostly his dog and me on the way here. Hello, again. How's the pooch?"

"What are the chances?" Foster said. "Well, this is a great start.

Pete has a hard-on for just about anything that could be remotely called organized— religion, crime, this paper. Isn't that right, Pete?"

"Fuck this paper."

"What did I tell you?" Foster said. "Gary's shown me some of your work, and we are proud to have you here. I like his idea of bringing you up our way, learning our aesthetic and maybe training to be his replacement in the event he topples over some day at the M&M or, perhaps, gets shot dead in his bare ass by yet another jealous husband."

Hands in my new pockets, I glanced at Gary. He kinked his neck.

"So, you will be learning newspaper layout, having a hand at photo editing, display ads, the whole enchilada—that is, when you're not working with this cantankerous bastard." He nodded toward Pete. Pete raised one finger.

"Pete spends face time with the people he writes about— the poor, the minorities and otherwise oppressed—and gets their side of the story. Then, he goes after the oppressors— sheriffs, the courts, politicians, the church. You'll accompany him on some of his trips to hear the stories first-hand. That will be the hardest part of this job, car time with Pete."

"Alright with the bullshit, Foster? I like this guy already, keeps his mouth shut, and if I have him pegged right, he's got mud on his shoes. Where you from Jim?" Pete said.

The temperature in the room had risen. "From the east coast, PA."

"What'd you do there, in P–A?"

"Built barns."

"Goddamn it!" He pulled his feet off the table and sat up. "See there? An honest-to-God, functioning human being. Surprised you hired one, Gary. Can I go now, Foster?" Strong hands pushed on the armrests, and he rose like a man who'd had too many bones broken. Probably six-two at one time, he was more like six-even, now.

"Yes, Pete, and thank you for gracing us with your humility."

Pete limped to the door, "Fuck you, Foster—you and your little orange Porsche."

"It is always a pleasure, Pete.

Well, that went better than I expected. It looks like you and Pete are a team, Jimmy. Or, is it Jim?" Foster asked.

"Either works. June calls me James."

"June?"

"His girl. Beautiful, strong and smart. They're all but married. Live in the Haight." Gary spread both arms across the back of the sofa. Wet pits.

"You've met her?" Foster asked.

"No. But he's told me a lot about her. Works retail. Goddamn goddess. They're head over heels."

The room was definitely hotter.

"I look forward to meeting her. If not before, surely at the holiday party. Gary has told you about that?"

Gary leaned forward, elbows on knees. "No, I'll fill him in —still got a month. He's going to be helping with some of the decorations."

"We've reserved Bimbo's 365 Club, James. It's going to be one heck of a night," Foster said.

"We probably ought to get back downstairs." Gary pushed himself up and off the sofa.

"Of course." Foster looked at his watch. "I have to run, too. I expect you to kick butt, James."

59

TAKE-A-LOOK

Pete and I were sitting on the packed dry earth beneath a concrete bridge. We were strobe lit by the flickering reflections off the water far below, and, three feet above us, city traffic pounded like a drum corps across tarred road seams. If I hadn't been there with him, I never would have known that part about the light. Aimless papers, bottles and clothing spilled from collapsed cardboard boxes, and all around, greasy sleeping bags scattered like napalmed bodies in that homeless hideout. Our subject hadn't once looked directly at us. He sat in front of us, cross-legged and in profile as Pete tried to get the story out of the man everyone called Take-a-Look. ". . . and, that's all I'm suh-suh-saying," he finished.

We'd overheard a few local kids talking about him at the hole-in-the-wall newsstand-café where Pete lunched on grilled cheese and a Diet Coke each day. Crowded little place, it was mostly a newsstand and there had to be a thousand magazine titles and newspapers represented in the shop. Small grill behind the counter where you ordered and it was all pre-made or grilled sandwiches at the newsstand.

Pete was about to bite into his grilled cheese. "You ever order anything else?" I said.

"Why?"

"I don't know, change things up once-in-a-while?"

"Why?"

"Vegetables, grains, fruit," I said.

"Why?"

"Never mind."

Three kids piled into the only other booth, behind Pete. Our cramped table and built-in seats shook. Pete grabbed his wobbling Coke glass.

"That was Take-a-Look. That was him, just now, across the street. Cleanest sidewalks in the city," the white kid said.

"You ever talk to him?"

"Yeah, me and Tony. He was bent over, digging shit out of the sidewalk cracks, and, like, I say, 'What's up, dude? Find anything cool?' And he glances at me then turns his head away, like he's really watching traffic—like seriously. So I say, 'You okay, man?' And I shit you not, he goes, 'Yes Raymond.'"

"So, like, who's Raymond?" the black kid said.

"My middle name. He called me by my middle name."

Pete stopped chewing.

"So, he knows you, or something?"

"Hell no! And, like, he called Tony by his middle name, too. The whole time he won't look at us."

"Whoa."

"Like he's all wizard, or something."

"Like a psychologist."

"They say it's ever since he tried to save a girl from being raped, got the shit kicked outta him and, like, got brain damage. Used to be a fireman."

Pete wiped his mouth, balled up the napkin and slid out of the booth. "Let's go."

There he was, across the street tilling sidewalk cracks— Take-a-Look. Giants cap, black overcoat and shoes turned up like a clown's. "Go on back to the paper. See what Gary has for you. I'm going to be awhile," Pete said.

Two weeks later, Pete's three-day, three-part-column was titled, *The Hero Among Us.* He took on the insurance companies, the city of San Francisco, the courts, the California State Fire Fighters Association, the ACLU, the medical community, pharmaceutical companies and Congress for sweeping the mentally ill out into the streets.

"The records show that the politicians were dogged by the image and financial problems posed by the state hospitals and that the scientific and medical establishment sold Congress and the state legislatures a quick (drug) fix for a complicated problem that was bought sight unseen."*

Pete had watched the action and interactions with Take-a-Look for the rest of that first afternoon and, as night set in, followed him to his bridge blocks away. Pete picked up his trail, again, the next day. He watched the man tender quarters into expired parking meters, pick up cigarette butts, papers and other trash and make countless trips to waste cans along his one-square-block daytime world. Near the end of the day, Pete got a few words out of him. Between that, his bird-dog nose and the paper's microfiche, it didn't take Pete long to glom the story together. I did three separate illustrations—an abbreviated beginning, middle and end approach. The last one showed us sitting face-to-face with the man in that eerie light beneath the bridge.

His name was Leland Gage, single and forty-three. Leland

had been a great fireman. In his years at the station, he'd saved lives, including the lives of two comrades.

Ten years ago, Leland had been out at Candlestick for a Giants game after which he came downtown to hit a few clubs. He was cutting through the Tehama Alley on his way to the Cadillac Bar & Grill when he heard a commotion and a muffled scream from the second deck of a parking garage. He charged up the ramp and ran right into a gang rape. He—and the girl—barely lived.

His shit-for-brains stepmother squatted in a Quonset hut in the forlorn and overlooked Hunters Point. His only kin, it was she who pocketed the one-time $5000 cash payout from the insurance company and to whose mailbox the monthly benefits checks came. A tidy cash cow, that stepson had turned out to be.

As a result of our column—Pete's column—Take-a-Look became a city movement. Donors mailed checks to the paper, others dropped off warm clothes and boxes of food. It was actually getting out of hand until a small phalanx of women from Glide Memorial Church showed up and offered to help. Arms crossed, and her back straighter than a broomstick, their leader stated, "Going forward, *we* will manage Mr. Gage's situation." And they did.

New York Times, Oct. 30, 1984

"So, Pete, I guess you did some good, made a difference," I said across the booth. The newsstand had a promotional poster featuring Pete's story tacked up over the grill.

He took another loopy-stringed bite, placed the grilled sandwich back on the plate with both hands, wiped his slick fingers on the napkin, chewed a couple times, leaned forward and sucked on the straw.

"You gonna say something, or what?" I said.

He chewed and swallowed. "What the hell am I supposed to say?" His snake eyes locked in on me. "We're just doing our job. They pay us to do this." He took another half-moon bite.

"A life is better because of what you wrote."

A lot of chewing, he finally swallowed. "It's just a fucking business, and we're cogs in the wheels. They have to sell papers —every day. Get it? The beast is insatiable." After a loud pull on the straw he sat back, palms on the table, swallowed and stared at crooked fingers. "Besides, there are thousands in this city living like him."

Saturday was Ram Van Day. We might have considered sealing up the van and donating it as a time capsule, encased in Plexiglas, set on a marble plinth, and a monument to transcontinental travel enshrined at the Palace of the Legion of Honor. Instead, we completely emptied, vacuumed, washed and waxed our starship. Black trash bags filled rapidly with peanuts, Snickers' wrappers, single socks, raisins, spent Kleenex, receipts, a couple moldy towels, crushed beer cans, a first volume of the *Encyclopedia Britannica* of which neither of us knew its origin—it had to be Tom's—and broken down, torn apart and shared paperbacks. That and a couple vacuum loads of White Dog fur. By late afternoon, it would have made Bobbi proud.

KANE'S LOST THE SCENT

The next morning rose crisp and cool. We pointed our pristine van north, past Crissy Field and up and out of the Presidio's stately groves and officers' quarters and directed our glasspacked rumble across the Golden Gate Bridge. We'd seen pictures of it plenty of times, but the scale! Who were the amazing, hardtack people who built this thing in the Thirties? About a mile long, a hundred feet wide and what, a thousand feet above the water? "Is that what it is?" June said. "A thousand feet?"

"Nah, that's not a thousand feet," I said. "Maybe two-hundred-and-forty. And, ladies and gentlemen, if you'll look to your left, Japan."

Off the north side of the bridge, we drove up into the rainbow tunnel and down into Marin County. We were out of the city and into the affluent countryside just like that—home to Jerry Garcia, George Lucas and four thousand inmates at San Quentin.

"Where are we going?" June said.

"Special place Pete told me about."

We passed the blue and white Sausalito's tall masts, its quaint streets speckled with galleries, restaurants and tourists, its elegant homes on the hill looking across the bay to the city, and we turned out of heavy traffic onto a narrow, winding Route 1. There, it was a serpentine crawl through our first ever, hallowed, redwood forest and out into twisted cypress stands and aromatic eucalyptus groves, past Nick's Cove and the waters of Tomales Bay. A stone's throw north, at the mouth of the bay, we got off the blacktop, doubled back and rolled slowly south on a dirt lane over bumps and ruts into Lawson's Landing. "Cows," June said. Mammoth sand dunes piled high to our right separated a flat green pasture and a widely-scattered herd of Angus and Hereford from the ocean. We followed tire tracks down through the pasture where kids flew kites and threw Frisbees between the cows. Parents, aunts and uncles grilled fresh-caught perch, pumped water and popped a few cold ones next to their campers. "What *is* this place?" June said. The van idled through what looked like an early Flemish painting scattered with RV's. "It has to be a movie set. Lucas and his crew are around here somewhere."

The lane gave out at a wide dirt lot. On one side, what looked to have been a great western barn from the last century now stood as a bait shop, general store and dry dock for marine repairs. Deep inside, welding sparks flew, and a heavy hammer bounced off ringing steel. An ancient sun-bleached boardwalk and rows of gray weathered docks edged the braided currents at the narrow mouth of the bay. The tide was changing. "End of the road," June said. We dropped out of the van.

It was a little-known place that made you feel like you could just hand in your keys, like you had finally arrived and had no reason to leave. Rural, quiet, now that the hammer had stopped, and not a soul to be seen. Far off, a dog. We walked to the end of the empty boardwalk, stepped down onto the wet gravel shoreline and strolled out the small peninsula. We passed a few spokes of dirt lanes rimming the area and leading through the dunes to the axle of the bait shop and store—lanes lined with an eclectic array of small and ramshackle trailer homes from the Fifties and Sixties. Another couple hundred yards along the water, and we were at the point.

"Look," I said.

She came up behind me, wrapped her arms around my shoulders, her chin on my head.

I scanned the narrow mouth of the bay. "Watch—out there." The surface rolled slowly. Small fussy waves licked at our feet. "There." First one, then many glistening heads popped to the surface. "Hold still." The closest was about twenty feet from us. Harbor Seals. A dozen watched. Polished, black eyes, their whiskers dripped, and they rocked gently with the waves. Now they stretched up and turned their attention to some-where behind us. We followed their gaze to a small herd of deer emerging from the tall grass of the dunes. Once the deer reached the water's edge, the mammals were just feet apart and curious.

"East meets West," June whispered. "And I think it's over, the running. Kane's stopped chasing us. I feel it, James. We have our lives back—beautiful city, I love my work, you're at that big fat *Chronicle* wearing city boy shoes and no more running."

Back at the docks, someone was trying to start a reluctant marine motor. There were rattles, grinding and a loud *POP!!* June jumped, then sucked a big breath. "Hey, you okay?" I said.

Her lips trembled like beginning a cry.

"Hey, it was a backfire." I hugged her, and she settled. "It's all good, right?"

"Right, right."

She leaned into me and relaxed some, her face against my

neck. Tears. A minute passed. Maybe she wasn't convinced the running was over, I thought. But she sure could tell herself a good story.

"June, you're doing that ear thing."

"I know."

"So, we're just going to do it here on the beach?"

"We can't be doin it in front of baby seals and Bambi." She straightened up. "C'mon, let's check out the gypsies."

"MARBLES TODAY"

Each trailer was its own sovereign nation. Some were decorated with prayer flags and bells, others with crossed swords and anchors, hub caps, road signs, Barbie Dolls, The Jolly Roger, driftwood sculptures, Mardi Gras beads and some with rooftop decks. My favorite was the rainbow trailer with tall swaying rods topped by kites, windsocks and spinners. The miniature coaches had been here awhile, sinking slowly into the sand for years. Many had extensive raised gardens— climbing bougainvillea, vegetables, succulents, herbs and cacti. A listing, hand-painted sign driven into the ground in front of one of the ancient rigs, its unpainted aluminum surface oxidized dull by the sea air, stopped us. "Marbles Today."

We were mulling over the marbles sign when the side door opened, and a pretty twenty-something in a long vapor of a dress, came out onto the little deck, scratched her stomach, raised one knee and let go a sonorous fart. "Yeowza!" She expressed what might have been pride or relief. She looked our way and reset the center of her horn-rims with one finger. "You like marbles?"

"Yeah. Says here you have some today," I said.

With serious concentration, she straightened her wide brim hat, pointed bare feet down the two steps, reached into her low neckline, adjusted something and opened the gate. It was waist high, to me, the gate. It was taller than that to her. "Veuillez venir dans," she smiled.

I deferred to June who went first. "You're a big one," the young woman said.

"A big what?" June said.

"Person. Like, whatta ya think? Tractor? I don't know if you're going to fit in our place. You might have to sit on the floor, if you can find space. Sorry, I'm not good about etiquette or housekeeping."

June lowered her head and entered.

"Showers, Dolly! You're also not good about showers!" a voice bellowed above the talk radio from somewhere in the back of the trailer. Close and dark, now that we were inside, Dolly opened tie-dyed curtains on the wall opposite the door exposing the neighbor's boarded up, flat black trailer, eight feet away.

"Please, find a seat," Dolly said. "I don't mind standing. Mom, do we have to?" she yelled at the low ceiling.

"You have to at least take a shower between boyfriends!"

"How would you know?" Dolly yelled.

"Christ, Doll, I can smell you from here!" Her mom came into the front room. She and Dolly were the same height. The mom, in a white terry robe, though, was more solidly built. The woman worked a large comb through long, wet, fragrant hair and dropped onto a pile of scattered mail on the loveseat. A cat screeched and bolted from beneath and disappeared.

June squatted on a footstool by the door, and I sat at the small built-in kitchen table. I slid some of the clutter back a few inches and leaned.

"You like strikers, sinkers, cats-eyes?" Dolly said.

"Yeah." I picked a few Cheerios off my forearm.

"Aggies, alleys, clearies?"

"Yep."

"Commies, corkscrews, swirls? Steelies?"

"I just want to play, again," I said. "Maybe play with June, here."

"It's all you boys want to do, is fuckin play."

"Wash your mouth out, Dolly!" her mom snapped.

Dolly whipped her hat off and slung it to the floor. She put her hands on her hips and stared at the ceiling.

"That's right," the mom said. "Little Miss Know-It-All, and who died and made you queen? Just sell the man some marbles, for Chrissake!"

June cracked the door open. In the trailer's brighter light, we saw that Dolly's five-gallon plastic buckets held marbles, clamshells, buttons, cookie cutters, alligator clips and thread spools. There was a bucket of beer caps and another of beer coasters. There was a single-shelf near the ceiling and running around three sides of the small room displaying hundreds of action figures. There were magazines tied in two-foot stacks on the floor. Atop the magazines were green and yellow milk crates of Hot Wheels, Legos, olive-green army men, tanks and trucks and her small refrigerator was covered in parrot magnets. In the tiny kitchen, a few long-ignored trays of cat litter overflowed, and they were choking us.

Dolly tromped out of the room and down the hall. Her mom smiled and demurely combed. We heard under-the-breath cursing and rummaging, and Dolly was back with a handful of cloth sacks. "Here, pick through the bucket, as many as you want. It's ten bucks a sack. Anyone want a drink? I'm having a Screwdriver."

"Uh, thanks, but we haven't had lunch," I said.

"I really don't know what that has to do with anything, but that's just me. Mom thinks I'm an alcoholic."

"You're not an alcoholic, Dolly. Look at you, you still put juice in your booze," her mom said. "And are you going to introduce us, or what? I'll have a Bloody Mary, while you're up."

So, it was Dolly and her mom, Raven. By the time I'd picked through the bucket and filled a sack, they were on their second drinks and well into their story, and June had propped the door wider against the breeze with her foot. The wind made dry noises, here—sand blew across the metal sides and roof.

Raven had been a roadie with The Dead whenever they were on the West Coast. On this coast the band drove wherever they went. She refused to fly. "It just don't make sense to me," she said. "Strapped into a tiny seat five miles up in the sky and 'In case of an emergency the little blue lights on the floor will save you?' I don't think so."

"I'm with you on that," June said. "Never flew, never will."

"When the boys were out truckin on the other coast or in Europe, I was Momma Central right back here in Marin. Someone needed a signature for a package? I signed for it. Jerry forgot his meds? I sent em." She emptied the last of her drink in one long gulp. "They were gone most of the time. Didn't call it 'The Endless Tour' for nothing." She said she supplemented things working weekends at The Sweetwater Saloon. "I was a generalist. I did whatever had to be done— bartend, cook, take tickets, wait tables, sound checks, security. There weren't many problems, though. It's a happy place." She chewed her celery.

"Then, one day Dolly just popped outta me bloody, head-first and hungry and things changed. No more road trips, I put down roots. Worked at The Sweetwater until Aunt Ollie passed away and left a small bundle and these buckets—enough to move out here and go into the marble business. Sure you two don't want a drink? Cute couple, where you from?"

"Oh, were kinda from all over," June said rising. She ducked and backed out into the sunlight. "I'm June and this is James." She beckoned me. "And he's promised to take me to lunch, and we really have to be going."

"Uh, yeah. Great place you have here. Nice to meet you. Boy, what a place, here along the ocean and all. Cool marbles, and thanks again." I handed Dolly a ten and followed June down the steps. Fresh air.

"Drop by again sometime," Raven called from inside.

Dolly leaned out the door and raised her glass, "Tah-tah."

June laced her fingers in mine as we walked back to the van. "Another trip through the looking glass," she said.

"Raven was young once. She did a lot of stuff, and now she's stopped, grown roots, she's lonely, and she'll die here."

"*That's* what you come away with?"

VENICE, CA, 2015

For a while there, Erskine sightings were infrequent. I assumed he was spending a lot of time at Annie's. When I did see him, it was at the deli locked into his laptop, pinched and intense, or we'd pass on the street with barely a nod. I expected him to be delirious—he and Annie in yippy puppy love. Yet he'd slip by, eyes averted, body slumped, head down.

I went to his cottage for the first time, ever. I knocked. A ghost opened the door, stepped back and waved me in.

"Hey Erskine. Coffee on?" I chirped. I figured it would pick him up, sound familiar, like something he'd said a hundred times at my place.

"Not really. Kitchen's there," he pointed. He wandered across the mirror-finished bamboo floor and dropped into a contemporary club chair. It was leather and looked to have been sewn and hand-rubbed by small women on the Amalfi coast. I looked around. Anal. Nothing out of place—a catalog photo.

I didn't know he read. He knew I read, having interrupted me countless times. But I never took him for a reader. Two walls in his pristine living room were floor-to-ceiling books. "Erskine, you read."

"Not really."

"All these books? You've read them?"

"Yeah."

I ran my fingers along their spines. "Biographies and histories."

"No shit."

There was Doris Kearns-Goodwin's *No Ordinary Time*, Jon Meacham, Walter Isaacson. Ron Chernow's *Hamilton*. There were Mary Frances Berry's *My Face Is Black Is True— Callie House and the Struggle for Ex-Slave Reparations*, and Linda Gordon's *A Life Beyond Limits*, and Bailyn's *The Ideological Origins of the American Revolution*.

"You're a history buff, Erskine."

"I'm not a buff anything."

"Mind if I look in your fridge? You got a beer, soda?"

"Go for it."

"You, too?" I said.

"Whatever."

I found a couple Pepsis and the opener. I passed on the perfectly-arranged crystal flutes behind glass cupboard doors.

"Coasters?" I said sitting across from him.

"In the drawer." He pointed to a very cool, hand-crafted side table—the proportions, the maple inlays.

I sat the coasters and bottles on thick Noguchi glass. "So, how you been?"

"Nothing to report."

"Haven't seen much of you lately," I said.

"Nothing left to see. I'm done. It's over. It's been a sham—the whole thing—my whole life. This is where I stop, where I just get the fuck off."

"Erskine, will you please cease with the violins and talk to me? You're getting dangerously close to dragging ass, here. What the hell's up? How's Annie for Chrissake?"

"Annie's good. I moved out."

"Why?" I took a sip. He hadn't touched his.

"I can't do this to her. She's so alive, such spirit. I can't do this to anyone, and why don't you just go and leave me alone, okay?"

"Can't do what, Mister Victim?"

"I'm serious this time. No shitting around."

"Okay. Serious about what, Erskine?"

"Cancer."

"You have—Hell, Erskine. I'm sorry. What's it about? I mean how bad, how far? Where, how long?"

"We don't know," he said.

I put the bottle down. "Then, you—wait. What? We don't know what? What do you mean? You have cancer."

"Yeah, I got it. That's about all we know."

"Where? What kind?" I said.

"Prostate."

"You have prostate cancer."

"I do. Slapped me down, midstride. When everything was looking up. The final insult. Goddamn biology. It fucking sneaks up on you. Eating right, doing the goddamn push-ups, then this."

"Wait a minute. Back up a second, here. You're sure. You've actually been to a doctor? You've had a biopsy?" I said.

"That's what that was? Him and his nurse sticking a dozen

needles as long as my arm up my crotch with me in stirrups like maybe I'm giving birth, and all the time they're arguing about last year's Super Bowl? That was a biopsy?"

"How bad? How far along?" I said.

"Early stages. Suppose to watch and wait."

"Watch and wait. Watch and wait? Hell, Erskine! We're all watching and waiting. Everyone our age has prostate cancer."

"Thank you, Mister Sensitive, but not like mine."

"Where's yours, in your nose?"

After getting Erskine's pins somewhat back under him, I'd gone home and contemplated my own prostate. Prostate, joint pain, tinnitus, gout . . . Life hitting the tilted tile floor a drop at a time —mortality leaking from the room.

Next afternoon, I went out the side door of the deli by the Rose Academy of Art—a short cut in the rain. It never rains in southern California? Guess what.

Edging close to the building and skirting the parking lot, I stepped into the shelter of a narrow, open, unaddressed doorway. The staccato muffle of leather hitting dense wood muttered out—a speed bag. I was dropped back forty years— that sound and the smells from that doorway—salt and vinegar, heat rub and mildew. I went in.

I stepped down two shallow steps, turned right into the corridor and was stopped by a low-on-the-nose, over-the-glasses stare. The gatekeeper. She sat at a desk, there, in the hallway—old computer, rolodex and scattered bills beneath a tortoise shell letter opener. A yellow pencil stuck out of an unwinding gray bun. Lips tight, she was framed by a collage of posters—Leonard, Mancini, Camacho, Patterson, Ali, Frazier, Foreman, Tex Cobb, Holmes. The bigs, and they were all there —the retired and the dead. Shoulders narrow, feet planted, crouched and ready, she was going to wait for me to make the first move.

"Hi, I heard the bag in there," I said and nodded down the hall. "Didn't know there was a gym, here. I boxed, back in the day, welterweight. Nothing special, I guess. Long time ago."

Chin low, she waited.

"Would it be okay to have a quick look?"

She stared. Her nose twitched. "What's that smell?" she jabbed.

"Oh, this," I grabbed at my shoulder bag. "From upstairs, tuna hoagie."

"Phew!"

"Sorry, yeah, kinda pungent. I just . . . sorry." I turned to leave.

"Follow me," she said.

The hallway opened to a mirrored room filled with a red and blue boxing ring. Outside of the ring, and squeezed into two sides of the gym, were heavy bags, speed bags, weights and a broken-down sofa. One tall, wiry, steel-and-cables kid worked out alone on a heavy bag in the far corner. He dropped his hands, shook sweat from his blond curls and looked over.

"Giovanni, can pops watch awhile?" she said.

He nodded and went back to work.

"Sit there." She pointed to the sofa. "Be quiet." She left.

He worked to an automatic timer, three-minute rounds. A couple rounds on speed bags, a couple on the heavy bags, shadow boxing, lightning-fast, tight left hook. Between rounds, he appeared to be spent, wasted and wrung out, not an ounce left, and I remembered feeling so flagged and nauseous way back when. At the buzzer, he was at it again, all speed, power and grit. It was cold, calculated mechanics. Two rounds per station, he worked his way down the wall toward me.

I hadn't had breakfast. I'd risen late and rushed out for

class. I don't know why I care about being there on time—none
of the students care. When they arrive, most busy themselves
with whatever food and drinks they stopped off for. That eats
another five minutes into class time. No harm in having my
sandwich here, I guessed. Saffron tuna salad with pickled egg,
pepper jack, lettuce, tomato, onion, oil and vinegar on a whole-
wheat garlic roll tightly wrapped in white butcher paper. A
one-pound, fermented, oozing torpedo. That and a Diet Snapple. I opened the hoagie quietly and bit into two-days-worth of
fleshy calories. He was, maybe, halfway into the next round
when the kid stopped, "What's that smell? That—!" He dashed
three steps to a plastic bucket and hurled his guts. From one
knee, he wiped his mouth on the back of a glove and looked up.

I wadded the sandwich back into my bag and, "Sorry, I'm
sorry," I left. On the armrest of the couch, the Snapple
remained.

* * *

I had just taken the last sip of the best cup of the morning. I
was at that crossroads—put the book down and get another cup
or continue to the next chapter. A knock at the door. Okay, that
sealed it. I marked the book, grabbed the cup and headed to the
door on my way to the kitchen. I opened to . . . "Erskine, you
knocked. Hey, come on in. I have coffee, and I think I have
sugar." I went out to the kitchen.

"We still on?" he said, closing the door.

"Yep. You're early, though. Probably ought to be heading
out in another fifteen minutes. Time for a coffee, if you
want it."

"I'm good," he said from my miniature living room. "Unless
you have donuts, or something. What's different in here? You
changed things."

"Not really." I took a plate with two of the deli's pie-size chocolate chip cookies in to him and went back out for the coffees.

"No, there's something different. Of course, you cleared this table, you picked up," he said.

"Yeah. Seeing your place the other day, and all—spotless." I put the cups on the weirdly naked table between us.

"I like things I can control, like cleanliness, punctuality, diet," he said. "It's things I can't control that put me on to boil. This prostate."

"We'll find out more about that this morning. Success stories, options, newest techniques."

"This is disappointing," he said.

"What?"

"I thought you said you had donuts."

"No, you asked for donuts, or something. I didn't say I had donuts."

"So you figured big-ass cookies?"

"You said, 'Or something.' "

The support group meets once a month at the Venice Community Center Annex at Third and Rose. Not much to write about as far as buildings go—single-story, flat roof, used to be a First African Baptist church. The steeple and cross were hit by lightning and destroyed six years ago in a freak Saturday afternoon storm—the dapper, fornicating preacher burned to a cinder. The small congregation got the hint and abandoned the God-forsaken place. A couple years later, the city took it over for a dime on a dollar.

I led Erskine up three concrete steps, through faded and peeling double doors and into the dull foyer. Two disagreeable-looking white-haired guys about our age in Polo shirts and khakis sat, arms folded and somewhat back-to-back at the greeter's table.

"Most hits of any player on record," one said. "They hate Pete Rose cause he's white. They'd never get away with this if he was black."

"Baseball's bigger than any one player," the other guy said. "They have to protect the integrity of the game."

"Integrity of the what? A game has integrity? Players like Rose, and there aren't many, make the game."

"Rose is a gambler. A fixer."

They moved their chairs farther apart.

"Amazing fielder, what an athlete."

"Cheater."

"Three series rings, two golden gloves."

"Tax evasion."

"Go to hell."

In front of them was the sign-in sheet and stacks of brochures on diet, mental health, yoga, pool therapy and an array of publications from The American Cancer Society. While the greeters argued, I signed in on lines forty-nine and fifty. Behind me, Erskine mumbled.

Another set of double doors and we entered what had been the sanctuary and was now a twenty-by-forty-foot resonant space with brown steel folding chairs arranged in arced rows. The rows were two-thirds full of gray, middle-aged, and older men. Empty seats were near the front. Erskine and I chose two in the fourth row and sat facing a mic'd lectern. Erskine sat straight, neck tense and stone-faced. His hands gripped his knees. I spread an arm over the empty chair next to me, slumped, turned and scanned the audience. Most must have been regulars, many were chatting. Not like chatting at a coffee shop or a baseball game, though. Somber, quiet chatting. None looked very happy. In the back corner, a line stood at the men's room door.

The mic popped and squealed. I turned front. He was tall, broad-shouldered in a madras shirt. Probably mid-sixties, moustache, eyebrows and thick, coiffed hair dyed black.

"Gentlemen, thank you for coming to this month's meeting of the Venice Prostate Cancer Support Group. I see a lot of familiar faces and a few new ones. Will you please raise your hand if this is your first time in attendance?"

I nudged Erskine.

"What?" he whispered.

"Raise your hand."

"No."

Our host scanned his audience from back to front and landed on Erskine and me. "Let's meet a new attendee. Here, in front. First time, sir?" he asked Erskine.

Erskine sagged and sighed. He looked up. "Yes."

"I'm Dan Thorkalson," the host said. "I was diagnosed seven years ago, underwent radiation therapy and have been cancer-free for six years." He knocked the wood of the lectern.

Erskine sighed and stood up. "I'm Erskine." He motioned toward me, "This is my neighbor, Jimmy. Jimmy was diagnosed a month ago and doesn't know what the hell to do next. Can't eat, can't sleep, he's been a nervous wreck. Look at him, red as a beet. His doc showed him a diagram of the situation, the tangled mess of nerves around the prostate and God's little joke of anatomy. Jimmy, here, sure as hell doesn't want some amped up Asian with a scalpel hacking away at that over-ripe cherry. And the thought of some zealous Israeli quack with a laser aimed at his ass isn't his idea of a great afternoon, either. So, I brought him down here to find out what's what. Maybe hear a couple success stories."

I stared up at him, open-mouthed.

"He looks old and dumpy, but he's spry for his age—still has a few rounds left in the chamber. You have any suggestions?"

In the back of the room, the toilet flushed. Someone came out, someone went in.

"Welcome, Jimmy, and thank you, Erskine. Jimmy, first-of-all, you're among friends. We've all been where you are, right now. What are your numbers?"

"Numbers?" I said. I looked at Erskine.

"I'm sorry," Dan said. "Your Gleason numbers."

"He's looking at a three, four," Erskine said and sat down.

"That's good news, Jimmy. Not so aggressive. Many options, and we can talk about that later. Right now, I'd like to introduce today's speaker."

I leaned into Erskine's shoulder. "What the hell is the matter with you?" I whispered. "Is this the only help you need? Has anyone ever suggested a brain scan?"

We left an hour later. We left a room of many incontinent, impotent and enduring men— men who'd had treatments years ago before less invasive procedures were available. Some had recurring bouts with the beast. We left them thinking how great for me that I had such low numbers and a peach of a neighbor.

* * *

"You have to sign the forms, Erskine. They say you understand there are always risks and that you're willing to undergo this procedure despite the risks."

"They should be signing this, not me. That *they're* aware there are risks, and if anything happens, *they're* responsible. Hell, I'll be asleep."

"Shall we just leave?"

"If I go under, I need back up," he said.

"Of course, you do. I've called the Secretary. The Navy has

sent a team. They're all over the roof with concussion grenades and ready to drop into surgery at my command."

"They won't respond to you, and how do you know about concussion grenades?" he said.

"Erskine, just fill out the forms, sign them and give them back to the nice nurse, here. Her name's Donna. Name, address, phone number . . ."

He shuffled the forms, spread them across the counter and began signing. "You think you know who your doctor is, then they put you under, and for all you know, they give the janitor a shot at it. The docs probably all love him, great guy."

"Erskine, you missed a line," I pointed.

"Janitor's probably some hairless Slovak named Vlado. They're teaching him English and surgery during their breaks in the lunchroom, and he's damned good. Takes to it damned fast. I can hear em now, 'That's right, Vlado, push the needle one more centimeter. Oops! Impotent. Oh, fucking shit! Ah, whatever, he signed the waiver.'"

62

BIMBO'S 365 CLUB

SAN FRANCISCO, 1990

I stepped into Bimbo's 365 Club through the kitchen entrance off Howard St. It was just after six, and the white shirt caterers were into full production, the countertops and stoves jammed, cutting boards clattered and pots boiled. One of the salad choppers pointed a knife toward the club's interior. Through the sprung doors and into the quiet dark, I followed plush carpeting and the dim orange glow of deco sconces past stars' photos and down a curving, narrow, time-warp that dropped me into a colorized Bogart film. The solid wood door at the end of the hall was cracked an inch. I knocked.

"What?" A voice from inside.

"I'm Jim. The paper? *The Chronicle* sent me over to take some measurements for our holiday party?" I said to the door.

"Sure, c'mon in."

His back to me, a glass desk top between us, he belonged in this movie. A small man, receding black hair, gray-at-the temples, he manipulated a spreadsheet on a Mac at the credenza. He spun around. He was maybe sixty, Italian. I stuck out my hand, "I guess you're the manager?"

"The paper. They still puttin that out—on paper? I mean, with all the young techies in this city and all of em online? AOL and a buncha young geek nerds from Cal, MIT and Stanford—great at math? Full'a scholarships, full'a brains, full'a themselves. Not one of em can find the handle on a shovel. But hey, they're loaded. Am I right? And I own the place so, yeah, you might say I'm the manager. Tony Caschera."

He leaned forward, and we shook.

"Have a seat, Jim. And you're not from around here. I can tell."

On the credenza behind him were signed photos of Tony and Ronald Reagan, Diane Feinstein, Lee Iacocca, Robin Williams, Michael Jackson, Tom Hanks, Pat Benatar, Elton John, Madonna, Van Morrison, Carlos Santana and a lot of important looking people I didn't recognize. He waited until I was done staring. "Yeah, our family's owned this club since the Thirties. Prohibition gin served in coffee cups, long-stemmed chorus girls hoofin it up includin a young Rita Cansino, and maybe you know her as Rita Hayworth. Herb used to be a regular and wrote about the club for the paper, talkin about the jugglers and dance teams, stand-up comics and Stage Door Johns. The place reads like the history of twentieth century entertainment. When I took over, I had to clear out a lot of the photos—Dad's. They're over at the house, now. You thirsty, hungry? We got a party here tonight, so we got a full kitchen and bar. C'mon, I'll show ya around."

We toured past the long-curved bar, the dance floor, the stage, backstage, the lighting, the dressing rooms and back into the kitchen. Tony offered me a deviled egg from a platter and stuck one in his mouth. "Yep, I could eat that whole damn plate," he said. "So, whatta ya wanna measure, Jim?"

"Maybe if we could go back out to the dance floor? Foster, the publisher, wants us to drop newspaper confetti from the ceiling at the end of the night. One of my jobs is to figure out how, and how much," I said.

"Sure, why not. We've seen it all, here. Not on the stage, though, right? Those lights are gonna be smokin hot by the end of the night, and I ain't burnin this place down. Also, Mr. Isaak —You're havin Chris Isaak, right? —Mr. Isaak isn't gonna to want stuff fallin out of the sky and all over his equipment. I know these guys."

"Yeah, Chris Isaak. My girl's crazy about him, really looking forward it."

"Show up an hour early, same way you came in today, and I'll see she meets him."

63

HONEY MUSTARD

S he was doing it, again, the boat-builder-to-goddess transformation. Just a couple hours ago, June got off early at Wasteland, jogged up the hill and burst sweating into our attic kitchen. "Par-tayh, James!"

I had been over at Bimbo's all morning with Gary, the rest of our crew and the HR department setting tables, stringing lights and generally fretting so everything would be perfect for the perfect evening. In just a few hours, the place would be jumping with more than six hundred parched, deadline-driven newspaper people in their Sunday finest—there to forget the office politics, bills and the kids for a few hours. It wouldn't seem that way at first. The first hour or so, there would be a veneer of decorum in the reception line. There, Foster and his parents and the paper's senior editors would greet each employee and their guest and hand out engraved, commemorative, gold-like-plated pens. There would be a quiet dash to "the best" tables and the setting up of territories—coats and jackets over chair backs, gloves and hats on chair seats. The second stop for most, though not all, would be the long, opulent bar where those who didn't give a damn where—or if—they sat, would already be ordering their second scotch.

I had just chomped into a chicken sandwich when June leaned down and kissed me between chews, "Ummm, honey mustard."

A CHEAP BLUE SUIT

Steam crept out beneath the bathroom door. Tonight, she was going to dazzle and stun. In heels, tight red satin, strategically accidental hair and dripping earrings, she'd be over six-feet of transformed, jaw-dropping woman. I'd have my hands full—keeping her attention, keeping her hand and keeping my cool as every other guy in the place would be eyes-all-over-her. I'd be the guy in the cheap blue suit, her Smurf friend. I was somewhat getting used to it, the size thing. I'd seen plenty of photos of shorter movie stars with taller women—Redford, Penn and Pacino, to name some. I was in good company.

VISITORS TO MEET MR. ISAAK

A few hours later, Bimbo's kitchen was on "Fast Forward." I stepped through the side door in my blue suit and was sideswiped by a guy hefting two large boxes of lettuce. Chopping blocks chattered, pans simmered, and the ovens glowed. Behind me, the transformed June stepped in and someone hit "Pause."

"Hi y'all," she said and flipped a wave and a grin.

Silence—until one of the cooks began a slow clap that gained speed, and the rest joined in with claps, shouts and whistles.

"Thank you, thank you," I bowed.

"Ass," June laughed.

"Come on, this way." I took her hand.

"Wow, what a place," she said.

I led down the hall to Tony's office, knocked, and we entered.

"Hey Jim, and . . ." Tony stood, took her hand and kissed it, "June. It is a pleasure and a privilege."

"Thank you. James has told me a lot about you and your beautiful club."

"Please, make it your home," he said. "And how bout I keep that promise and introduce you to Mr. Isaak before it's too late? This way, kids."

Tony led briskly. June leaned over and whispered to me, "All this attention. Maybe I wasn't ready for it."

"You love it and you know it, and your feet are still big," I whispered.

"Prick."

Four bartenders stopped their preparations and tracked us—June—as we passed through and into a curtained doorway to the backstage. Tony knocked on the dressing room door. "Visitors to meet Mr. Isaak." He turned and left. "Have fun."

A large cowboy of a man opened the door, grinned a row of piano keys and motioned us in. "How y'all doin? C'mon in, and take a load off." He pointed to a sofa and took one of two side chairs facing it.

Mirrors, lights, a wide countertop and eight chairs extended the length of one side of the room. Two musicians were busy fixing and fussing at the mirror. Two were playing *Fish*. The opposite wall was rolling racks of suits, instruments, boots, straps and belts.

June shook his hand, "I'm June, and this is James, and you're Kenny Dale Johnson, the drummer, aren't you?"

"Of the Borger, Texas Johnsons, yes ma'am."

"Phew," she said looking around. "You've played with everybody. This is so cool. I mean, we're sitting talking to you. And, is Chris here?"

Water ran behind a small door at the far end of the room. Behind Kenny Dale, the door opened, and there he was—a square-shouldered Adonis in a turquoise suit, black piping and a line of hazelnut-sized chrome beads running up both sleeves and down his legs.

June sprang from the sofa, fingers spread at her temples. "Oh! My! God!"

"Hey, you must be Jim and June. Tony said you'd be coming." He was casual with his walk over to June. She froze. He hugged her and kept her hand in his as we shook. "So, Merry Christmas." He grinned. "Please, have a seat."

"Great suit," I said.

"I brought a bunch—I switch em around. For somebody who grew up wearing clothes from the Salvation Army, it's my way of feeling 'big time,' " he said with his fingers. "I have suits with rhinestones and colors that Liberace might have turned down." Kenny Dale nodded and laughed. "My brother, Nick, says it's important to have dazzle as well as talent. He says there's nothing I can do about the talent, but I can buy a flashy suit."

June reached over and squeezed his thighs. "No, Sugar, you've got the suits and the talent."

Shit, there she goes, I thought.

Chris gave Kenny a backhand slap on the arm, "Kenny, would you get Nick in here to hear this? So what are you two doing for the holidays?"

"We just got into town, so we're still kind of settling in. All our family is back East, except June's dad's in Alaska. We'll probably make a meal, eat in, sightsee around our new city," I said. "How about you?"

"I plan to see my mom. Every Christmas, she makes ravioli. Mom's Italian and can really cook." He unbuttoned his jacket and leaned back. "When my mom puts the ravioli on the table, everything stops."

"June's the great cook for us."

"Beautiful *and* she can cook," Chris said. "Marry her."

June looked at me and raised an eyebrow. I swallowed.

"You going to be seeing your dad?" Chris said.

June looked at me, then to Chris, "Definitely. Next summer, definitely."

There was a knock at the door. Kenny rose and opened to Tony. "Hey kids, time to go. The Farallons and the bosses are here. Doors are opening."

June and I slipped back through the kitchen and out to Howard Street. Seeing hundreds of newspaper people in the reception line trailing outside the club, we took a stroll up Columbus Avenue. She caught my hand. "If we went home right now, I've had a great night," she said.

The city was glowing. We passed the Indonesian Consulate, went as far as Bay Street and turned to start back. "June, I absolutely fly with you. I fly, I slam dunk like MJ, and you make me speak French." She backed out of her heels and, arms around my waist, pulled me in. Horns honked as we kissed long and soft.

Arms still around me, she pulled away, "Then, you love me like I love you."

"Parlez-vous francais?" I said.

White teeth flashed, then, "Huh."

"What?"

"Still can't say it."

"What, June?"

"Let's go fix my make-up."

VENICE, CA, 2015

Things had come together so positively, so quickly once we arrived in San Francisco—finding a place, landing jobs. Yep, we were on a roll. It's times like that many of us are prone to forget, or ignore, some of the predictable characteristics of the natural world. Newton's Third Law is one I should have recalled upon meeting Foster Farallon. Maybe you remember it from high school physics. According to Newton, the force exerted by object *one* upon object *two* is equal in magnitude, and opposite in direction, to the force exerted by object *two* upon object *one*. There was some giving and taking about to happen in my life, and I hadn't seen it coming.

GODDAMN GOTHAM ADORATION

SAN FRANCISCO, 1990

At the end of the reception line, and finally inside the club, we were within sight of the Farallons—Foster and his parents. Foster looked our way between handshakes and back pats, then looked again. He checked his watch, ran a hand through curly, gelled hair, straightened his tie and looked once more. June stood half-a-head above everyone in front of us, and he wasn't checking me out. We moved up, and it was our turn.

"Hey James, great decorations," Foster said to June's eyes. "Here's a pen." His eyes didn't leave her. She in heels, he was still an inch taller. He took her hand in both of his, "June, such a pleasure. Welcome. I look forward to spending some time together."

June's smile was soaring in goddamn Gotham adoration. Her eyes sparked. I was glad when the Farallons finally drifted out of sight with opening celebratory responsibilities. We made our way, squeezing sideways between partiers, to the bar, she above the gathering green cloud over me. Foster was on the stage. The band's equipment behind and all around him, he was comfortable in the rockstar lights. After a sermon about the strength of newspapers, this paper in particular, their Pulitzers and a few local feel-good stories, he took off his tie and draped it around his neck. "It's time people. Have at it and, believe it or not," he waved a long arm to the wings, "Chris Isaak and Silvertone!"

We stood at the bar, June in Wonderland and me on shrinking ice. What was this funk I was getting into? I didn't belong here. It was a ruse—all these suits, decorations, the money spent. To make us, what, feel sophisticated and important? Two bar stools opened as if Moses had commanded and we climbed aboard. The band took the stage as bands take stages—Kenny Dale moved the high hat closer, adjusted his mic, the overhead stage lights and the color spots from the back corners of the room glistened on steel and chrome, and Chris, up and ready and his Gibson's strap over his shoulder, kicked into, *"Well she was just seventeen—"* then stopped. He pulled the mic in and laughed, "Got ya. Thought it was the lads from Liverpool, didn't ya. Nope, I'm from down the road in Stockton, and you're just going to have to deal with that."

"So cool, James," she said. "Are we going to dance? I mean, I can't just sit here like these paper people."

"I don't know. How long do you think we should stay?"

"Alright, folks," Chris said. "We're going to slip into our own skins now. Here's one from our latest CD and, June and Jim, this one's for you." The band lit up, *Don't Make Me Dream About You.*

"That's it." She took my hand. "We're on." Out through the tables, onto the empty center floor and close to the stage. Chris sent a wink down to us. June can dance anywhere, anyway, anytime. This moment, she chose a kind of country swing. It was an easy, greasy, hip-hugging and small stepping kind of thing with some pro wrestling moves thrown in—expanding, contracting, sliding and fluid. I was just shy of a half-step-behind following her and starting to get into it. Okay, I thought, maybe it's not so bad. Like, we're pretty cool together. And we must have looked great from the cheap seats. At the end of the number, as we left the floor to refuel, we got quite the applause, including from the band. Next song, the floor was packed.

Funny how bartenders protect and preserve their bars when it comes to beautiful women. Our seats had remained empty among legions of groundlings.

I nudged June and nodded toward the dancers. Gary was out there bouncing and spinning in his white-man's interpretation of a James Brown Funkadelic with one of the women from advertising. She was cute, half his age and likely wondering what she was missing on television. He looked like he was due for a change in his medication. His shirttail was out, sweat flew, and his previously slicked hair had reached that lunatic-scramble. Across the room, Pete was bored. He sat alone at one of the large round tables. One arm spread across the chair next to him, he tapped a spoon.

"Shall we hit the buffet?" I said.

"Not hungry, James. You go ahead."

"Back in a flash." I swung wide around the back of the room and dropped by to see Pete. "You're alone at the holiday bash," I said.

"Not for long, and not for long," he said.

"Huh?"

"Not at the holiday bash for long, and not alone for long. Got a date at a bookstore in about thirty minutes. She's off at eight, and we're going to catch a movie."

"What's playing?"

"*Awakenings*, De Niro. I'd pay to mow his lawn. And there she goes." He nodded toward the bar.

Foster escorted June to a spot deep in the dance crowd.

"Guy's a piece of work, Jim. Listens to his dick, and you'd best watch your back."

"She's a big girl. She'll take care of things. Woman just loves to dance."

"Uh-huh. Well, I guess you were on your way to the food." He rose slowly. "Let's eat."

Pete and I ate at the empty table. He left, and I wandered back up to the bar. June's stool was still open. Mine wasn't. The bartender slid a drink toward me, and maybe I drank it too fast. No sign of Foster and June in the dance crowd. The band was great, running through the entirety of *Heart Shaped World*. So how long's it takes to play a whole CD? About an hour? That would say they've been dancing for what, twenty-five, thirty minutes? I told the bartender, "I'll be right back." He shrugged.

I went to the end of the carpet, stretched up on my toes and scanned. Huh. I wove out through hips, shoes and shoulders to near the center of the floor. I did a slow three-sixty—not a sign. I looked up at the band, and, mid-chorus, Chris nodded toward the kitchen. "Really?" I mouthed. He nodded.

I arrived at the kitchen doors as they swung wide, and three tray-wielding servers strafed past in a dive pattern to the buffet. I stepped in. A cook at one of the stoves pointed a long spoon to the back door. "Shit."

There was one parking space behind the club lit by a mercury vapor light's cold glow. The orange Porsche was just turning out onto Howard Street.

I sat at the edge of that empty space on a low concrete wall. My chest in a knot. "What the hell, June?" I whispered. I closed the jacket lapels to my neck. The world reduced to nearly black and white in that light, and, quiet and slow, a moth crisscrossed up and floated away. Behind me, from inside, a muted ballad, *"It hurts to watch her laugh at you, with someone new . . ."* I got up, stabbed my hands into my pockets and walked out to the street. Not much traffic, shops closed, lights in the apartment windows above. Saturday night, Chinese take-out and TV, I guessed. I stood there looking up at the normal lives, then remembered to breathe.

VENICE, CA, 2015

Looking back on it, how long could it be until June realized that I was the dull side of the coin? Come on, Charlie Watts, Ruth Pointer, Foster Farallon? That night, it had happened, and it hadn't taken long. And what is it with women leaving me? Margaret a total misfire, Natalie, rest her soul, Eva counting push-ups, and June taking off with Foster? I thought she'd probably forgotten all about White Dog, too. I hated him back then, my mortal enemy—Farallon and his toy car. Foster. What kind of name was Foster? Okay, it was just going to be me alone—me alone, White Dog and the Ram Van. She wouldn't be needing that anymore. What was she thinking? What was she doing to me—to us?

I'd felt bloodless. Weak. Then enraged at that sonofabitch and his car!

But it wasn't him. It was June. She was just his next thing. The next thing he wanted, and he always got everything he wanted, and every childhood birthday he'd been all dressed up and leaped with joy and clapped his hands, and she could have said, "No." It wasn't him, it was June, and she could have said, "No," and she didn't, and there was nothing I could do about it. I was going off like fireworks, fierce blasts of rage. Then empty silence. We'd started fresh, June and I. Been through a lot and it was real—forever. A fresh start with love like I'd never known, like we'd never known.

67

YOU GET THE NUMBER?

SAN FRANCISCO, 1990

In the black and white fizz of the alley light, I thought, damn, June, and what the hell? Then Nature spoke, and I had to take a piss. I pulled the cold steel handle and went back in through the kitchen.

Out of the restroom, I drifted on empty down the hall to Tony's office and knocked.

"Yes?"

I stepped in. "Hey."

"You get the number?" he said.

"Huh?"

"The truck that hit you."

"June took off with Foster."

"No way, kid."

"I saw them leave."

"Has to be somethin innocent—a miscalculation. Have a seat. You want a drink? I got bourbon and scotch."

"Yeah, whatever," I said.

"Scotch then."

He pulled the bottle and two glasses from the bottom of the credenza, poured and handed me one. "To the power of love."

"Huh?"

"Jim," he reached behind him and picked a small silver frame from the collection. "This is my mother. From Genoa. See her here, still young, so pretty? June's age. One day, during the war, shortly after they were married—a small ceremony, his family would not attend—police broke into their house. My father, a Jew, was arrested and transported to a concentration camp near Salerno, nearly five hundred miles from their home. She was heartbroken, cried all night. The rest of the family and the neighbors tried to console her, but there was nothin they could do. The next morning, exhausted with no sleep and little food, she began walkin south."

"Walking?"

He waved his hand, "Sure, sure there were cars and trains, but it was the war—there was no fuel." He poured me another scotch. "Under bridges, she slept and in barns. Sometimes strangers were kind and gave her a lift on a grain cart, let her sleep in their homes. She was a beautiful young woman in need of assistance at every turn, and there were soldiers everywhere. We'll never know how many times her vulnerability was exploited during her journey, but she never wavered in her mission. Walked five hundred miles in extreme conditions to once again be near the one she loved." He took a sip.

"But he was in a concentration camp. They couldn't be together," I said.

"Turns out it was more like a resort. Ya know the Roman Empire didn't just happen. It wasn't built by idiots. They were protectin their Jews from the Nazis." He sat back, hands behind his head and smiled.

"Tony, that's a wonderful story, amazing story, really. Why'd you tell me that just now?"

He sat forward, "Beautiful country girl comes to the city and maybe gets a lot of attention from a tall, handsome, rich guy. Maybe her vulnerability is exploited."

My cheeks burned. My hands felt huge. "But your mother didn't leave him," I said. "It's just the opposite."

"That's not the point. The point is, there's some things we'll never know about our loved ones, should never ask, don't want to know. The point is that there's always the next day. The point is we should never underestimate the power of love. C'mon, let's go back to the party, see what's up."

Tony's hand on my shoulder encouraged me up the hall. My legs were wood. The band was on break, and in this thick, dull light, the silent hallway could have been mistaken for a funeral home's—dim sconces, slow deep carpet, dark trim. Come to think of it, most of the celebrities in the photos were dead. We emerged to the bar, and I stalled mid-step. I couldn't do this. The next few minutes of looking around, asking around, were only going to humiliate me. "Tony, I can't."

I got out of the cab having no recollection of getting in. No lights in the house, everyone out in The Haight on a Saturday night. In our attic, I dropped my jacket and tie by the door and disappeared into the dark crummy depths of the beaten sofa. No tear-stained songs, just freefall. And I could see it clearly—

His house was steel and glass, and the 180-degree view of the city reflected off the calm of the bay. He brought drinks out to the deck. He'd worked with the architect for a year designing the house and had suffered, believe it or not, through another five years of permits and inspections. "Phew, getting things done in this city!" Part of the issue was his blocking a couple of the neighbors' views. He'd made some concessions and volunteered to pay for upgrades and improvements to their properties, and didn't that just topple the budget. But, it all worked out, and he'd finally moved in eight months ago. The art? Oh, the art. He'd been a collector even as a child. He'd bought his first substantial piece, the one by the door, the small linoleum engraving, a Matisse, when he was ten. Since then, he just couldn't stop. This wasn't the entirety of his collection. With all this glass, there wasn't enough wall space. He limited this house to The Fauvists and Neo-Impressionists. Say, wasn't it getting cooler? Should they go inside? Maybe make a fire?

I never realized that the stove clock ticked. Small, it was a faraway sound, like when I'd lay my head down on my watch in high school. You hear things in the dark. Once in a while, a car horn. Heels and a laugh from the sidewalk below. Music from the park drifted in and out depending on the breeze. The bus stops down at the corner nearly every twenty minutes—but not every—half-a-block away. I lost track of how many buses. That and my heart. Not that I checked, but I'm sure it was irregular, too. There was a throbbing in my chest, short breaths, a pulse, and white foam rushed to my ears, then a nauseous whooshing away. The receding tide leaves the sand flat and dark, and birds scurry in to dig out, kill and devour whatever life is left. I drifted off.

68

THE LIGHTS, THE ATTENTION, THE MONEY

The cushions sagged. I hadn't heard her come in. Her thigh was warm tight satin against my cheek. Her hand lighted on my chest in the dark. She whispered, "I'm sorry."

I yanked off the sofa and up to the window. Out there was a head-lit city of ants, all racing in triple lines—Oak Street one way, Fell Street the other, and for what?

"What's going on, June? You left. That's what's going on! It's hard for me to believe, and maybe you can't believe it either, but you really did. You left. You left with that asshole and his fucking car!"

"James, I—"

"Are we done? Is that it? Have you buried us, here? Like, this is really it? Like, *Bang?*" I slapped the molding, "And, see ya?"

"I'm sorry. I got caught up in it—the lights, the attention, the money."

I turned to her. She sat straight on the couch, hands folded on her lap. "Like, I should beg? I think I should. I think I should definitely beg. Yeah, cause if I don't, I'll always wish I had, and

I'll be looking back on these years from now and wondering why I didn't beg you to stay."

"James, we were just going out to see his car. Then a little ride around the block."

"And now you're leaving?"

"No. I just got caught—for a moment."

"He's tall and rich," I said.

"Yes, he is."

"He's tall and rich and he looks like a model."

"Yes."

"You spent the night. Is it morning? What time is it?"

"After one."

"How fucking mad should I be, June?"

"Mad, but not very."

69
HOW BAD IS IT?

I couldn't eat. For days, I felt my way through the motions of shower, stairs, sidewalk, bus, stairs, work, and I stayed late those first few nights. I didn't want to talk to her, and maybe she'd be asleep when I got home. Each time Pete's and my path crossed, black, steel eyes scanned my face, then passed in silence. He was the only one in my small circle who knew what happened. Thursday noon, Pete stopped me on the sidewalk in front of the paper.

"You eat?" he said.

"Not hungry. Goin for a walk."

"Come watch me eat." He started up the street to the newsstand café. He stopped and turned, "Well? C'mon." Hands in my pockets, I followed. At the newsstand's counter, he placed his order, "The same but double—two cheeses, two diets."

"Pete, I'm not hungry."

"Just in case. Pick a booth." There were only two and one was occupied. We slid in. "Your tail's between your legs, Jim. Has she come back?" He stared at his folded hands on the table.

"She came back that night."

"How bad is it?" he said.

"Says it was a mistake. Says she just got caught up in the moment."

"How bad is it?"

"It sucks. What do you think?"

"Her—what she did. How bad?" he said.

"I said, already. A mistake."

"How big?"

"She says, 'Not very.' Not very big."

The sandwiches and Cokes arrived. Pete bit the corner off his grilled cheese, chewed four times and took a pull on the straw. He hadn't looked me in the eye since we sat down. "Eat something. You're starting to look like your little sister," he said.

"You know my sister?"

"Didn't know you had a sister, but she's probably starving herself."

"She calls it 'trim.' "

"Eat."

Now that we were here, with food in front of us and him eating, maybe I *was* hungry. I took a hell-fire-hot bite of what Pete called his soul food—crisp on the outside, creamy, salty and molten inside.

"So a mistake, a not very big mistake, and she came back that night," he said.

"Yeah." Swollen tongue, I chewed.

"You guys talk this out? She's sorry and you forgave?"

"She's sorry," I said.

Now he looked at me and it was intense. "But you're withholding the forgiving? Making her pay the price? Making her miserable, making yourself miserable, hell, making *me* miserable seeing you drag your self-pitying ass all over town?!" When Pete got wound up, he didn't care who heard.

"I—"

The people in the booth behind us left.

"'I,' shit! 'I' is one goddamn lonely man, Jim! 'I' is you sitting alone at night watching the goddamn television and wondering what the hell you did to drive the one you loved, the one who loved you, away forever. This is a 'we' thing, Jim. Are you two a 'we,' or not? If you are, then you're goddamn lucky, and you'd best stop screwing around with this as I did—and fuck that! This is about you, Christopher Robin! Are you two a 'we,' an 'us?' " He ripped another chunk out of his sandwich. The cheese stretched and raked over his knuckles and stuck to his chin. His jaw moved like it was crushing rocks.

"Yeah, we're us. June and me, we're us."

He unlocked his eyes, wiped his chin with a paper napkin and took a pull on the straw. His hands relaxed, and he picked at the cheese strings. Walnut knuckles and squared off nails, cracked, never bitten. "Then go up to Wasteland right now. Ask her out onto the sidewalk, into the Panhandle's sunshine, and tell her so. Tell her, 'June, you and me, we're us.' Have you ever told her flat out you love her?"

"I, sure—of course."

"Bullshit!"

70

NOT WHAT I WANT TO HEAR

"Bullshit, James! It took me running off with Foster to finally wake you up. Then you played martyr for a week while I twisted in the breeze waiting to see which way it was going to go!"

Ten feet away, June was looking for something to throw at me—I could tell. "I came back, damnit! I came back that night before the total shit hit the fan after which there'd *be* no coming back!"

It was sunny in the Panhandle, but this wasn't going the way Pete had in mind.

"What the hell is it with you, James? Commitment? 'Love' was always too tough a word?"

"We've been running your plan all the way, June. We left our jobs, Prairie in Maryland, Tom in Nebraska and came here. I came west with you. We made it, June."

"That's not what I want to hear!"

"We're family. We're us," I said.

"You can't say it?"

"Say what?"

"You can't say you love me!"

I threw my hands up and watched traffic a few seconds. I turned back and she was walking away—fast.

"Wait. June, wait." I followed after her.

"Say it," she called over her shoulder.

"June—"

"Say it white bread!"

"What? I'm *what*?"

"Say it!"

"Fuck!" I stopped.

She was out of sight on the crowded walks.

VENICE, CA, 2015

I realize now the part I had feared, the part that could hurt most was being surfaced. The part where you commit your love, go all in, then maybe get slapped down and cast out by the hand that feeds you. I wasn't kidding anyone. Of course, I loved her. But if I didn't say it, there remained that veil of protection. I hadn't told her that day on Haight Street and I hadn't told her months before—that night back in Maryland, when she was getting ready to go out with Tom and Prair to The Boat House. She'd held my face in her rough hands and said she thought she loved me, and I made a joke. Fool.

WHITE MAN PROBLEM

SAN FRANCISCO, 1990

Depeche Mode bumped through the speakers at Wasteland—*Personal Jesus*. A few of the women straightened racks, shoes and purses. The manager was behind the counter. He nodded, "You okay? Lookin pale, dude."

"Yeah, white man problem. Is she here?"

"Nope. Blew through like a bad storm. Said she was taking a few and split."

"You think she meant a few minutes?" I said.

"You know her, man. What do you think?"

"Hell, if I know."

"When you see her, tell her I need her back here," he said.

"Yeah, me too."

EXPECTING SOMEONE?

I hauled a loaded bag of take-out up the steps to our attic. She had to come back—White Dog, her clothes, and, if for nothing else, to punch me in the face. I emptied the paper boxes into separate bowls, covered them and put the bowls in the oven on "Warm." I had candles, wine and flowers, too. I set the table.

God, this place is small. I can stand in the middle and nearly touch each wall. We live like this? Out the windows, where the view had been, was fog, and it was damn cold. I pulled on one of June's flannel shirts.

Her key in the lock, the door swung open.

"Hey, you're here," I said.

She threw her jacket on the dump of a couch and slipped past me, "Nice table. Expecting someone?" She closed the bathroom door.

"June," I went to the door. There was a rustling on the other side, then quiet. "June, I—"

She turned the water on—loud. "You say something?"

"Yeah, June," I said to the door. "I say something. I say, 'I'm sorry.' I say, 'I've been a white bread asshole.' I love you, June. I say, 'Heart and soul.'"

Water off, she opened the door and stared at me for too long. "I'm sorry, the door was closed. What did you say?" She pushed me aside and went to the table and sat.

Okay, take a breath. My eyes stung. Like, what the hell? I blinked a couple times and wiped my nose on my sleeve—her sleeve. "Like I was saying, I've been an ass, okay? I love you. Yeah, there. I do. I loved you back in Maryland, Ashtabula, Ohio, and Norfolk, Nebraska. I love you here, and wherever's next. It's like, I've never known anything like this, okay? So helpless in love."

"I can't help you," she said.

"What do you mean?"

"If you're helpless, in love. I can't help that. You have to be strong in your love—in me."

"But you love me, right?"

Thirty minutes later I picked up the chairs and reset the table. June sat in a puddle of flowers on the floor and buttoned up. I lit the candles.

"What's in the oven, James?"

"Thai. Probably dry Thai."

"Perfect," she said.

73

MILK AND COOKIES

For the next few months, we flew high in the city. She loved her work, the people she worked with and our neighborhood. We had moved into a storybook first floor with window flower boxes and a tiny garden. My work was intense, challenging, and the pay had taken a jump. They were making an investment in me, and, being aware of my incredible luck, I was going to see that it continued. There were six-day weeks, but June and I always had at least one full day together to explore or chill. We had more money than ever, I had benefits, and I found my favorite bicycle shop. We were frequent visitors and got to know the proprietor as a friend. The Ram Van was conscripted to street parking, and the single garage at the back of our narrow lot became the bike club—two bikes, bike stands, tools, compressor, shoes, helmets, posters and memorabilia.

Pete's mid-seventies, once-proud, bronze, and now shit-brown and bent, Ford F-150 rolled up our alley one Saturday. Our garage doors swung wide, and June, her hair in a long, braided weave, and I were wrenching at the bike stands. He pulled in close to our neighbor's garage and climbed painfully out through his window. "Looks like those bikes own you."

"Hey, Pete. What's with your door?" I asked.

"Been meaning to fix that. Ever think of maybe getting one sports car instead of two of those things?" he asked.

"Matter of economics. Can't afford a Porsche like friggin Foster's," I said.

"Nah, Pete. He's a bike guy, and determined to make me one. Actually, I'm kinda diggin it. Great way to see the area— Mt. Tam, Diablo—the descents are killer."

White Dog bounded into the garage and, front paws on Pete's chest, was making a big fuss. "Hey buddy! What's shakin in the hood? You been eatin squirrels?" He gave White Dog a hug.

"Made some cookies, Pete." June returned an Allen wrench to its set. "Cookies and milk if you want?"

"Well yeah, June, that'd be great, thanks."

"Back in a few."

Pete went over to June's bike and gave the front wheel a spin. "So, June's a good rider?"

"Strong, go figure," I said.

"You might try to think of something you could do that might not have as many consequences as getting June hit by a truck."

"We're going to try and avoid that, Pete."

"You descend fast, don't you—really push the envelope."

"Well, that's kinda the idea," I said. "Maybe June'll think I got some Rambo in me."

He squeezed the brake lever, the wheel stopped. "What are you running from?"

"Whatta ya mean? Not running from anything."

"Something's driving you two. Either running from or to something like a goddamn freight. Like the runaway kids down there on the street. Sitting on the sidewalks in rag-tag clusters smokin dope and pan-handling and running off to hippy nirvana to escape who-the-hell-knows-what back in Bumfuck, USA. You two have that same look, only deeper, Jim. It peeks out, there, from behind your eyes—both of you."

"Maybe it's just the shock of being here, the city, everything happening so fast—falling into place."

He took a slow lap around June's bike. "Bullshit."

June was back. She sat a plate of cookies on the bench and handed Pete a tall glass. "To your health, Pete."

"Well thanks, June." He stared hard at me, then her and raised the glass, "To yours."

74

HOW LONG DOES IT TAKE TO
GET TO SEWARD?

SAN FRANCISCO, 1991

We spent a lot of saddle time finding the city's nooks and crannies, everything new to us, flashing, on the move and on the make. A favorite cheap lunch was at Red's Java House beneath the Bay Bridge. Red's served food not found in the world's finest restaurants including breakfast of a Burger and a Beer, $4.50. There were also the Dog and a Beer and Double Burger and a Beer. Red, himself, tended the grill, and Red was an impatient man. He wasn't there for the scenery. Time was money, there were only so many minutes in a day and, "Whatta ya want, kid?" It probably started when he was a commission-driven boy hustling newspapers to the longshoremen. You had about two seconds to tell Red what you wanted before he lost interest and moved on to the next customer. It was all bike messengers, truck drivers, dockworkers and June and me sitting outside the shack in the sun on thick rope coils and stacks of heavy deck planks.

June chomped into her sandwich. "How old is Pete?"

"Forty-fifty-something? I don't know. Why?"

"Keeps to himself, doesn't he."

"And?" I said.

"Like, he must have secrets—his limp, his scars."

"Yeah, his body tells stories. He thinks we have secrets. Says we're running from something."

"You are, James."

"We are."

"Kane's lost the scent. I'm not running."

"So it's just us? Home safe?" I asked.

"You don't have a home, my love."

"Shit, too."

She swirled the straw in her can. "If I was your perfect woman, who would I be?"

"You *are* my perfect woman."

"No, c'mon, really. I'd be shorter, right?"

"Wouldn't change a thing," I said.

"You always say my feet are big."

"They are."

"So, maybe I'd at least have smaller feet."

"I never said they're *too* big."

"C'mon, Jim-Jiminy. Think of all the women in the world. All the women who—"

"Okay, Demi Moore."

"Who? That, friggin Demi, white-teeth, white-bread Moore? You gotta be kidding me!"

"Yeah, Demi Moore, but a half-breed."

"Huh." She scowled.

"So, okay, like, if I was your perfect guy, I'd be, like, tall? Like Foster?"

"You're not?"

"You must have noticed."

"Don't count for much, my man."

"So, I'd be my size but cool?"

"Earth to Jiminy?"

"Like Tom Cruise or that guy from *Ghost*?" I said.

"Patrick Swayze."

"He's small. You like how he dances, like in *Dirty Dancing*," I said.

"Hell yeah!"

"So, I'd be him, if you had your way?"

"Hell no," she said.

"Then what?"

"I don't know. Maybe you'd square off and show some color. Maybe get pissed off at me more often."

"For what?"

"How about my flirting?"

"Yeah, that pisses me off."

"Leaving you at the club," she said.

"Can we not talk about that? That hurt, okay?"

"I don't want to hurt you, but I want you to want me. Passionately."

"I love you . . . passionately," I said.

"There, you said it again, and, look, your nose didn't bleed."

"Maybe your feet *are* too big."

"Prick."

"June shifted her weight to the other cheek and took a sip through her straw, "This summer, James? We vacation in Alaska?"

"Sounds like a plan. I mean, we have our jobs and all, but we can probably get some time off."

"Might need a week or more," she said.

"Shit, I'm a mess!" Ketchup and mustard glopped onto my

shoe. I wiped it off, spread my feet and leaned forward for the next burger bite.

"How long do you think?" she asked.

"What?"

"To get to Seward. How long?"

"Hell, I don't know. Couple days?"

75

PUT A STAR NEXT TO YOUR NAME

G ary was the perfect boss when it came to hiring people better than himself, delegating, and he was a devious piece of work. He took me under his wing—not all good. "You're going to be my guy, Skeeter. Most of these slugs have been here too long, too many bad habits, long lunches and phoning it in. You're my man, fresh from the farm, my eyes and ears." He'd been at the paper for nearly thirty years, had dirt on all the other department heads and pretty much came and went with impunity. Mostly, he went. His brief weekly staff meetings always ended with some variation of, "I have a busy week ahead, way over-booked, a lot of meetings to attend, a lot of irons in the fire. My job's to make sure there are no surprises, no ambushes, scout ahead, look after your best interests. When I'm not here, and you need something, ask Jimmy. He'll know where to find me." I rarely did.

"Got an idea, Skeeter. Here's what I'm thinking—photo editor." He leaned back in his chair, tie to one side of his gut, hands behind his head. Two of his shirt buttons were about to launch. "Haven't found anyone I like. It's been months. Time to up your game. Whatta ya think?"

"You want me in that slot? Photo editor? Of the *San Francisco Chronicle*? Mind if I sit?" Like, a job for life and benefits and retirement and car payments and a commute from the suburbs and a mortgage and a lawn and the neighbors and barbeques and June and me and the kids and PTA and birthday parties and holidays and graduations?

"Sure, have a seat. It's time to bring you into upper-middle management—put a star next to your name."

I took a couple breaths. Think money, I thought. No, think position, think title, think San Francisco, and this is it? Where it ends? Like, this is what June meant? Me squaring off?

76

WATCHES AND HAIRCUTS

S pring waned, and we'd been talking about Seward each night for the past few weeks. The time had come. If we were going, I had to ask for a month off.

"I don't think this will fly, June. I haven't been at the paper that long, you know? And being a new editor, and all . . ." I leaned, hands on the back of a kitchen chair.

She sat on the counter, arms crossed and dug in. "It's why we came west. To go to Alaska—my dad."

"No, you said, 'Adventure, to see where Janis lived.'"

"I know what I said, James! Don't *tell* me what I said!"

"Things change. Like, this job, you know?"

"I'm going. I sure as hell don't want to go alone, but I will."

"What is this, this either or? Can we find a way to make both happen? Does it have to be right now? What about waiting one more cycle, hold out until next summer. Write to him. Tell him we're coming next year. No hurt, no foul."

"I'm not putting this off, and we've talked about it."

"Okay. How about we fly up and back over a long weekend?"

"No."

"Why?"

"I won't fly *ever*, I'm driving, and I'm not rushing this, James. It's too important."

I spun the chair around, thought about sitting, then didn't. I leaned again.

"June, this isn't just a job. C'mon, look where we live—how we live."

"No."

"I'll know the ropes in a year. I can set things up way ahead, so I won't be missed. So I have coverage."

"You told me Pete said it's just a business. Pete hates business. What's happening to you? You hate business. You hate their soft hands, their suits, their shoes. You hate their stupid watches and haircuts. I'll go alone, James. That's it. I'm going alone."

And then what? I thought. I wake up here hollow each morning in this empty house and go off to the paper and sit at a desk—my oh so big-and-important desk—for money, and for what? And you're driving three-thousand miles alone and anxious, and maybe you find your dad and maybe you don't, and if you don't then you drive all the way back here alone and sick to your soul, and I'm still sitting at that goddamn desk? I should have stayed at the M&M. "You're not going alone. Not after all this. I'm in, June—all in. And Pete's like one of the biggest columnists in the country. Pete can say anything. And . . . their *haircuts*?"

"I'm going. Alone."

"You can't."

"I can."

"No." I said.

"Why?"

I let go of the chair and stood straight. "You need me, that's why. I'm the guy that's got your back, your beginning and your end, your sweet and creamy, warm and yummy vanilla custard filling."

She uncrossed her arms, hands on her knees.

"You want to smile, don't you? I can see it. You're about to burst, June, I can tell."

She grinned, slow and small. It spread wide, and she jumped my ass and threw me to the floor. She had me pinned and slapped at me. "Take time off. Fight for it, you shit!" I howled in laughter. The next day, neighbors asked if we'd heard the coyotes.

77

I DIDN'T KNOW YOU HAD A CAT

Gary sat straight in his green leather chair, arms folded, head back slightly and snored. I took a seat across the desk from him and cleared my throat. He jerked slightly, recovered and opened his eyes. They were red. "Yes?"

"Hey Gary, got a minute?"

He looked at his watch, leaned forward, pulled his pen from its holder and scribbled something on his empty day-planner. "I've got a couple, then I'm needed upstairs. Whatta ya have?"

"This is awkward, but I'd like to put in for some time off. Like, July."

He tapped his pen point twice, "Done deal. Couple days? Three? Four?"

"The month, actually."

He placed his pen in the spine of the book. "Heh, heh . . . No, really, how long?"

"June and I have to go to Alaska. We're going to find her dad. She hasn't seen him in twenty years."

He took off his glasses and leaned forward, "You haven't asked about my cat."

"Huh?"

He replaced his glasses. "What? You don't care about my cat—about his hemorrhoids?"

"I guess I didn't know you had a cat."

"I don't. But if I did, would you give a flying fuck?"

"Gary, I—"

He came out from behind his desk and paced behind me. "This is a newspaper. Every night, three in the morning, drivers from as far away as Modesto show up here to drive all over Northern California to drop off bundles with ten thousand resounding thuds to hundreds of locations so local carriers can drive, bike and walk those papers to a half-a-million-doorsteps in hamlets we can't even imagine so grandma can read *Dear Abby*, and jocks can check the scores, and the goddamn mayor's mom can cut pictures of his largess from the front page of 'State and Local News.' "

"Yeah, I—"

"There are some fifteen-hundred full-time employees showing up here every day to write, photograph, edit, layout, print, fold, sort and distribute what the hell's going on in the world this very minute so state, national and world leaders can decide which sleeping village to bomb next." He was back in his chair. He scribbled a flourish into his day-planner. I was on the steep part of the slope and sliding out of control. I knew what lay ahead, and this was going to be an ugly finish.

"No one gets a month off. I don't, Pete doesn't, and the goddamn publisher doesn't! Move to plan B, cause nobody gets a month off, and we've spent enough time on this. What do you have on that new 'Entertainment Section' concept?"

"Gary, I know you took a chance with me, and I owe you everything here at the paper."

"The 'Entertainment Section?' I believe we've moved on to that?" He came out from his desk, took his jacket from the hook and pulled it on.

"I'm grateful to—"

He closed the door as he left.

CAN'T ROLL FOREVER

ROAD TO ALASKA, 1991

E ight months in San Francisco and we'd found the promise of the rest of our lives. The paper and I had been granted cartooning's Berryman Award for the work I did on Pete's column, I had the start of a career I could never have imagined, life was spinning on ceramic bearings, and June was happy. Then she'd committed to finding her dad that very next summer and it was probably her talking to Chris Isaak I had to thank for that and Gary was understandably immoveable on a month off but reluctantly generous with two weeks.

Over the Willamette River and around Portland, right through the middle of wet and sockeye Seattle, and we entered the eight-hundred-mile open grandeur of British Columbia. June nested with one hand on the wheel, the other on her knee, her bare foot on the dash. The tires droned, and I found a comfortable spot with a pillow against the glass.

This country, the mountains and forests, looked like Pennsylvania when I was five. Seeing it with older eyes, I realized how small my world had been compared to this. As kids, we were in the woods every chance we got, sunup to sundown— exploring, following animal tracks, coming upon fresh cool springs, building lean-tos. We made maps, blazed trails, set snares and did uncountable damage in our explorations. In what we thought to be endless wilderness laid the great mystery and promise of the unknown. Our destiny was to come upon sights never-before seen by mankind, unearth fossils and dinosaur bones and to be ever wary of bears and snakes. Crossing through British Columbia, that feeling returned, and I loved the promise and the threat and the not knowing what laid ahead.

"You think he'll want to come back with us?" I said.

"Why would he? He has his life up there."

"But, he said he's about done with it."

"He wouldn't like San Francisco," she said.

"You think we'll really stay there forever? Like, San Francisco?"

"Can't just keep rolling, James. Gotta finally put down somewhere, and what we have there is as good as it gets."

"Right."

"You *are* running. Running from something—maybe everything," she said.

"I just don't want to get bored, June."

"And I'll bore you because I've stopped?"

"We're on our way to Alaska, June. Running to Alaska to find your dad. You haven't stopped."

Passing into Yukon Territory at daybreak, we saw a sign for the capital, Whitehorse, and The Klondike Restaurant. "Just another seven-hundred miles to Anchorage, James. You like wolverine with your eggs?"

79

I HAVE SOMETHING TO
TELL YOU

ANCHORAGE, JULY, 1991

I was into the third cup of coffee as we waited for our orders, well, my order. It was Sunday morning, and we were awarded the last booth at The Old Alaska Restaurant. With an upstairs and downstairs, I think it seated two hundred. June had as much of a breakfast as she was going to have—tea and toast. She hadn't been feeling well the past week, or so. The place was jammed and clattered with dishes, squawking chair legs and boisterous conversations. She started to say something, and I leaned in. "Sorry?"

Our waitress dropped a steaming platter between us that would have fed Take-a-Look for a week. I picked up the orange slice and brought it to my mouth. June curled her nose. I replaced the slice, moved the plate to one side and leaned back in, "What, June?"

"I have something to tell you."

I finished the last of the cup, rubbed my face with both hands and spread my elbows on the table.

"Ready?" she asked.

"Yep."

She looked side-to-side and leaned in closer to me. "I—"

Televisions blared from four corners. The game was coming on.

"What? Say again?" Distracted by the TVs, I picked the orange slice from my plate, brought it halfway to my mouth.

"James! Look at me!"

I returned it to the plate.

"I said, I missed my period. It's been three weeks." Her eyes raced over my face.

That fight-or-flight lump jumped to my throat.

"I've never missed it before—a first."

I sat back and took a couple sips of water. I leaned back in, "So, like, I mean—"

"I might be pregnant. I'm pretty sure I am."

"Yeah, right. I was going to say that. Like, pregnant." I took a deep breath and tried for calm, but my heart wasn't hearing it.

"I got a test kit. It was positive."

"But they're not always right," I said.

"Ninety-nine percent."

"Of course." I sat back, reached over to my plate, picked up the orange slice and stuck it in the ketchup cup. Like, those test kits? They come in boxes? Boxes like hair color kits? They probably have pen & ink illustrations and directions in two languages and clear, stretchy rubber gloves so you don't contaminate the, what, the sample? "So, maybe we're having a baby? Like, you and me? Like how?"

"We kissed, remember? I want to know what you think, James. I want to know what you want."

I looked around at the other tables—a lot of large guys in flannel shirts and beards, mothers, daughters, fussing toddlers and above, ceiling fans going round and round and round, and I was getting short of breath.

"June, I have medical at the paper. But it's just for *me*. What's a baby cost? We'd probably need a bigger place. Place for a crib and stuff. Diapers. I mean, can we afford it? I mean, regarding a baby we got nothing."

June stirred honey into her tea. "We have nothing?"

A cheer went up at the other end of the room.

"No, I mean, we do. We have everything. I mean we just don't have insurance for a baby and all the other stuff. I mean, have you been to a doctor? No insurance, you probably haven't been to a doctor, and we got no space."

"So?" She took a sip, placed the cup back onto its saucer and kept her finger curled in the cup's handle. Her head cocked. "What do you want, James?"

"Okay, give me a second." I'd hit redline. I put both hands up. "This is a lot, like, the thing you had to tell me. You know?" Air. "It's hot in here and that coffee—it's got coke in it, and I had three cups. Like, that's a really big thing you had to say."

She nodded.

There was a lumberjack's breakfast cooling at my left elbow—three-egg cheese, onion and broccoli omelet, breakfast potatoes, crispy bacon and homemade herb toast, and it looked awful. I wiped my forehead with my sleeve. "I'm just going to get a breath outside—just a second. I'll be right back. I'm happy for us. Really, I am. It's all good." I slid out from the booth and took quick steps to the front door, out to the wet cool of the parking lot. At the curb, I looked left, then right. I chose left and walked up past the K-Mart—up to the red light and did a few deep knee bends.

Down. What are you afraid of?

Up. You have it all jerk.

Down. I'm not a father.

Up. Guess again.

Down. I don't know how to be a father.

Up. You had one.

Down. He didn't know how either.

I jogged along with traffic back to the restaurant. Back in through the front door and back to the booth. Her finger was still there, in the cup handle. My scalp itched. Hell, my teeth itched. I ran my fingers through sweaty hair and stared as her image receded to the other end of the tunnel. She watched me with a small off-center grin. I tapped the table. "Really, I'll be right back, just, I don't know—the restroom." I dodged waitresses and busboys and found my way. It was locked, being cleaned or something, and so what. My orifices were so salt-puckered, I couldn't go if I had to. I weaved through the dining room traffic, made a wrong turn, came back out of the kitchen, back to June and fell into the booth.

She leaned in, "Is this our moment? I'm all in. I want our baby, James. I need you to want our baby."

I leaned in closer, "You said I could keep my soul. You said you didn't need anything. You said I only had to give my heart, but you have them both."

"And I love you, more," she said.

"Shit, too."

"Don't change the subject."

80

GOOD GOD GIRL!

"I have to do this alone, James."

"So. This is it, then?" I said.

She took a deep breath, and we stood. "Yeah, this is it." She squeezed my hand and kissed me long. She left the little coffee shop's door open as she crossed the street toward the hotel.

"I'm here. I got your back, momma," I called from the table.

She looked taller, now. Lean, her steps smooth, assured. Her hands glided at her sides with purpose and connected her to the next moment with muscle and steel. Her fingers flexed— a panther.

The Seward Hotel sat at the bottom of the town, a three-story clapboard Victorian by the water. There was a small maritime interpretive center on one side and, beyond that, a line of mom-and-pops running up the grade, a tiny chapel and a spotting of underfed bed-and-breakfasts.

This could explode, I thought. This whole thing could blow

up. Her dad might not be here. I moseyed over and leaned in the doorway.

She dug strong, blunt nails into her palms. Over her shoulder, "Alone, James." She started up the steps.

Two motorcycles clattered around the corner, bumped their noses diagonally into the curb and shuddered to a stop. The old guy on the rusted out, zip-tied Honda 750 looked like Eddie Rickenbacker in goggles, flight cap and jodhpurs. An aged hippy couple was on the dripping, fifties-vintage Triumph with a bloodhound and a sloshing jerry can chained-up in their plywood and wire-cobbled sidecar. They lit three joints and crossed the street to the hotel. Both of us held up at the curb, the hound and I stared at each other. He read my mind. How long was I going to wait? I crossed the street.

The bell above the door binged as June entered the set of single-light, rose-glass doors marked "Hotel Entrance." An identical set farther down the long porch said "Restaurant & Bar." She closed the door quietly behind her.

I was on the porch, at the half-open window in seconds. I'm an ass, I thought. She said, "Alone," and here I am, a stalker. No, I'm backup—I'm here as backup.

It was a ghost town of a lobby. High, pressed tin ceiling and a brass bell at a dark, varnished front desk. Random pine floor, wainscoting and pink plaster walls hung with ancient hunting trophies. Heavy, primitive furniture stumbled about like it was lost. The escaping window draft smelled of old books and soot from ten thousand fires on the hearth. She rang the bell.

The manager entered through the door behind her and dried his hands with a small towel. "Hello there, and welcome to Seward." He edged behind the counter and flipped the towel onto his shoulder. He rolled his sleeves down and buttoned them. "Need a room? We have a few." Fifty-something, he had the look of a maybe part-time cop. He slid a laminated room rate card across to her—gold pinky ring.

"Yeah, I guess. I come a long way to see a tall man looks somethin like me. Dark. You see one?"

"Can't say."

"Well, then, I guess I'll just have a room." She pulled a small pack of cash.

"We like cash, hon."

"I hear he looks like me about once a year for maybe fifteen years, now. Down from Prudhoe Bay for the sun and the salmon. Says he stays here."

"None of my business. You check the bar?"

"You think I should?"

"Up to you, hon. Here's your key and call down for anything—just to talk, a friend, massage. I'm here all night."

Damn, she's coming out, probably headed over to the bar. I hopped off the porch and skinnied down the side of the building. There, at the back, was a high, small, louvered window. I peered through and on into the restaurant from the top of a garbage can. From my perch, I could see the length of the bar. The hippy bikers were there, at the corner near the front door. They were having a great time. Back lit in the front window, the hippy woman was spinning to Canned Heat on the jukebox like the Summer of Love. The rest of the bar was empty but for two guys at the taps. Behind the hippies, the front doors swung wide, those tall rose-glass doors. I saw her in silhouette—June. The two guys in the middle of the bar looked to the doors. The moment suspended, the hippy lady slowed, the music drifted into the dust rays. One of the shadowed figures at the taps, the thinner of the two, stepped out tall and slow from the bar and moved toward her. His was a deep, resonant, "June!"

Her brow screwed tight, eyes intense like they searched for

what?, and her breath looked to be sucked from her chest. She held onto the edges of those doors like crutches.

She backed out into the gray light of the hotel porch. Her father followed, hands open, head cocked to one side, "You came," he said. "Good God, girl!"

She was at the edge of the porch and a deep drop to the top step. Her dad. To be sure, it was overwhelming for her. Beyond what she expected. What *had* she expected? Too soon, too fast? He held his hands out. She took them. He had to be whiskey and beer, tobacco and long-worn wool. They embraced. He kissed her forehead. I know she just wanted to collapse there, tired, surrendered and six, again. She wanted to burrow into his jacket and nap. She wanted him to tell her a story while she fell asleep, to hear all about his life. To wake up and make him coffee, tell him of all the things she had done, about living alone, growing up on her own and how well she'd done. About me and Tom and Prairie. About the governor and Chief and— Mom. Mom left me, Dad! They held each other long and tight. She looked up at him, there, him with his eyes locked shut and his nose running and the lines on his face pulling in on themselves and his lit, crooked smile like hers. She looked over his shoulder, back through her tears and the double doors. His friend sat at the bar and stared. She must have thought she was dreaming. He raised his glass to them. With finger and thumb, she wiped her eyes. She squeezed the bridge of her nose, sick and weak with baby and adrenalin. Nodding, the friend turned back to the bar. He nodded and chuckled.

81

WHERE'D THEY GO?

She'd made it. She found her dad, and she was in shock. I jumped off the trashcan laughing like a leprechaun. It toppled, and things that end up in cans like that erupted around me. Hell, then, get most of the crap back into the can, and give June and her dad time alone before swinging around front to join them. Empty motor oils, frozen food trays, eggshells, coffee grounds, fish heads and a lot of plate scrapings. People around here really liked T-bones. I scooped up as much of the kitchen mess as I could with the food trays. Lid back in place, I rinsed my hands at the hose and hustled up the side of the building and around front.

Okay, where'd they go? I popped up the steps and checked inside. Three old hippies dancing and the guy in the center of the bar—big guy, hat pulled low and surrounded in darkness. A warning ran up my back. I took a breath, collected my shit and started his way. Barely a glance and he stood, kept his back to me and crossed through to the hotel lobby.

I hustled back out to the middle of the street. Nothing. Not a car in either direction, including the Ram Van. I swear we parked it right in front of that pick-up, at that corner by the jewelry store. What the . . . ?

82

GET IN THE VAN!

Seward's laid out like a small stovetop grill, a perfect rectangular grid running precisely north and south, east and west. There's no heading west from Seward unless you're a goat, and going east, you'll need a sturdy sea vessel. Route 9 leads in from The North and dead ends at the water, just yards past the hotel. Standing in the middle of the street I gazed north. Alone. Gulls shrieked overhead, and the occasional echo of a sea lion glanced across the water and rumbled off the hotel. Suspended, I felt like the movies, after, "The End." Before the credits ran.

Duel glass packs. The Ram Van barely made the corner and slid up to me. "Get in!"

"S'up, June?" I grinned.

"Get the fuck in the van!"

I ran around to the passenger side, and her dad pointed to the back. I climbed in the side door and rolled into White Dog as June floored it. White Dog and I struggled for balance against the back doors. "What the hell, June?"

"Kane!"

"That was him?"

Her dad turned and looked back over his shoulder. "That's what she says. I know him as Lionel. Been working with him for a while, now. Always call him Lionel. Everyone does." He turned to June. "So, he's a killer, and he's after you—or me, you say—cause you're in with this guy?"

"James, Dad. This is James. Because we're bat shit in love and Kane thinks he owns me and he's intent on taking us both out and I took his truck money."

"You stole from the man?"

"He owes more than I took. Also, you're going to be a grandpa." She swerved to miss a pedestrian.

"Damn, girl! When you show up all kinda stuff happens! I'm going to have a grandchild!" He was beaming. "When? I mean, you don't look to be in a birthing way."

"I'm a couple-a-three months in." She glanced at me in the mirror. "And now, we're all going to get the fuck out of here."

"Okay. Okay, I believe you. Pull in here at the harbor. I'll get my stuff off the boat, and we're goin. Where to, by the way?"

83

TOO FAST FOR A BIG GUY

The crowded harbor held enough small boats to evacuate the entire town, one per boat. June and her dad had gone out to the end of a dock for his gear, and I hustled back up the lot to the bait shop to buy drinks and a few sandwiches for the road. I was tense. Kane was here. Returning with the food, my senses peaked as I approached the van. Guys celebrating their catch echoed up and over the bank. Below, a small radio played country. It was colder this close to the bay—fuel and salt water stung the air. One of the van's rear doors was open. The van rocked slightly, the door swayed. June stared straight ahead behind the wheel, her dad, bolt upright in the passenger seat.

June's dead eyes moved toward me. A single, small shake of her head. I backed away from her window and slowly approached the open door at the back of the van. In the spark of a second, I saw White Dog dead on the floor and June's dad's hand pressed to the side of his head, blood on the passenger window. Behind him a crouched dark figure. Too fast for a big guy, he swung round and something hit me cold stop.

. . .

gray cod, halibut, black cod. They're unloaded from tenders at the harbor. Halibut are individually gaffed off the fishing lines and can go as much as 250 pounds. In summer, it's silver salmon at the head of the bay that move right into the harbor where they can be caught from shore. In the open sea, silvers are often caught with a sharp hook baited with cut plug or strip herring bait. The technique is called mooching. "Gaffed," and "mooching," now, there are a couple words.

84

GRAVITY DOUBLED

The blackout couldn't have lasted long. I was somewhat crawling out of the hole as the floor rocked, and doors clicked shut. It was a few more minutes until I fully emerged to conscious—the stringent metallic dark and wet of the van—blood everywhere. Throbbing nose, loose teeth and a paralyzed left arm. Just White Dog and me—good-bye, friend.

Gravity had doubled. I ratcheted up to my knees and got a back door open. I pulled the bow from the rack and stepped onto the dirt. An unsteady sunset shadow. A weapon? I'd never again . . . A weapon.

They had launched a white, twenty-foot skiff. The water rolled slow. Cerulean and white churned at the prop. The wake spread. June stood at the console in the center of the hull, one hand wrapped in a bloody towel. Kane sat in the stern, her dad slumped in front of him. Steel stairs led me down to the floating dock. Eyes fixed to the far side of the tilting bay, I fought for vision. Nauseous, I wove to the end of the dock. They were maybe thirty yards out and pulling away, the motor's rhythm like padded thumps on a rawhide drum. I loaded Chief's razor hunting point onto the bow, dropped to my knees and sat on my heels. I sucked hard and raised the bow. Multiple boats and spinning vision, a bloody, unsure grip. I didn't have the strength, couldn't draw the bow. Nolan's Zen words came back—*Don't think of what you have to do, don't think of how to carry it out.*

June looked back over her shoulder, her eyes animal terror. She saw me and turned to the wind, away from whatever was going to happen next.

The target got smaller. *This, then, is what counts—a lightning reaction which has no further need of conscious observation.* In one quick motion, I drew the arrow to the corner of my mouth. White pain stabbed my eyes. I was going to pass out.

It was a God moment. The cold wind across the dock, a dark forest cathedral and deep ribbons of granite dropped straight into three sides of Resurrection Bay. A bald eagle shrieked above the shore, boats lapped and pulled at their cleats, lanyards clanged against masts. Behind me, otters barked for handouts at the cleaning station. Eerie and slow, blue megaton ice sheared from glaciers at the far end of the bay and dropped into the sea as three humpback whales swelled the surface. The shot was low. It sliced through Kane's carotid artery and struck deep into her father's skull. He died instantly. Minutes later, Kane.

VENICE, CA, 2015

You might think this whole thing to be fiction. I might, too. It's been enough years that I've rolled it around, retold it to myself until either end could be up—the bluegrass concert, the little one-armed prick, the shot. In twenty-five years, the whole thing's likely evolved from what actually happened to the story you just read.

It's quiet here this morning, my tiny suitcase by the door. I've poured the last cup, dumped the filter and rinsed the pot. I unplugged the toaster, and I haven't a clue why. Just sitting, now, I wait for the cab.

Looking back on that day, it left us empty, so deep in our shock and despair that no counseling would reach, no friend could console. Her bottomless loss, our mirrored anguish and guilt's cell door slammed on me. We needed each other more than ever but couldn't bear it.

The sun had nearly set. The temperature fell, and grief-struck shadows unwound, dropped low and laid on the water. June brought the boat back to the dock. She stayed there—on the boat. She had shoved Kane's body off the seat into the hull and cradled her dad in her arms. She kissed his cheek, his lips, and silently cried. She looked up at me briefly—a face I had never seen. Her fingers drifted down his chest, her tears pooled in his eyes. I kneeled, blood-choked. Weak. Dark. As they arrived, we were lit by EMT vans and police cars. One crew dealt tenderly to June's father, another hustled her off to the med center. If they spoke to me as they irrigated, stuffed and bound my shoulder, I didn't hear. I was pulled to my feet, restrained on a gurney and taken away.

TWENTY-FIVE YARDS AND
TWENTY-FIVE YEARS

Getting through the legal system was surreal. I rarely saw her those months—she was showing by then and each glimpse a wind-deadened bell. We were kept apart. They needn't have been concerned about that. In our shock we were self-canceling—our life forces, our losses so equally strong, so repellant. When it was over, and I saw her that last time, it was as if she was lifted away on the fog. That morning in Seward, the sky dropped heavy and low through town painting blocks invisible then revealing fragments of trees, cars and single-story doorways before covering them again. I stood on snow-dusted ground at a small rise in the park. Across the street, her gloved, cuffed hands lay flat on the roof of an unmarked car. She stared at me through the roiling mist, no expression, and I was lost.

My face wet then, it is now. Twenty-five yards and twenty-five years apart, and I feel the weight in her eyes.

A muted voice from within the car, she released her stare and stepped into the back. They disappeared north.

AUNT JUNIE'S SECRET TAHINI DRESSING

Annie and Erskine will watch the house, check in on it every couple weeks, if it *is* that long. They're down in Solana Beach most of the time, healthy and tan, just up here for a trip to Harvelle's to catch a band once in a while. They love to dress up, Erskine in his pointed, two-tone shoes, pleated trousers and suspenders—Annie's spiked heels laced up past her ankles, a short skirt. I went with them a couple months ago. The band took up a third of the club, thirteen pieces, horns to the side and girls out front—Blowin Smoke and the Nickettes. There are some things I like about LA. I sat at the bar while they danced—Erskine and Annie. Quite something to see. The young applauded. Easy, fluid and flawless, they danced until the band went home.

I'll fly from LAX to Bangor, rent a car and drive twenty-some miles toward the coast. I'll find the general store where she stops in, and I'll ask around. It has to be this way, she's off the grid. Those were Tom's words, "She's off the grid, Jimbo." As much a victim as anything else, and after some legalese with the state of Florida, June was released in Anchorage. Tom says she lives alone in Maine now. A place without an address, without a phone, on a lake in a cottage she built—never remarried.

I'd tracked Tom and Perri down long-distance starting at the med school in Omaha. I dialed and entered the auto voice system. Finally, a live operator and she was Nebraska-polite in her young voice, "Yes, Doctor Perri Hardware is on our board."

"Mrs. Thomas Hardware?" I asked.

"I'm sorry, but I must ask what these concerns?"

"You've gotta be kidding! Do you know she may be the second-best barrel racer ever raced?"

June, too, about a year ago, had found Tom. She called from a pay phone at the general store. Yes, he and Perri were happy, mad about each other, their two kids and three grandkids— loved the fishing in Nebraska. No, hadn't a clue, hadn't heard from ol Jimbo all these years.

Tom told me our son, Aaron, is in Northern California. He's a handsome, strapping man—June's genes—writing for a Ferrari magazine. He's in Italy frequently, track-testing cars, and we have a grandson. Would I ever meet him, them? Would they want to meet me? I felt like I was standing outside my own life and looking in.

The only way June will know I'm coming is if she calls Tom again. Would she? Not likely. That she called Tom to begin with, that she asked about me after all this time—I'll take that. Has she combed through that year of our love as often as I have, looking for a bit we missed, overlooked, or if we'd found it, failed to act upon? A way in which we might have stayed together in Seward, San Francisco, in Maine? Does she still make Aunt Junie's secret tahini dressing?

Ah, here's the cab. I shouldn't get my hopes up. But honest to God? They are.

ACKNOWLEDGMENTS

I am thankful for the encouragement, suggestions, criticism, and, in some cases, blind faith from the following: Mitch Allen, Jane Burton (my wife and acid-bath critic), Mary Leigh Hennings, Lisa Kastner (my publisher), Sacha Kawaichi, Ammi Keller, Phillip Laird, Margaret Lent, Nate McFadden, Camille Minichino, Robin Olsen, Howard Rappaport, Malena Watrous, Peter A. Wright (my editor) . . . and June, wherever you are.

Running Wild Press publishes stories that cross genres with great stories and writing. RIZE publishes great genre stories written by people of color and by authors who identify with other marginalized groups. Our team consists of:

Lisa Diane Kastner, Founder and Executive Editor
Cody Sisco, Acquisitions Editor, RIZE
Benjamin White, Acquisition Editor, Running Wild
Peter A. Wright, Acquisition Editor, Running Wild
Resa Alboher, Editor
Angela Andrews, Editor
Sandra Bush, Editor
Ashley Crantas, Editor
Rebecca Dimyan, Editor
Abigail Efird, Editor
Aimee Hardy, Editor
Henry L. Herz, Editor
Cecilia Kennedy, Editor
Barbara Lockwood, Editor
Scott Schultz, Editor

Evangeline Estropia, Product Manager
Kimberly Ligutan, Product Manager
Lara Macaione, Marketing Director
Joelle Mitchell, Licensing and Strategy Lead
Pulp Art Studios, Cover Design
Standout Books, Interior Design
Polgarus Studios, Interior Design

Learn more about us and our stories at www.runningwild-press.com.

Loved this story and want more? Follow us at www.runningwildpress.com, www.facebook.com/runningwild press, on Twitter @lisadkastner @RunWildBooks